Trapped in Pairadice

....

Becky Bronson

Rebecca Bronson, Publisher

Rebecca Bronson, Publisher
Westford, MA USA
www.beckybronson.com
Copyright © 2022 by Rebecca Bronson

Printed in the United States of America
Library of Congress Control Number: 2022910715
First Printing, July 2022

ISBN 978-1-7348551-4-2
Cover design by Rose Miller:

https://fiverr.com/rose_miller

Dear Gambling—
I wish we'd never met.
I remember the day I first learned of you...

One

- -

CARA SULKED IN THE back seat of the car. Her dad was
such a jerk! Arms crossed, she stared out the window. At
twelve years old, she should have more independence. She
had been looking forward to spending the afternoon with
her best friend, Stacey, but her dad had other ideas.

"You can play with Stacey any day of the week," he told
her. "I only get to see you on Saturdays."

As far as Cara was concerned, this new arrangement
sucked. Her dad had moved out a week ago, and though
she missed having him around during the week, she didn't
understand why she needed to jump through hoops to
accommodate him.

"Where are we going?" Brady piped up from the front
seat. Two weeks ago, on Brady's 7th birthday, their parents
had gifted him front seat car privileges. Cara hadn't been
allowed in the front seat until age 8, but that decision was
based on size rather than age and Brady grew faster than
she did. So now she shared the honor of the front seat

with her little brother. Added to that, his incessant chatter and clear adoration of their dad was getting on her nerves. More reasons for her to be annoyed. "We're going for ice cream, but first I have to make a quick stop," her dad said.

Cara snorted. "What if I don't want ice cream?"

"You can get something else," Brady said matter-of-factly. "I LOVE ice cream. Can I get a sundae? With hot fudge and whipped cream?" he asked.

"Anything you want," Dad answered. "As long as you promise not to tell Mom…"

"I promise," Brady said solemnly, as Cara stewed even more. She and Stacey had planned to bike to the local park and meet up with some friends from school. Secretly, she hoped Patrick would be there. She and Patrick had been best friends since pre-school. Or maybe even pre-pre-school. They had been school bus seatmates and recess playmates until second grade, when most girls and boys drifted apart. Recently, however, Patrick had caught her eye, and she found herself wishing they could spend more time together. The last thing she wanted to do was go for ice cream with her dad and little brother, when it might mean she'd miss spending time with Patrick.

She opened her mouth to object as her dad turned the car into a large, almost empty, parking lot. An enormous building with a gold dome and huge golden doors to match loomed in the distance. It looked like a scene out of a fairy tale.

"What is this place?" she asked.

"It's called 'Nuggets.' I have to talk to someone here for a minute. I'll be back before you can blink." He flashed them a big smile as he got out of the car. "You two wait here."

Cara and Brady waited. And waited some more. After a while, Brady climbed into the back seat.

"Those doors sure look cool. I wonder if they're made of real gold. What do you think Dad's doing in there?" Brady asked.

"I don't know and I don't care," said Cara. She wished Brady would shut up. She wished her dad would hurry back. Maybe, if they went for ice cream soon, she could get back in time to meet up with her friends.

The minutes ticked by, and Dad didn't come back in a flash as he'd promised. Underneath her anger, Cara worried. Brady bounced up and down in the front seat, then crawled to the back and started play-punching her. Cara cast about for ways to entertain him. They played patty-cake. Then she made up fairy tales about the castle in the distance. She hoped Brady couldn't tell by her voice that she was feeling panicked their dad might never come back.

"I need to pee!" Brady whimpered.

"Great!" hissed Cara under her breath. "Guess we have to find a bathroom."

"In there?" Brady pointed to the castle-like building.

"Where else, dummy?" she asked.

Cara held Brady's hand as they walked to the gilded front door of the palatial building. They peeked through the window, jumping back as the door opened with a loud creak. A security guard stood just inside the entryway. Behind him they glimpsed a vast, neon-lit room with red-and-black checkerboard patterned carpeting. He beckoned them in, and they stared in awe at the countless machines lining the walls, with pictures in constant motion. Bells clanged, merging with the sound of clinking coins falling through the chutes of the machines into the trays below. People milled about without seeming to go anywhere. Brady gazed up at the domed ceiling, entranced, but Cara looked down at the patterned carpeting. To her, it felt suffocating. This was where their father had been all this time?

The security guard guided them to the coat check desk, where a matronly woman sat on a stool.

"Who do you belong to?" she asked.

"My daddy is Clyde Davenport," whispered Cara, still not looking up. "He's in here somewhere."

The woman groaned. "A'right. You wait here and I'll go find him on the floor. He's probably at the wheel. Good thing we're not too busy right now." She called out to the security guard, "Jackson, watch these two 'til I get back!" With that, she bustled off.

Cara glanced at Brady, who stared, mesmerized, at the blinking lights. Then she remembered he needed to use a bathroom. Could she let him go alone in this place? Tears formed in her eyes as she struggled to figure out what to do. A moment later her father showed up, trailed by the coat check clerk. "You oughtta be ashamed!" she berated him as she pushed him toward the children.

"Okay, you two!" he exclaimed, rubbing his hands together. "Let's go get some pizza and ice cream!"

Cara stared at him. Did he even realize he had abandoned them all afternoon?

"I need to pee!" cried Brady.

"Okay, buddy. I'll take you to do that, and then we can get our ice cream. Cara, you wait right here."

She looked away and nodded, hoping he would be quick this time. Out of the corner of her eye, she saw the woman at the coat check desk shaking her head.

"It's wrong, what he's doing to y'all," she muttered. "He should know better."

Cara stared again at the checkerboard carpeting, fighting back her tears. She heard them returning before she saw them. He was holding Brady's hand, and Brady skipped alongside, looking up at him adoringly.

A short time later, as they enjoyed enormous ice cream sundaes, Cara asked, "Daddy, what's the wheel?"

Her dad almost choked on his ice cream. "The wheel of destruction," he muttered. "It's the devil in disguise, Cara! Forget you ever heard about it. In fact, forget about everything that happened today. Let's just keep it a secret between us. Your mom doesn't need to know where we were. She'll just yell at me and we don't want that, do we?" Cara and Brady both shook their heads no.

"Our little secret, right, Dad?" Brady said with a grin.

Cara stared at the two of them. Deep down, she knew it was wrong, but she also knew she wouldn't tell their mom. Mom was mad enough at Dad already, and Cara didn't want to make things worse between her parents. If she kept quiet, maybe they'd get back together. She sank down in her chair, wishing she was anywhere else in the world.

GERALDINE MAJOR STARED AT the plot of earth in front of her. Though her father had been sick for the better part of the past year, she still couldn't believe he was gone. How was she supposed to follow in his footsteps? True, he had given her a crash course on the business and she was a quick study, but at the moment, all she felt was despair.

She thought back to the first time he had brought her to the casino ten years ago. She was ten years old and the memory of that day was seared into her mind forever. After a fight with a girl at school, which turned physical, she ended up in the principal's office and was picked up by her dad. The principal berated her (and her dad) for her nasty temper and then suspended her from school for three days.

"I suggest you ground her, Mr. Major," the principal said as they left the school. Geraldine slid her father a look, praying he wouldn't be angry with her, though she was more concerned about what her mom would think. As she climbed into the car, it seemed her prayers were answered when her dad spoke.

"I'll bring you to work for a few days. Your mom doesn't need to know about this. It'll just upset her."

She sat beside her dad in the car and stared at the gi-gantic building in the distance. An enormous sign, "Pair o' Dice," graced the front of the building. It looked like a castle, and she imagined her father must be the King.

A doorman with a long, sharp nose opened the doors and bowed to her father. "Good morning, Mr. Major," he said. "And who might this be?" He pointed his nose down at Geraldine.

"This is my daughter, Geraldine. She is home-schooled by her mother, who is feeling somewhat indisposed today. We thought it best if Geraldine came to work with me. She's going to sit in my office and read."

Geraldine gazed around the room, captivated by the blinking lights. At this early hour, there were few people around, but the room didn't *feel* empty. The entire space was in perpetual motion. Slot machines lined the walls, and the pictures inside them moved, whether or not a player sat in front of them. Even the card tables, neatly arranged in the center of the room, seemed to undulate as dealers shuffled and reshuffled cards. She laughed in delight at the sound of a loud bell, followed by the deafening sound of dropping coins. Her father pointed across the room at a woman who raised her hands in celebration with a loud shriek. Geraldine watched in fascination as the woman poured all the coins she'd won into a bucket, then resumed staring at the machine, pulling the lever like a zombie. Her father nodded and smiled as he watched the scene unfold. The sights and sounds of this magical place enchanted her. She *belonged* here. She had never felt surer of anything in her life.

Geraldine followed her father down a red-carpeted hallway to a set of large doors. He pushed a button, and the doors slid open, revealing a cozy office with an oversized desk. There was a small sofa in the corner, and she sat there all day, listening to the muffled sounds of the casino, which increased as the day progressed.

"Daddy, why do you sit in here all day while everyone out there is having fun playing games?" she asked. It made no sense to her.

Her father studied her, his dark eyes penetrating into her. "They're playing games all right, but don't mistake that for having fun. It's a temporary pleasure. The house ALWAYS wins, and I'm the house. I own this place. I will always come out ahead, but only because I never play. And some day, maybe you'll own this place, but you need to remember what I'm telling you now. This may be your playground, but it's not your place to play in. Those people out there are like hamsters, mindlessly spinning on a wheel. Watch when we leave here and notice if any of them are smiling."

"But why are they here?" she asked innocently.

Sighing, her father took hold of her arms. "Most people come here to escape the pressures of everyday life. And for them, I suppose it is fun." He paused for a moment, deep in thought. "I'll tell you a little secret—just between you and me, okay?" She nodded and stared back at him, her big brown eyes wide open.

"I can watch them have fun and not feel like I have to be there playing. But some people can't stop playing, and they're the ones who drive our business. They're called addicts. Remember that, but don't tell anyone. It's our little secret. We try to help addicts by supporting programs to assist them. But underneath it all, we want them to keep coming. We want their business more than anything. Understood?"

She nodded again, not sure she understood, but willing to go along with what he said. He seemed so serious when he was talking to her and it made her feel so grown up. As they walked out at the end of the day, she gazed at all the people lined up at the machines. She wondered how many of them were addicts. "Like hamsters," her father had said, though to her they looked more like robots, mechanically inserting tokens and pulling the levers to make the pictures spin. Her father was right about one thing though... she didn't see a genuine smile on anyone's face, except for brief moments when the bells clanged and coins dropped after a big win.

"Remember, the house always wins. We don't need to play these games the way they do to have fun. We make plenty of money off those who come here. Casinos aren't built by luck. They're built by understanding and exploiting the weaknesses of other people. Addiction is one of those weaknesses. We don't force addicts to come here. It's their choice."

As she stood at her father's graveside, a voice jolted her back to the present. "I'm sorry for your loss." She looked up to see one of her father's business associates, Senator Richard Bly. "Your father ran quite an operation. We will all miss him." He smiled down at her.

She looked off in the distance, avoiding the Senator's gaze. "Yes, well, I'm sure you will all manage. He put a lot of things in place so his business could continue."

"I understand you will be in charge of his major holdings," Bly pressed. "Please, feel free to call on me if you need any advice." He gave her a weak smile, which didn't quite cover the patronizing look on his face.

She glanced at him, wondering at his use of the word "major." Was that an intentional snipe at her dad's name and legacy? Her dad had named his corporation "Majority Rules" as a way to incorporate his own name into his life's work. She remembered her dad's recent words to her. "Others may not think you can run this company, but I know you can do it. Go out and make our name great." Her dad had also told her that some politicians may seem arrogant, but they were important people in this business. She needed to make sure she could call in a few favors if needed.

She had learned from an early age that gambling was a business, and she now needed to rely on the countless hours of training her dad had provided. He had put his faith in her to carry on his legacy, and she wasn't about to let him down. Perhaps others thought she couldn't do it. If so, she would have to prove them wrong.

She pasted her best smile on her face and made direct eye contact, exactly as her dad had taught her. "Thank you for your kind words. I'll remember that. Good day, Senator."

Two

GERALDINE STOOD IN HER father's penthouse office overlooking the city and the bay, cigarette in hand. *Her* office now, she mused. Her empire. Such a beautiful place. She had worked damn hard to get here, and she intended to stay in control.

Her father had trained her well. He wanted her to be prepared—and prepared she was, though the pain of losing him still burned within her even after all these years. She would carry on with his legacy and make him proud. She recalled his words to her at the very end of his life when he knew his battle was over: "Show them Majority Rules!" he had said.

She liked that. It had been a driving force for her since she took control of the corporation seven years ago. She had recently branded a new line of casinos with that name, though she also had her own idea of another direction for the company. Her father had built his dynasty with brick-and-mortar casinos, but she was banking far more on the online business.

She had the best minds in the business working on the development of a new platform, and the sky was the limit. She even had a name picked out. "Pairadice," she would call it. She let the name roll around on her tongue.

She could taste the success of it, though two recent reports from the Center for Disease Control in Atlanta linking online gambling to suicide had her worried. *I must stop this before it takes root,* she thought, staring at the glowing tip of her cigarette. A careless bit of ash landing on dry tinder might turn into a wildfire in a matter of hours. She would not allow this minor flare to escalate that way. She needed to snuff it out at its source before it could take root. Angrily, she ground out the cigarette she was holding. Though she knew smoking was a nasty habit, it was the only indulgence she allowed herself. Much to her father's chagrin, addiction to cigarettes was one of the few traits she had inherited from her mother. As she contemplated wildfires and cigarettes, she pondered how the tobacco industry grew, despite clear evidence of the dangers. A germ of an idea formed in her mind. Maybe she needed to fight fire with fire....

Geraldine had always been a bit manic. Once she got an idea, nothing kept her from exploring it fully. She could disappear into research for weeks at a time, barely surfacing for meals and occasional catnaps. She set her phone to "Do Not Disturb," then opened a new file on her laptop, labeling it "Tobacco Industry." Closing her eyes, she pondered the question: How did that industry flourish despite the growing awareness of public health danger, and what ultimately caused its failure?

For days, she sat at her computer, consumed by the desire to understand the tobacco industry, poring through advertisements, government documents, and lawsuits. Through her research, she discovered the blueprint was there. Her pulse quickened as she realized her intuition was right. Everything she needed was already laid out. Three weeks later, she had enough information to create a plan. She sent an encrypted email to several prominent politicians and investors, all of whom had substantial investments in the online gambling industry. She wanted to meet with them while this latest situation at the CDC was fresh in their minds. They would come, she mused. Two weeks from now, she would launch her campaign.

SEATED AT THE HEAD of a long conference table, surrounded by some of the wealthiest people in the world, Geraldine was well aware of being the only female in the room. She thought back to one of her father's favorite sayings. "Keep your friends close and your enemies closer." These men all acted like they were her friends, but she knew better. Each of them had the power to destroy her if they felt it was in their best interests. She needed to impress them and offer them something of value. "Gentlemen," she began. "Thank you all for coming on such short notice. I know your time is valuable and I wouldn't have called you here if it wasn't an emergency. I chose you because you are the best minds in the industry and I am confident we can work together. Your businesses are all on the line here, so it is critical you recognize that what we say in this room stays in this room. Can everyone agree with that?" She gazed around the room, making eye contact with each of the six men: two U.S. Senators, two prominent business executives, and two prominent scientists, all of whom either owned casinos or had major shares in them. All of whom stood to lose billions of dollars if the gambling industry faltered. Her gaze lingered on Senator Bly as the men all nodded in agreement.

"I'm sure by now you've read the documents circulating around—the ones drafted by a couple of presumptuous researchers at the CDC attempting to draw a connection between online gambling and suicide." She paused as a few of the men shifted uncomfortably in their seats.

"The fact is, our industry is under siege. There's plenty of money for us all, as long as people keep gambling. There is no shortage of customers in the world for us. If we want to survive, we cannot view one another as competitors. Our real enemy is science. We cannot let the scientists of the world, and particularly the United States CDC, interfere in our business. We need to sow confusion in the public mind—to tell people, 'We know this may bewilder you and we're looking into it. You can trust us.'"

"Who's 'we'?" asked Senator Bly. As a member of the U.S. senate, he was on the governing board of the appropriations committee and wielded substantial power in Washington D.C. His committee set budgets for all U.S. Federal Organizations, chief among them the CDC. *What was Bly to her?* Not an enemy exactly, but a friend who needed to be watched closely.

"Ah... a brilliant question! I'm glad you asked! We are all founding members of a new organization: The Gambling Industry Research Institute. Our sole purpose is to be the public face of gambling research in the United States. Together, we will show the public that we are interested in public health. Our businesses are not injurious to health; rather, we provide a way for people to escape the everyday stresses of their lives. Our group always has and always will cooperate with those whose task it is to safeguard public health."

She displayed a slide on the gigantic wall monitor for all to see. "Our mission is to inform the public of the following:

1. Gambling, and especially online gambling, is a safe and effective tool to promote relaxation and reduce stress—far safer and more effective than alcohol or mind-altering drugs.
2. There is no conclusive scientific proof of a link between gambling and suicide. Both medical and psychological research point to many probable causes of suicide.
3. Only a tiny percentage of people are true gambling addicts, and gambling addiction is often secondary to other addictions. We will join with other industries to finance addiction treatment programs, but we need to

make it clear to the public that our industry is not one of the leading causes of addiction.

4. We can reassure the millions of people who derive pleasure and satisfaction from gambling that this issue is being researched extensively by prominent scientists, who will reveal all the facts as they become available.

Once we have the public's trust, we can launch a new era in online gambling. I propose to develop the technology of Virtual Reality so people will flock to our sites. Brick and mortar casinos are a thing of the past. Think of all the money we will save in overhead! This will be the crowning glory of our industry. No one will be able to resist this form of entertainment, and that will translate into billions of dollars in our pockets."

Richard Cox cleared his throat. He was a scientist by background, though he owed his fortune to his shares in her company. "I'm a bit worried we are rushing into this Virtual Reality technology. We are playing with people's minds by blurring the lines between fantasy and reality. I'm not sure there are enough safeguards in place yet to protect people if they stay in these sites for too long. It might be possible for a person, especially someone prone to addiction, to get trapped in a dream state. In layman's terms, that could cause a person to lose their mind."

"We'll run psychological tests with our Beta Testers and make sure it's safe," she countered. "And we can put out disclaimers, advising people not to stay in for long periods of time. After all, people are constantly told to drink responsibly. Why not tell people to gamble responsibly?"

She stared at Senator Bly. "We can do all this as long as we have control over what the CDC publishes. Senator Bly, do you have any thoughts on that?"

Bly squirmed under her gaze. "You say gambling is secondary to other addictions, but there are some published studies showing that it can be a primary addiction...." His voice trailed off as he looked at Geraldine's scowling face.

"We need to refute those studies—in particular, the articles from the CDC! We must discredit the authors and put the focus of addiction research squarely on drugs and alcohol," she said.

Bly looked down at his hands. "I can do a little damage control by talking to the CDC director. We may be able to restrict those reports. After reading them, I did some digging and discovered the two researchers, Hynes and Lawdly, work in the Office of Education and Curriculum Development. Their direct boss is Gloria Spiegelman, daughter of a former top military commander. She is ultra-conservative and operates her office 'by the book.' She is a rule follower. If her boss tells her to do something, you can consider it done. She is the ideal person to keep close tabs on these two scientists. And if she can't, then I'm sure we can figure out a way to cut them out of the organization."

"That's good, though we need to be very careful about this," Geraldine said. "I repeat what I said earlier: nothing said in this room is for public consumption. No one can know we are behind this campaign. We need to develop a unified strategy and we need to develop it fast. I'm counting on all of you to draw up some ad campaigns that will promote our goals." With that, she left the room, confident these men would do her bidding. They all had known her father and owed much of their past business successes to him. More importantly, they all would suffer substantial losses if the industry nosedived.

If someone had asked her in that moment if she had any ethical concerns at all, she would have laughed at the idea. She didn't see this as deception or fraud. It was merely giving the public what they most wanted—fun and instant gratification—while putting money in her pocket and in the pockets of those in her inner circle.

Three

CARA STARED AT THE email on her screen. *Patrick*, she thought as a tear dripped onto her desk. *Why you?*

He was her childhood friend and first crush. Though she had only seen him a few times since graduating high school, she still remembered the countless hours they played together as kids. True, they drifted apart in their elementary school years, but then they reconnected in high school and became best friends. He was an anchor she counted on during her stormy teenage years, when she often clashed with her parents.

Last year, when her father passed away from a heart attack, Patrick provided a much-needed shoulder to cry on. He helped her sort out her conflicting feelings about her dad, with whom she had a complex relationship.

Always the listener, she thought now. She recalled how Patrick had also supported her when her college boyfriend, Ben, died by suicide. Patrick listened to her for hours on the phone as she struggled to understand why, lamenting her inability to recognize the warning signs and prevent it.

At 23 years old, Cara was now an analyst at the CDC in Atlanta, working in the office of Education and Curriculum Development. A large part of her job involved providing statistics on teen and young adult suicide to help develop educational programs in schools across the country. She took the job as a way to deal with Ben's suicide, hoping to do something meaningful to stop this epidemic. She knew it was a national crisis. Now, however, as she stared at the email from her high school friend Stacey, she was shaken to her core. This was not just another statistic; it was her oldest friend. Whose shoulder would she cry on now?

Stacey included few details—a memorial service Sunday afternoon, a smaller vigil Saturday afternoon and evening, and then another get-together Sunday evening. "Can you come?" Stacey asked in her email.

Sighing, Cara looked at the calendar. If she planned it right, she could fly out Saturday morning and only miss one day of work on Monday. She had just started her new job at the CDC, and it might be tricky to take time off. She wondered how her supervisor, Gloria, would respond. So far, she liked the job, but she was not so sure she liked her boss. Gloria was hard to read, and Cara was a bit intimidated by her. The quick trip would be expensive, but she didn't see how she could not go.

She dashed off a quick email to Stacey and then set to work researching flight options, her mood darkening further as she realized the cost. She could save about $500.00 if she stayed an extra day. She had money stashed away in a trust fund from her dad, but she didn't want to tap into that unless it was absolutely necessary. If she did this, she would miss two full days of work, which Gloria might object to.

She looked at the screen again. *Buy now! Only 1 ticket left at this price!* Should she do it? What if her boss said no? She didn't consider herself impulsive, but sometimes that urge to act rashly was hard to resist. She brushed her long bangs from her forehead, weighing the pros and cons. *Buy now!* flashed front and center on the screen with the cursor hovering over it.

"Hell with it!" she thought aloud as she clicked on the link. "I may regret it tomorrow, but I need to be there!"

SHE ARRIVED EARLY TO work the next morning, hoping to get on Gloria's good side before asking for time off. Unfortunately, she could hear Gloria's bad side reverberating down the hallway as she walked toward her office. Gloria had the body of a bull and a voice to match.

"I want this done yesterday," Gloria screamed at Henry. Cara cringed. Henry was a junior researcher, hired just a few weeks prior to her. He was unassertive and short, with unruly, dirty blond hair and a scraggly beard that looked as if it hadn't been touched in weeks. Cara wondered if Gloria might be more sympathetic to him if he cut his hair and shaved. He blinked rapidly and his face was contorting—a facial tic he displayed when stressed. Cara pitied him for being on the receiving end of Gloria's wrath. Perhaps this was not the best time to ask for time off, but she had to do it today to comply with institute guidelines to submit requests for leave at least two weeks in advance.

She worked without a break all day, hoping to make a good impression. By 4:00 pm, Gloria's mood had improved—or at least it seemed so to Cara, as Gloria had been quiet for the past hour. Cara felt it was time to make her move. With a quick, silent prayer, she knocked on Gloria's office door.

"What now?" snapped the voice on the other side of the door.

"May I come in?" Cara asked, opening the door a crack and peeking in. Gloria beckoned her in with a wave.

"I hope you're here to tell me you finished the statistical analysis I sent you."

"It's all done and uploaded," Cara replied as she entered the office. "It's as complete as I can get it with the information available. There are still a few holes in it, but I'm sure we can get those answers tomorrow."

"Humph," grunted Gloria, looking at her screen. "Looks like you still have a bit of work to do."

"I do, but I'm waiting to get information from the library. I can't find some of these sources online, so I need to look at the actual microfilms. The librarian is searching for them now." Cara thought it odd that one of the premier government institutions in the world still had resources that were micro-filmed and not available online, but this was not unusual at the CDC.

"I'll call the library and make sure you can get what you need. What else do you want from me?" asked Gloria gruffly.

"Um, I was wondering if I could talk to you about something else," she began, brushing her jet-black bangs from in front of her eyes. *I need to get a haircut*, she thought.

Annoyed, Gloria glanced up from her screen, peering at her over the top of her dark-rimmed glasses. Cara hadn't experienced that look since she was a schoolgirl. She pressed on. "Last night I learned a close childhood friend of mine passed away, and there is a memorial service in two weeks that I would like to go to. Would it be possible for me to take a couple of days off work to attend that?"

Gloria narrowed her eyes. "A couple of days? For a memorial service? How come so much time?"

"It's in New Hampshire, and when I checked on flights, there is a huge price difference if I stay an extra day."

"Company policy is that you get no time off until you have been here at least six months. You've been here a little over four. I do like the work you've done so far, though. Maybe I can work out something so you can take unpaid emergency leave. That's the best I can do for you."

Inwardly, Cara flinched. *There goes the airline savings.* She was rapidly reassessing her initial impression of Gloria from hard-to-read to downright bitchy.

"I'll get back to you tomorrow, though if I were you, I'd wait to purchase that plane ticket until you get the final okay from the Personnel Office. Is there anything else?"

Cara shook her head slowly, trying to hide the tears forming in her eyes. She needn't have bothered; Gloria was already immersed in her screen. If ever she needed to lean on Patrick, it was now.

Four

It was good to be back among old friends. Cara forced herself to focus on the positive, though she was still angry with Gloria for docking her pay by two days. With the memorial service and prayer vigil over, she was glad for the chance to re-connect with her high school classmates. Funny how six years could seem like nothing. In some ways, it felt like high school all over again—the way they all lounged around in Stacey's basement. It was comforting to still feel part of this group, though she looked and felt totally different with her hair now cut short. Her long, jet-black hair had been such a source of pride in high school, but after deciding that braiding and styling it was a waste of time, she now kept it as short as possible. She wondered what else about herself had changed.

"I still can't believe Patrick would do something like this," said Audrey. "We dated a little during the first part of senior year and I never thought he was depressed. Did I miss something?"

"No," said Stacey. "He wasn't depressed at the beginning of the year. But at some point, he disappeared. He didn't come to any of our year-end parties." Cara nodded in agreement. At the time, no one had paid much attention, but now she wondered if there were warning signs along the way.

"Remember all our poker games?" said Billy. "Damn, that was fun!"

"Yeah. Patrick was the superstar," said Jimmy. "Seemed like he won most of the time."

"Not quite," said George. "I recall you often walked away with some pretty large pots."

"Yeah," replied Jimmy. "It was a pretty big thrill. We'd each put in just $10.00, and if we had a good turnout, I remember walking home with $150.00."

"Seriously?" said Stacey. "I never realized you guys played for that much! That's a boatload of money for a high school kid to win."

"Yeah, well, most of the time we didn't have a huge group, and the pot was a lot smaller, but we had fun playing together. Even those of us who lost all the time," said George.

Cara pondered this. She recalled Patrick bragging a few times about winning money from his friends. "Well, maybe those of you who lost ended up winning in the long run," she mused.

"What do you mean?" asked Jimmy.

"You all gave it up and moved on. You realized it was fun to be with friends and that was it. But I wonder if Patrick kept gambling. We stayed in touch during the last few years, and several times he told me he had won a lot of money. Maybe that all caught up with him and he got into enormous debt and felt trapped. I mean, wouldn't that explain things?"

"I don't think so, Cara," said Billy. "What happened to Patrick is sad, but gambling wasn't a problem for him. He wasn't an addict. No way. He was always a straight arrow."

"Agreed," said Audrey. "He stayed away from drugs and alcohol because he knew they were addictive habits. He enjoyed winning at poker, but he wasn't obsessed with it. I don't know—maybe it was my teenage romantic side, but I always felt like there was so much he wouldn't talk about. Like he was sad, but not really sad. I can't quite explain it, but I never would have thought he'd die by suicide."

"I remember he was pretty funny. Or maybe witty is a better word. He always had a clever thing to say," said Stacey.

"We sure had some good times," said Jimmy. "Remember our junior year ski trip?"

"All I remember is Patrick sitting in the hot tub and then jumping into a snowbank! I kept wondering why anyone would do something like that."

"Yeah—and then he spent the rest of the night shivering. We tried to get him to go back into the hot tub to warm up, but he wouldn't do it. Even then, it seemed he had a bit of a death wish," said George.

The room became silent, everyone lost in their thoughts of Patrick. *Did he have a death wish back in high school?* Cara pondered this. At first, she would have said of course not, but now, hearing all his friends talk about him, she wondered. *What possessed him to resort to suicide?*

This was the same question that had plagued her when her college boyfriend, Ben, died. Since Ben's death, she had studied and learned as much as she could about suicide. She knew the warning signs: being isolated, increased anxiety, feeling trapped or in unbearable pain. If Patrick had experienced any of that, he hadn't reached out to her. True, they had drifted apart in the past few months, yet still she felt he was a close friend and thought he had felt the same. When Ben took his own life, Patrick was the one she turned to. He had been there to console her. Surely, he would have known he could have turned to her if he were desperate. Yet, he didn't ask for her help and now she wondered if she could have been a better friend. Perhaps if she had stayed in touch more and not taken the friendship for granted, Patrick might have opened up to her and let her know he was hurting.

She wanted answers and sadly, she thought, she wouldn't be able to get them. As a statistician, she knew the numbers, but still didn't fully understand the motivation. With suicide, there were no simple answers. And Cara, for all her academic knowledge, still couldn't fathom how anyone could feel so much despair that they would take their own life.

THE FOLLOWING MORNING, CARA'S mom Sally arranged to go to work late so she and Cara could have time to catch up. It was the first chance they had to connect since Cara had arrived two days ago, as Cara had been with her friends all weekend.

It had been a long time since they had shared a meal together, and Cara felt she could use some mothering. The trauma of losing two close friends to suicide had her reeling. She hoped her mom could help her sort out some of those feelings, but as she looked at her mom now, she wondered if she should burden her with that. Sally seemed far more fragile than Cara remembered. She had always seemed solid to Cara, yet now she looked as if a feather could knock her over.

"Are you doing okay?" Cara asked. She knew money was tight and her mom fretted about it, but the worry lines etched into Sally's face seemed deeper than Cara remembered.

"We're managing," Sally answered. "I'm just glad you're able to support yourself and have that trust fund to fall back on. I think I can scrape together enough for Brady to go to the state university, assuming he gets in. Your dad left a trust fund for him also, which he can use after he turns 18. I'm meeting with my accountant soon to see how we can manage that."

"How's Brady doing? Is he showing an interest in school?" Brady had gone through a major depression when their father died, and Cara had tried to be there for him, but the distance made it hard. At first they had talked endlessly on the phone, though that tapered off as Brady seemed more like himself. Now, she had a gnawing feeling she should do more, a feeling intensified by her guilt over drifting apart from Patrick.

Sally hesitated. "We've had our rough spots lately. Honestly, we don't talk much. We're more like housemates than family. It works as long as I don't do any real parenting. At least he's doing okay in school and going to all his classes now. He missed a lot of school days last year because he wouldn't get up in the morning, but he seems to have gotten past that." She paused. "He's a good kid. As far as I can tell, he's not into drugs or anything like that. He pretty much keeps to himself, and when he spends time with friends, they seem like a decent group."

"So were Patrick's friends, and look what good it did him," said Cara quietly.

"Cara, you can't save everyone," her mom replied. "I know you and Patrick were close growing up, but people change. They do weird things. Lord knows, your father sure did."

"What do you mean?" asked Cara. Though it had been a year since her father's death, simply hearing her mom mention him was painful. "What does Dad have to do with this?" As she studied her mom, she saw the tired lines under her eyes, the look of defeat.

Sally hesitated. "It's nothing, really. I just mean you can't control other people's behavior. You aren't responsible for what happened to Patrick. He made his own choices."

"Okay... so why talk about Dad?" Cara repeated.

Sally sighed. "I didn't mean anything by that. I don't want to burden you..." she began.

Cara shook her head. "Don't hide things from me, Mom! I'm not a little girl anymore, and if there's something going on, tell me! Especially if it concerns Dad."

Sally looked down at her clasped hands, avoiding Cara's gaze. "What are your best memories of your father? When do you remember him being happiest?"

Cara pictured her dad for a moment. In her mind, he was always a carefree guy. When was he happiest? "I suppose it was the times we were together as a family," she murmured. She felt a sharp pang of guilt when she said that. After a brief separation when she was twelve years old, her parents had re-committed to their marriage and her father always pushed them to have family time. To Cara, that often felt suffocating.

"Okay," her mom prodded. "When was that, and what were we usually doing during those times?"

Cara squeezed her eyes shut. She had to admit she had very few happy memories of her dad in recent years. Since she left for college six years ago, it seemed her father was distracted and distant whenever she saw him. "My best memories are from a long time ago. I suppose he was always happiest playing cards with us. He was so excited to teach us a new card game."

Sally stared at her. "You're right. He played cards incessantly, with us and without. He was happiest with a deck in his hand, or more recently, when he had his phone in hand and was logged into a gambling site."

Cara narrowed her eyes. "What are you saying, Mom?" she asked.

Sally took a deep breath and looked at her daughter. "Cara, your father was a gambling addict."

Cara stood up and glared at her mom. "You're lying!" she cried. "No way was he an addict! How could you say that about him?"

"I wish I were lying. I tried to deny it for years while he was alive, but as more and more debts surfaced over the past year, I can't hide from the truth. His gambling became worse when he discovered online casinos and ran up debt from the comfort of home. That was what really destroyed him."

"I don't believe it! Sure, he gambled. We all knew that. But he did it for fun! He was just trying to escape from the stress of everyday living!" she added, quoting directly from the huge billboard advertisement for a new casino she'd noticed in the airport. She remembered the name: "Majority Rules." The ad touted all the benefits of gambling.

"No, Cara, he didn't do it for fun or to relieve stress. Well, maybe he did at first, but eventually, he did it because he was possessed by the idea that he could win back whatever he lost the day before."

Cara slumped back down, conjuring an image of her father in her mind. As much as she hated to admit it, she saw now how preoccupied he was during her last few visits home. She recalled coming home for the holidays during her freshman year in college, brimming with stories to tell her parents about campus life, only to find her dad sequestered in his home office for the entire week, uninterested in being with her. When she told her mom she felt he was hiding from them, Sally brushed it off, saying he was just going through a bit of a mid-life crisis and things would improve. Only they didn't. After that time, she came home for a few brief visits, and each time she sensed he was not fully there. And then he was gone for good. Still, she couldn't bring herself to admit he was an addict.

"There's more to tell you," Sally said, pulling Cara out of her memories. Gently, she placed her hands on top of Cara's. "I didn't want to tell you this, but I think you need to know."

"What else could there be?" Cara asked. She tried to pull her hands away, but her mother tightened her grip.

"Your father didn't die of a heart attack."

"What do you mean? Of course he did!"

"No, he didn't. He took his own life. He *faked* a heart attack by overdosing on a medication that made it look like one." Sally had tears in her eyes now.

Cara stared at her mom, speechless. "He died by *suicide?* How long have you known? Why didn't you tell me?"

"I suspected something initially, but wasn't sure," responded Sally, focusing on the table to avoid eye contact with Cara. "I didn't want to speculate, and I didn't want to say anything to you or anyone else because I wasn't sure. But I know now. He had massive debts he couldn't handle and thought by doing this we could collect life insurance and we'd be okay."

Cara stared at her mom. Sally started to pull her hands away, but now it was Cara's turn to hold tight. Right now, they both needed that connection. Another suicide, she thought. Another statistic. "Mom, I am so sorry. I had no idea. You're not responsible for all his debts, are you?"

Sally hesitated. "Mostly, no, though there are a few credit card bills I am still contesting. They will be settled, but it's going to damage my credit for a long time. It's just that he left us with very little money, and since they have ruled his death a suicide, we can't collect on the life insurance. My job is stable, but it's barely enough to cover our mortgage. Added to that, I'm worried about Brady. He's due to get a large sum of money of his own soon from that stupid trust fund your dad set up years ago. I'm meeting with my accountant to see if I can control that to keep him from gambling with it, but I'm not ready to tell Brady any of this yet."

Once again, Cara thought of her 17-year-old brother. "He's old enough to know what happened. Why the secrecy? Are you ashamed of Dad?"

"I'm not ashamed of him, but there is such a stigma attached to suicide, and I don't want Brady to feel that. Your brother idolized your father, even more than you did. He was so despondent last year. I told you it was a struggle to get him out of bed and off to school. He's doing better now, but he's still fragile. If I tell him all this, it could be a major setback for him, and I don't want to go back to living with that depression again."

Cara nodded slowly, remembering the dark depression that had overtaken Brady during the last year. It bothered her that her mom felt that stigma, but she understood it. Suicide wasn't something people talked easily about. "Is there anything I can do to help?" she asked.

"Maybe talk to him. Brady's at that age where he will do everything possible to annoy me. Without telling him too much detail, I want him to understand we must watch our spending right now. No more dinners out, and I want him to stay away from gambling. That's truly my biggest fear. But I need you to promise me you won't tell him why. Don't tell him about the trust fund either. He needs more time to heal before he receives a large amount of money. Living through that depression with him was terrifying for me. Every day, I worried he might do something to harm himself. I can't go through that again."

Cara hesitated. She was happy to talk with her younger brother, yet was uncomfortable with promising to keep these secrets. Though five years separated them, she and Brady had a special bond. Ironically, she now realized she had taken on the role of Brady's parent several times over the years. A long-buried memory surfaced. It was during her parent's brief separation, when her father took her and Brady to a casino.

"I'll be back in a flash," he'd said with a big smile as he got out of the car. "You two wait here."

With complete clarity, she remembered her dad telling them to forget about everything that had happened that day.

"Let's just keep it a secret between us," he had said. "Your mom doesn't need to know where we were today. She'll just yell at me and we don't want that, do we?"

At the time, both Cara and Brady shook their heads no, and Cara now found herself shaking her head at the memory as she sat across from her mom. *Who leaves a 7-year-old and a 12-year-old in a car when he hasn't seen his kids all week?* Neither she nor Brady ever said a word. As far as Cara knew, her mom was completely unaware of what had happened.

The memory shocked her. Did Brady remember it as well? They had never discussed it.

Lately, her new job had so dominated her life that she and Brady barely spoke. She promised herself she would set aside some time for him and was glad for the extra day here. Maybe she could catch him after school.

"I'll try to talk to him this afternoon," she said. "Patrick's mom asked me to come by, and I'd like to do that this morning."

Sally nodded. "We'll be okay, Cara. It's good you're moving forward with your life. I know how hard the last few years have been for you."

"I'm good. Really, I am," she replied. "I just have a witch of a boss to deal with, but otherwise, my job is great."

"Well, I'm proud of you. Speaking of work, though, I need to get into my office. I told my boss I'd be late so you and I could have a little time together, but work is busy right now. I don't want to jeopardize this job. It's my only lifeline at the moment."

As Cara hugged her mom goodbye, she realized their roles were reversing. *So much for getting a little mothering.* She had hoped her mom could provide her with some solace, but instead felt more burdened than ever.

She stared out the window as her mom backed the car out of the driveway. How many times had she watched that same driveway growing up, waiting for her dad to come home? It seemed surreal. Her image of her dad as competent and successful was crumbling, though she realized now it was just that—an image. Still, she had trouble grasping this new reality. She wiped the tears from her eyes, trying to reconcile her mind to the fact that her dad was not who she thought he was.

Her thoughts turned to Patrick. This was as good a time as any to visit his mom, Lena. With all the time she spent at Patrick's house growing up, Lena had been a second mom to her. She wished Lena could play that role now, but realized this wasn't the time for that. Like her mom, Lena was the one who needed consoling. Cara hoped she could offer something that would help ease Lena's pain.

"CARA, THANK YOU FOR coming! It's so good to see you!" Patrick's mother stood in the doorway of her house, looking small and forlorn. During the service the day before, Lena had put forth a show of strength, but here, alone in her house, she looked defeated. Cara blinked back tears as she saw how much Lena had aged.

"I'm so sorry for your loss! I can't believe he's really gone," Cara said as she pulled Lena in for a tight hug. They stood for a moment, allowing the embrace to span the distance the past ten years had put between them.

Slowly, Lena let go and led Cara into Patrick's childhood home—a home that had once been as familiar to her as her own. The furniture was exactly the same as it had been when she last set foot in that house years ago.

"We have so much catching up to do!" said Lena with forced brightness. "Patrick told me you had a new job working at the CDC in Atlanta. Tell me about it."

Cara swallowed. Somehow, telling Patrick's mom that her new job involved research into suicide didn't seem like the best idea. Her mom's earlier comment about feeling there was a stigma attached to suicide made her hesitate.

What if Lena felt the same way? She tried to think of what she could say to avoid the topic.

"Um, I'm just a statistician there. I'm helping to create a curriculum for middle schools and high schools, high-lighting the dangers of drug and alcohol addiction."

"Good for you! I'm sure your mom is very proud of you."

Cara squirmed, still searching for a way to change the subject. Finally, she blurted out, "I never saw this com-ing. With Patrick, I mean. We weren't in touch as much after college, but we talked a little during the last year. He seemed good a month ago, the last time we spoke. I never knew he was depressed or anything." She paused, feeling foolish for making this about herself. "I'm sorry! I should be the one consoling you. If you can't talk about it, I understand..."

"It's okay," said Lena slowly. "It helps me to talk about Patrick. You're right—he was doing well a month ago. But he lived a bit of a double life. He struggled with depression on and off but would never let on there was a problem and was very good at hiding behind a cheery outer face. In his mind, there was no problem. Things spun out of control before he had time to ask for help." Cara looked at her questioningly.

"Oh, I wish we could turn the clock back 20 years!" Lena exclaimed. "I remember the two of you running around together day after day. You know Patrick consid-ered you his best friend for years, right?"

Cara blushed. "Yeah, until about second grade. We reached an age where it was no longer cool for us to hang out together. I wish we had stayed in closer touch. If I had talked with him more during the last couple of months, maybe he would have reached out to me when he needed help."

"I doubt it would have made a difference," said Lena. "He didn't think he had a problem. At least most of the time. But I suppose that's true of all addicts..." Her voice trailed off.

"What do you mean? Patrick wasn't an addict, was he? I'm sure I would have known if he was into drugs."

Lena sighed, wiping the tears from her eyes. "He was. Not drugs or alcohol, though. Gambling, mostly. He just couldn't stop. We tried to help him, but there was only so much we could do."

For a moment, Cara was speechless. She stared in amazement before finding her voice. "Gambling? I never knew...."

"Of course not. How would you? It was a secret life, a separate existence. Something he could do in the privacy of his own room. He started playing poker with friends in high school and then expanded to casinos after he turned 18. That was bad enough, but it was the online platforms that ruined him."

Cara blinked. *Online platforms ruined him*. Didn't her mom say the same thing about her dad? Cara wondered if Lena knew of what really went on in her family. *So many secrets*, she thought. She wished she could tell Lena about her dad, but she was afraid her mom would disapprove. That was just how her mom was. Family stuff stayed in the family. Always.

Cara turned away for a moment. How was it possible that both her father and her oldest friend were both gambling addicts and she never knew? Was she that blind? *Just breathe*, she said to herself as she turned back to look at Lena.

"One of his friends introduced him to it, and once he started, he couldn't stop. We tried to get him treatment for years, but there are few programs for gambling addiction, and nothing specifically for online gambling. To medical professionals, all addiction is the same, and it's all treated identically." She spoke with a trace of bitterness in her voice.

Cara thought of her work. Developing more options for treatment and prevention of drug and alcohol addiction was her job. What about treatment and prevention of online gambling? Was that included in her job description as well? She wondered if the CDC guidelines considered gambling a disease in its own right. Or, as Lena said, was it simply lumped in with substance addiction? And was addiction to online gambling the same as addiction to gambling in a casino in terms of how it should be treated? She had never considered that question, but both her mom and Lena seemed to think it was different.

She again recalled the billboard ad she had seen in the airport. It had promoted both a new casino and the idea of gambling from the comfort of your own home:

Escape from the stress of everyday life...
Enjoy a slice of Pairadice

Cara's mind reeled as she tried to focus on what Lena was saying. "With online gambling, there's no regulation, and most sites are based in foreign countries. Plus, there's no preventative education in high school. It shouldn't be that way."

She thought of the programs she was developing nationally and her own high school experience. With all the education highlighting the dangers of drug and alcohol abuse, was any type of gambling ever mentioned? If so, it was only in passing. Would Patrick have avoided gambling altogether if he had more information, or would he still have dabbled in it, as so many other kids did with drugs and alcohol during their teen years? Slowly, she shook her head. It was so easy to second guess everything. The fact was, that message was never conveyed in high school. Patrick didn't have any kind of support system, and he ended his life.

She wished she could go back in time and talk to Patrick. Though what would she say? Would he even talk to her about his gambling if she pressed him? Probably not, she thought slowly. Although she hated to admit it, Cara realized her mother was right. She couldn't save the world. Although now that she knew both Patrick and her dad were gambling addicts and died by suicide, she wondered whether there was a true correlation between gambling and suicide, or if it was merely a coincidence in her own life.

She placed her hand on Lena's shoulder and looked directly into her eyes. "This must be so hard for you. I wish there was some way I could help."

"Just you being here helps," said Lena sadly. "You were a good friend, and for that, I'm grateful. You brightened Patrick's life and mine as well." She forced a weak smile, then looked away to hide her tears.

Cara thought back to her childhood days. At times, Lena had been more available to her than her own mom.

She recalled coming home from school one day to a locked house when she was about seven years old. She panicked and ran to Patrick's house, thinking something dreadful had happened to her mother. When her mom got home, she had some excuse that involved losing track of time, though Cara never quite understood how that could happen. Thinking back on it now, she was grateful she had a place to go. "It worked both ways," she told Lena. "You were always here for me, even when my mom wasn't."

"Your mom may not have been perfect, but she did the best she could," said Lena. "Don't be so hard on her. Let go of the past. What she did years ago was done. She has struggled since your dad died. She needs you, but doesn't want to burden you."

Cara sighed. Lena was right, but Cara still felt a little adrift. "I know she needs me. Brady needs me as well. I'm just not sure I'm ready to take all that on."

"You're strong, Cara," said Lena, giving her a hug. "Your mom and Brady are lucky to have you."

"Thank you," she said, returning the hug. "You're strong, too. I can't even imagine how you keep going."

"I just put one foot in front of the other and keep walking. Visits like this help a lot. Stay in touch, okay?"

Cara nodded as she left the house. She walked home, mulling over what she had learned about her father and Patrick in a few brief hours. Surely, they weren't the only people affected by this. Perhaps she could look into the CDC records to learn more about online gambling and what was being done about it. If there was information about this, the CDC archives should have it. It wouldn't bring Patrick or her dad back, but if she could prevent a few young kids from going down a path to addiction, that would be a worthwhile goal.

It was innocent enough at first. A few poker games with friends broke the monotony of growing up in a small town where everyone knew everyone else's business. It didn't take long for me to figure out that poker involved much more skill than luck, and I was skilled. I studied hard, and you rewarded me with your riches. I was unbeatable... or so I thought.

Five

THAT AFTERNOON, AS CARA waited for Brady to come home from school, she pondered the revelations of the past few days. Both her father and Patrick—gambling addicts and victims of suicide. How could she not have known? She wondered about her college boyfriend, Ben. Had he been gambling online as well? Now as she thought about it, she recalled often catching him engrossed with his phone. When she tried to talk to him at those times, he wouldn't engage with her. Added to that, he was always anxious about money, more so than most of her other classmates. She had thought that a little odd at the time—they lived on campus with all their expenses prepaid and he came from an affluent family—but she never questioned it. Was it possible he was gambling and couldn't control his spending?

She thought of the promise made to her mom to keep her dad's gambling addiction and suicide a secret from Brady. She hated secrets, and these were both big ones.

Perhaps Brady was fragile, but she wasn't convinced silence was the best policy. She wondered what her mom was really worried about. Was it the stigma of suicide? Or of gambling? Or both? Cara thought Brady could handle that knowledge, but she *had* promised, even if it was nonverbal, and for now at least, she needed to be careful about what she said to her brother.

The door slammed, and Brady came sauntering into the room. "Hi!" he smiled at her. Tossing down his backpack, he made a beeline for the refrigerator. He pulled out a large hunk of cheddar cheese and a loaf of bread. "I'm glad you stuck around an extra day. I feel like we barely saw each other over the weekend. Sorry about Patrick, by the way."

"Thanks and hi back," she said as she studied her brother. He had filled out considerably, and his bright red hair hung in curls down to his shoulders. He looked so much like their father, she mused. She had loved her dad's red hair and wished he had passed it on to her instead of Brady. Instead, she took after her mother with jet black hair that always fell in soft waves down her back.

"How are you doing?" she asked, expecting the typical high school response of "Okay."

"Great," Brady beamed. This was the last thing she expected to hear from her usually reticent brother. "I aced a math test. We're studying statistics and it's awesome. I feel like I'm finally learning something useful. Saturday night, I won $100.00 playing poker with some friends. They are all so stupid. We just learned this stuff in class, and none of them even thought to apply it."

Uh-oh, Cara thought to herself. *This could be tricky.* Aloud, she said, "You won $100.00? From friends?"

"Yeah, how awesome is that?" Brady asked, taking a bite of his sandwich. "We've been playing pickup games for a while now. I remember everything Dad ever taught me about cards, and it's paying off."

Alarm bells of worry rang in Cara's head. Of course, now that Brady mentioned it, she remembered countless times when her dad talked numbers and cards with them. It was part of the fabric of growing up in their household, just as playing poker in high school was embedded into their small town. The warning signs were all over the place, but she never saw them. And why should she have? No one told them their father's behavior was unusual. Yet now that she knew, it seemed so obvious. And she had to communicate this to Brady without revealing a huge family secret.

"You know, Brady," she said, choosing her words with care. "There's more to life than playing cards. I know you love to be with your friends and play, and I understand it connects you to Dad as well, but too much of it could be dangerous."

"What do you mean, dangerous?" bristled Brady. "Please don't lecture me about this. Mom already tried that. I'm having fun. We don't drink or use drugs. We sit around and laugh and have a good time! Just like our family used to do when Dad was alive."

"Brady, I know you can't see this, but gambling is risky..." Cara began.

"It's not gambling!" he threw back. "It's poker! There's a strategy to it! And I'm winning. A lot."

"I agree. $100.00 is a lot. And I understand there is a strategy for what you're doing right now. But you can't count on always winning."

"I know that!" Brady snorted, grabbing a drink from the refrigerator. "But I sure am having a good time trying!"

Cara took a deep breath. "Brady, I learned something this morning that I need to talk to you about."

Brady turned and looked at her. He put down his drink. "This sounds serious. Is everything okay?"

"You know Patrick died by suicide, right?"

"Yeah, I know. I heard he was depressed for a while."

"Well, maybe so, but there's more to the story. Today I visited his mom, and she told me Patrick was a gambling addict, online gambling mostly. He got in way over his head and took his own life. His mom thinks he couldn't deal with the debts and the shame of it."

Brady stared at her. "You're kidding, right?" he asked.

"I wish I were, but no, I'm not. He had an addiction to online gambling and couldn't break away from it, no matter how hard he tried." She looked straight at Brady. "It started with poker in high school."

"I don't believe it," Brady shot back. "And besides, I'm not doing the online stuff. Some of my friends tried it, and I think it's lame. Don't worry about me so much. I know what I'm doing."

Cara blew out a breath. Though she wanted to say more, she didn't want to alienate her brother. At least she had planted a seed, she thought.

"Tell me what else is going on in your life. You dating any girls?" she asked teasingly.

"Not really. There's no one I'm that interested in right now. How about you? Are you seeing anyone?"

"Are you kidding? With this new job, I'm expected to put in 60 hours a week. I have a witch of a boss who tracks my hours like a hawk. I don't have time for dating. Take my advice and have a social life while you can!" Brady blushed as she paused.

Still wanting to keep the conversation going, she continued, "I'm glad you're interested in school again. Are things okay here between you and Mom?"

"Yeah, as long as she leaves me alone. Occasionally, she gets on my case about getting a part-time job, but I just don't see the point. I mean, it's not like we really need the money, right? Mom told me a while ago that Dad had a massive life insurance policy, but she has become a huge tightwad in the last year. Now she's telling me I can only apply to state schools, and I shouldn't set my sights too high. What's up with that?"

Once again, Cara considered her words carefully. "You know, Brady, she doesn't want to worry you, but I think she got less than she expected from Dad's estate."

"What do you mean?" asked Brady. "She told me the life insurance would cover everything, and we didn't have to worry."

Cara hesitated. "I think there are some... restrictions on that. She hasn't been able to collect on it, and it worries her."

"What do you mean, restrictions?" Brady eyed her with suspicion. "What did she tell you?"

"Look, just be supportive of her, okay? She's doing the best she can, and she wants to provide for you as much as possible. Things will work out, but for now, you need to be careful with your spending and maybe save a little money for college as well. You'll feel better if you have some spending money at school and don't have to rely on Mom for that. Maybe a job would be a good idea, if only to ease her mind."

"I'll think about it," said Brady, though Cara could tell he probably wouldn't. Why would he want to work at a minimum wage job when he could walk away with $100.00 after an evening of playing cards with friends?

There was a knock at the door. It was Stacey, coming to pick her up for dinner.

"Listen, Stacey and I may be out late, and I'm leaving early tomorrow morning, so I may not see you again before I go. I know I haven't been in touch much lately, but let's talk more on the phone. And in the meantime, lay off the cards a bit, okay?"

Brady shrugged and turned his attention back to his sandwich, leaving Cara to wonder whether anything she had said to him had made a difference. Clearly, one conversation wouldn't change him, but at least he hadn't shut her out the way he used to when he was depressed. She knew from experience how defensive he could get. She made another promise to herself to stay in better touch with him in the coming weeks.

Six

EARLY THE NEXT MORNING, Cara sat at the airport gate awaiting her departing flight. The quiet of the airport surprised her, given the pressure she had felt to buy her plane ticket a week ago. Based on the ad, she had assumed the flight would be full. She looked around, once again noticing the enormous billboard for the Majority Rules Casino and the new online platform called Pairadice. She shook her head. Were people stupid enough to think gambling could solve their everyday problems?

She glanced at her phone, noticing an article from the Washington Post. "You've Been Scammed!" screamed the headline, but that wasn't what grabbed her attention. It was the byline: Libby Lewis. Cara smiled. Her college roommate, Emiline Jackson, was now an investigative reporter for a premier newspaper. Emiline had made up the pen name 'Libby Lewis' in college. Most people knew her as Em. Good for her! Cara thought now. She finally landed her dream job.

Their friendship had not started out on the best terms. Cara had grown up in a predominantly white middle-class suburban town while Em had grown up in a black inner-city neighborhood. Although Em had an older brother, she was the first member of her family to enroll in college.

Cara remembered arriving at her dorm room on the first day of school and seeing Em sitting on a bed, with all her belongings already stowed away. To Cara, it seemed Em had taken the nicer bed by the window. She hadn't been sure what to expect, but thought they could have at least had a conversation about how to arrange the room.

Em waved a hand in greeting as she bit into an apple. "The room's not huge, but it's all we've got," she said, staring at all the stuff Cara had left in the hallway. Then she put on some headphones and wrote in a journal. Cara set about unpacking her things, wondering if she had brought too much.

For most of their freshman year, they tolerated each other, but things changed when Cara's boyfriend, Ben, killed himself. As Cara struggled to deal with the loss of her boyfriend, Em opened up about her childhood.

"I kind of know how you're feeling," she told Cara a few days after Ben's suicide. "I lost a friend once. Not a boyfriend, but a close childhood friend. Her name was Libby."

"What happened to her?" asked Cara.

Em closed her eyes for a moment. When she opened them, Cara could see her pain. "We were playing in my driveway, and a car sped by. Someone fired a gun—a gang fight, I think. A stray bullet hit her."

"That's horrible!" exclaimed Cara. She shuddered, thinking about how hard that must have been for Emiline.

"She was one of my best friends. Her life was cut short for no reason. I could never understand it. It seemed so random."

Cara was quiet for a moment. "What helped you get through that?"

"Writing," said Em. "It still does. She speaks to me when I write. Sometimes, if I can't decide something, I'll ask myself 'What would Libby do?' and she'll give me the answer in writing. That's why I want to go into journalism. If I ever start publishing my writing, I'm going to do it in Libby's name. I want to be her voice because she can't speak for herself."

"I wish I could be Ben's voice," said Cara. "But I don't even know what he'd want to say."

"Well, maybe that's for you to figure out. Maybe your calling in life is to study psychology and help other people so they don't go down the same path."

Cara recalled that conversation now as she perused the front-page article of the Post. She hadn't realized it at the time, but Em's suggestion had been the reason she minored in psychology. Now, with her job at the CDC, she felt she was gaining even more knowledge about suicide trends in the country. Maybe she could do something to prevent some future tragedies.

The article exposed deceptive advertising practices on the internet, highlighting how various industries were flooding the internet with targeted marketing campaigns. Em described the use of mind-bending tools, which enticed people to make impulsive purchases. It captivated Cara immediately.

With a twinge of guilt, Cara realized she hadn't spoken to her friend in over four months. She made a mental note to call her in the next couple of days to catch up and compare notes about their respective new jobs.

As she boarded the plane, Cara noticed the nearly empty cabin and considered her own recent purchase of this airline ticket. "Buy Now!" the website had said. "Only 1 ticket left at this price!" Now she wondered if that was true. She hadn't bothered to look any further. Had she been a victim of a simple marketing scheme? How many of her decisions were based on free choice, and how many were guided by pressure from an outside source? She shook her head. The mere thought of this depressed her.

Back at home that evening, she called Em to congratulate her on her feature article.

"Libby Lewis!" Cara exclaimed. "I was so surprised to see your byline! When did you get that job?"

"I started three months ago, and this was my first big break," said Em. "Honestly, I wasn't sure they'd run it given all the industry pressure around here. The amount of lobbying that goes on in D.C. is crazy, and sometimes it can be super hard to expose. I'm hoping these articles can pave the way for some laws to change, but it's a slow process."

"I think you are incredibly brave to stand up to it all," replied Cara. "But is it safe? Are you worried you might get death threats?"

Em laughed. "The bigger the risk, the bigger the payout! Yes, I have to be careful, but that's why I write under a pen name. No one else knows my true identity."

"How does that work at your job? Are you Libby Lewis at work?" asked Cara.

"Not exactly," replied Em. "They hired me as Emiline Jackson, and I write mundane stuff about fashion and restaurants. But when I write about social issues or anything controversial, I use the name Libby Lewis. No one except my direct boss knows I am the one writing as Libby. Not even upper management at the paper. That way, I'm protected, even if Libby gets death threats. I'm counting on you to keep it a secret!"

"That's a little scary," said Cara. "I'm glad I knew your alias today. I thought your article was superb. After reading it, I wondered if I was scammed when I bought my plane ticket online. The 'Buy Now' ad grabbed my attention, and I didn't even bother to look for other deals."

Em sighed. "You aren't the only one. I'm trying to make people aware so they can become more savvy shoppers. It's getting harder and harder to navigate all this."

"That's for sure," agreed Cara. "Maybe we can talk more about it in person. There is a conference in Washington D.C. that I may go to. I haven't confirmed it with my boss and given the fact that I'm not on her good side at the moment, she may have changed her mind about sending me, but if I go, let's get together for dinner."

"Sure!" said Em. "The last time we talked, you had just started at the CDC. It'll be great to catch up."

"Yes, we have a lot of catching up to do," said Cara. "I'll let you know my plans as soon as I can."

She smiled as she clicked her phone off. With all the upheaval in her life right now, it felt good to have a friend she could count on. She hoped Gloria would approve her trip in the next few days.

Seven

CARA RETURNED TO WORK the next day to find Gloria in an exceptionally good mood. "What's up with her?" she asked her co-worker Henry.

"I'm not sure, but I think the Director praised her about how well things are running in this department. She went to a dinner Saturday night with several other senior directors and she's been in a great mood ever since. She hasn't criticized me at all in the last two days, and every time she's walked by my desk, she's flashed me a big smile."

"That's good!" Cara said. "Did she mention anything more about that symposium in D.C. next month?"

"She did, in fact. I think she wants you to go rather than me. There's going to be a comprehensive middle school curriculum-building workshop centering on alcohol and drug abuse and suicide prevention. The suicide piece fits in better with your background than with my research. Plus, I think she doesn't like me. I'm not sure why, but nothing I do seems to satisfy her." Henry looked at her morosely. Once again, Cara felt sorry for him and a little guilty as well. Gloria did seem to favor her over him much of the time. She shook off the feeling as Henry continued. "At any rate, given her good mood, today would be a good day for you to ask about it if she doesn't bring it up first."

"Thanks, I may do that," said Cara, hoping Gloria would be the one to broach the subject. A few minutes later, it looked like her wish might come true, as Gloria summoned her into her office with her usual text: *"pls see me."* Rising from her desk, she whispered to Henry, "Wish me luck."

Before she could knock, she heard Gloria's voice from beyond. "Come on in!" Cara stepped inside and stood timidly in the open doorway. "Close the door."

As Cara sat, Gloria peered at her over her glasses. "Now that your friend is buried six feet under, are you ready to focus on your work here?"

Cara looked at her, speechless. Was there an appropriate response to that?

"Sorry to be so crass, but we have some deadlines here and I need to know you are ready to work. This symposium in Washington D.C. is turning out to be much bigger than I expected. A lot of our funding depends on this. I need you to represent us there and be up to speed with all the latest research. You'll have three weeks to prepare. Do you have a problem with that?"

Cara blinked. "It's no problem at all," she said, finding her tongue. "I would love to present this."

"Great," said Gloria. "You'll need access to the restricted microfilm stacks again for some of these papers. I told

Abigail to allow you to look at these last week, but I'll make sure she knows what to give you." She sighed and shook her head. "So much research related to suicide is kept under close surveillance here. I expect a written rough draft of your presentation by next Monday, and an initial run-through by the end of next week. Here's the name of the travel agent we work with to make all plane and hotel reservations." She handed Cara a business card. "Call her today so she can set you up for the trip."

Cara nodded, unsure of what else to say. Should she just get up and leave? With Gloria, she never quite knew where she stood. She rose from her chair uncertainly as Gloria dismissed her with a wave of her hand. "That's all. You can go now."

She left the office with Gloria's earlier comment rattling in her head. "So much research related to suicide is kept under close surveillance..." *Why would that be?* she wondered. *Why put old research papers on microfilm and lock them in the library, rather than publish them on the internet?* Cara found that strange, but it was common practice here.

Back at her desk, Cara rolled her head and neck, trying to ease the tension she felt after meeting with her boss. She wished Gloria wasn't so mean, but given the deadline, she couldn't dwell on that right now. She needed to get to work and decided to plunge in with a trip to the library.

It was her second time there, and she dreaded it. Located in the bowels of the building, the library felt like the set of a Halloween horror movie. She wished Henry could go with her, but he didn't have authorization to look at the restricted microfilms.

Access to the library required use of a special elevator. Squaring her shoulders, she exited the elevator in
the sub-basement and walked down the dimly lit, ce-
ment-walled corridor, her footsteps echoing in the hallway. She imagined the dungeon of a medieval castle might
be like this, save for the occasional video cameras along
the ceiling and the high-tech card reader outside the library door. With a shudder, she noticed graffiti scrawled
in yellow paint high on the cement wall. The wet paint
had dripped from the bottom of the letters toward the
doorway like giant tentacles.

CARMEN WAS HERE: 1994

Shaking her head, she flashed her ID and the heavy steel
door creaked open. A young, bored librarian sat behind a
large metal counter reading a worn paperback novel, her
glasses carelessly tossed on the counter. Cara peered at her
ID badge. **ABIGAIL**, it said in big block letters.

The woman glanced up and grabbed her round glasses.
She peered out from behind them at Cara. "How can I
help you?" she asked curtly.

"I'm here to collect some papers for the symposium
next month on drug and alcohol addiction. Gloria told
me she called down to give me clearance."

Cara looked around the dingy room while she waited
for Abigail to collect the films. Dull green paint covered
the walls and there were splotches of it on the untreated
cement floor. Cara shivered again. She imagined the inside
of a prison cell must look like this. On returning, Abigail
buzzed her in behind the counter, beckoning her into a

private room with a microfilm reader where she was free to browse through the articles.

"You can read these in here. If you want any printed, let me know and I'll do that for you," Abigail said as she walked out of the room.

Cara shook her head as she gazed at the decrepit microfilm viewer. It was at least 30 years old, and it seemed so implausible to her that an organization as high-ranking as the CDC would still use this outdated technology. She glanced at the pile of films Abigail gave her. The articles were all written by CDC researchers and labeled "For Internal CDC use only." Several were for background information, and Cara perused them briefly, taking a few notes on a pad of paper Abigail had provided. Six key articles formed the basis of her report, and she scrutinized each one. It was an incredibly tedious way to do research. She was just finishing up the last one when she noticed a citation at the end: "Correlation between online gambling and suicide" by A. J. Lawdly and R. C. Hynes.

She caught her breath, and her heart skipped a beat. Searching the archives for this might be easier than she had thought. She glanced at the rest of the citations and saw two more articles by the same authors that appeared to cover similar material. She was about to ask Abigail to get these articles for her when the librarian entered the room. "It's closing time." Abigail announced.

"Oh, I didn't realize how late it was! I'm sorry! I can finish up tomorrow. Could you find these other three microfilms for me tomorrow morning?" Cara handed Abigail the titles scribbled on a scrap of paper.

Abigail glanced at the paper, then looked at the floor. "Come by about 10:00 tomorrow," she mumbled. "You can leave all your stuff in the room overnight. No one ever comes down here off-hours." With that, she pointed to the door, clearly wanting to lock up and leave.

Grabbing her phone, Cara made her way out the door and down the dim hallway. When she reached the elevator, she wondered if she should hold it for the librarian. On the one hand, Abigail said no one ever came down here after hours, but there were several janitors' closets, so surely the cleaning staff used the hallway. She hated to leave another woman down here alone in this dingy space, even if that woman seemed to dislike her.

The elevator door buzzed and Cara held it open as she heard footsteps clicking on the cement floor of the hallway. Abigail trotted into the waiting elevator without a word. When they reached the lobby, she hastily disappeared into the crowd.

THE FOLLOWING MORNING, CARA showed up at the library hoping to collect her papers and look at the three new ones. Everything was on the table, exactly as she had left it the day before. "Which ones do you want printed?" asked Abigail curtly.

Cara handed her the films she wanted copies of. "Were you able to find those other titles?" she asked.

"No. They're not available."

"Not available? What do you mean?"

"I mean, not available. I can't get them." Cara sensed Abigail's annoyance. She wondered if that meant they were not there, or if someone had blocked her access to them. Either explanation made no sense. She'd have to ask Gloria about it.

Back at her desk upstairs, she was getting up the nerve to knock on Gloria's door when she got a now familiar text: "*pls see me.*" Entering Gloria's office, she had the distinct impression Gloria's mood had shifted from the previous day. The woman scowled at her as she stood in the doorway.

"It's come to my attention that you were looking for some papers that had nothing to do with the symposium research," Gloria began.

Cara's jaw dropped in surprise. "What...?" she began.

"You asked for some titles about gambling. The symposium is covering drug abuse and alcohol addiction. Period. Gambling is not at all part of that. Gambling addiction falls under the jurisdiction of the Gambling Industry Research Institute. I told you yesterday I need your FULL attention on this project, to the exclusion of everything else. If you have other interests, you need to put them aside. Your job is to gather as much information as you can on these topics so you can make a clear presentation in less than three weeks. Is that clear?"

"Yes, but...."

"No buts!" Gloria slammed her fist on the desk, making Cara jump. "You need to stay focused on the work assigned to you."

Gloria turned her attention back to her screen. It was clear Cara was dismissed. Shaking her head, she backed out of the office slowly. She hated being bullied, but this was her job, and she needed to do what Gloria expected if she was going to keep it. Perhaps she could investigate gambling addiction later, once the symposium was over.

CARA WORKED FEVERISHLY FOR the next several days to put together a program for the upcoming symposium as Gloria's words played over and over in her mind: "*So much research related to suicide is kept under close surveillance....*" Was there something hidden in those papers that Gloria didn't want her to see? Though she tried to put it out of her mind, it gnawed at her. Maybe she could do a little sleuthing on her own time at home. Even though she didn't get the papers, she had the names of the two lead authors. They might very well be doing research and publishing papers in the public sector now.

At home, she spent the better part of the next weekend trying to locate the two authors, but there was no public record of either of them. Finally, she enlisted the help of her college roommate, Em. As an investigative reporter, Em had access to tools unavailable to Cara.

"I can't make any guarantees, but I'll try to find a way of contacting them," Em promised. "The papers were internal documents, so these men must have worked there.

I should be able to follow a paper trail. In the meantime, take your boss's advice. It sounds like there are people at the CDC who don't want you pursuing this line of research. For now, prepare a killer presentation! No pun intended there...."

Cara laughed. "We have a lot of excellent information to present. I hope we can put gambling in there as well. I feel like it's an addiction that's being ignored."

"Maybe so, but it's not worth losing your job over it," said Em.

Eight

Two weeks later, as Cara packed for the conference, Em called. "I have news for you," she said. "I located Ron Hynes, one of the two researchers who wrote those papers. He was hard to find, and you may have to be careful in how you approach him. It looks like he severed ties with the CDC and keeps an extremely low profile. He may not be too keen on talking to you."

"I wonder why that would be," Cara mused.

"I don't know, but I'm willing to bet if you call him and tell him you're from the CDC, he'll hang up on you."

"So, what do you suggest?" asked Cara. "How should I approach him?"

"If I were you, I'd wait and pay a visit to the school where he works. He teaches at a community college just outside of D.C."

Cara stared at the phone for a few minutes after hanging up from Em. She now had his phone number and work address. She could wait to visit him in person, but after two weeks of searching through whatever records she could find, she felt increasingly frustrated. What had started as a quest for more information on her part had turned into an obsession over the past few weeks. This man held the key to information that she wanted. What would be the harm in a simple phone call? She took a deep breath in, then blew it out and keyed in the number. She was about to hang up after several rings, but when the phone went to voice mail, she surprised herself by leaving a message.

"My name is Cara Davenport and I work at the CDC. I understand you used to work there and I have a few questions for you. I would appreciate a call back if you have the time."

She clicked off her phone and buried her head in her hands, wondering if she had just done the stupidest thing in the world. Why hadn't she taken Libby's advice and been patient? Of course he wouldn't return her call! What had possessed her to think he might? And now, if she tried to see him, he would know ahead of time she was from the CDC. If he left the CDC on bad terms, he'd probably refuse to talk to her. She wished she could travel back in time and erase the last five minutes of her life.

As she sat there berating herself, she thought of her father and Patrick, both gambling addicts and victims of suicide. And a man who had written a paper on the correlation between those two things. Maybe she had been impulsive in wanting to talk to him, but she couldn't let that deter her. One way or another, she was going to track him down to get some answers to her questions.

After a busy morning of presentations at the symposium, participants had some leisure time to enjoy lunch and take a guided tour of the city. Cara opted out of the tour and instead, pulled out the paper with Ron's work address scribbled on it. She summoned an Uber and headed off to the community college where he taught psychology. She hoped to catch him unawares between classes. Thankfully, the campus was a short distance from the symposium meeting site, and within minutes, she was standing in front of a brick administration building. *I can do this*, she said to herself as she entered the building and walked to the reception desk.

"May I help you?" asked the clerk.

"I'm looking for Professor Ronald Hynes," she began.

The receptionist hesitated. "May I ask who you are?"

Damn, thought Cara, completely flustered. *He knows. I bet he put the entire school staff on alert to look for me.*

"Libby Lewis," she blurted impulsively. "I'm a journalist for the *Post* newspaper."

The desk clerk's eyes widened. "The same Libby Lewis that wrote that article about being scammed? I look for her articles every week!" Cara nodded, wondering why she had used her friend Em's pen name and already regretting it. *Best not to say anything more.* The woman behind the desk checked her computer screen and then turned to Cara. "I just *love* reading your stuff! You seem to get right to the heart of things. And here you are, in person! Okay—here... he's in a class right now that should finish up in about 15 minutes. It's in the Bullfinch Building, across the quad. You can find him there when he gets out." She handed Cara a map and sent her on her way.

As Cara exited the building, she heard the receptionist behind her. "Libby Lewis! Here, in person! Imagine that!" She felt a twinge of guilt and wondered if using Libby's name was a bad idea. *Too late to change it now,* she thought. She sent a silent prayer of thanks (along with an apology) to Em for the use of her alias. That would not work for Professor Hynes, though. She needed to let him know who she was if she wished to get any answers from him. She hoped he wouldn't turn her away.

Her timing was perfect. She found the building and walked inside, just as a group of students was leaving. The hallway outside the classroom was dark, and she waited a few moments until all the students had left, then peeked in the door. He was at his desk, tidying up papers with swift movements, a tall, slight man with a shock of dark hair falling in the middle of his forehead. Slowly, she pushed open the door. He looked up, startled.

"Professor Hynes?" she asked tentatively from the doorway.

He glowered at her, clearly annoyed at being interrupted. "Who wants to know?"

"I'm Cara Davenport. I tried to call you a couple of days ago...."

He hastened to the door and motioned her to follow him out of the room. Once in the hallway, he looked around. "Are you on official business with the CDC?" he asked quietly.

Cara shook her head. "No, I–"

"Then you should leave." He turned to go back into his room. Cara stared at him. He looked back at her with piercing eyes.

"I told you to leave," he said.

He walked back into the room, leaving Cara perplexed in the hallway. *Should she go?* After a few minutes, she figured she had no choice. "I just had a couple of quick questions to ask you," she called out. "I'm tired of being stonewalled!" She walked outside and started toward the street.

As she approached the street, she heard footsteps behind her. He caught up with her and walked alongside. "Look, I'm sorry to put you off, but I'm not supposed to associate unofficially with anyone from the CDC."

"Will you at least answer a couple of questions?" Cara asked.

He blew out a breath in frustration and glanced around nervously. "Maybe, but first I need to know who sent you."

"No one sent me! In fact, my boss would likely fire me if she knew I was here. I just want some answers!"

Ron was silent for a moment. "Your boss... a woman?" he asked. Cara nodded and could see he was pondering how to respond. He looked straight ahead with his hands in his pockets. "Okay, I have a little time to talk now. On the other side of the quad, across the street from the school and behind a coffee shop, there's a playground with some picnic tables around it. Walk around the outer perimeter of the campus." He pointed toward the street, away from the building they had exited. "Meet me there in ten minutes—and make sure no one is following you." With that, he strode off, leaving Cara staring after him.

Cara watched him disappear back into his classroom building, then took out the campus map the receptionist had given her. The campus was small, and it didn't take her long to figure out where he wanted to meet. When she arrived, Ron was already seated at a table on the edge of the woods, a cup of steaming coffee in front of him. Apparently, he had cut across the campus quad.

She slid onto the wooden bench and faced him. He was younger than she expected, probably in his mid-thirties. She had to admit he looked kind of cute with that lock of hair that kept falling into his eyes. And what eyes he had! She felt she was staring into the depths of the ocean. She'd have to be careful around him, she thought.

"So, Ms. 'not officially from the CDC'," he began. "What do you want from me?"

Cara blinked in surprise. She hadn't expected him to be so direct. So much for small talk. She took a breath. "My name is Cara, and I've been working at the CDC for a couple of months. I'm here in D.C. for the National Conference on Addiction."

"I'm well aware of that conference," he said curtly. "There's big money riding on the decisions made there."

"Yes, there is, and that's why I'm there. I'm presenting data on alcohol and drug abuse in teens to help develop a national curriculum on suicide prevention." She paused, and he motioned for her to continue. "I was working in the CDC library a few weeks ago and came across three references to internal papers by CDC researchers connecting suicide to gambling addiction. I wanted to pursue that line of research, but when I asked to see the original articles, my boss blocked me. In very direct terms, she told me those documents were off limits and I shouldn't look for them." She paused again, waiting for him to pick up the thread.

He said, "This is all off the record, correct?" Cara nodded. "Let me guess... one of those documents referenced my name, right?" Cara nodded again.

"Why the secrecy?" she asked. "My boss told me all research into gambling addiction is off limits."

Ron gave a wan smile. "Your boss... let me guess. Is she Gloria Spiegelman, by any chance?" Cara's eyes widened in surprise. His smile broadened. "Is she still summoning workers to her office by writing 'pls see me' on post-it notes?"

Cara laughed. "Not post-it notes, but texts. I have more of those summons on my phone than I can count right now."

"Oh, so she's graduated to the age of technology. Good for her!"

"So, you worked there, right?" she said, leaning forward. "And you wrote those papers?"

He fixed his gaze on her, his deep blue eyes burning into her. "Let me tell you something straight, Cara. Yes, I worked there. And yes, I wrote those papers. But that is as far as this goes. You are entering some extremely dangerous territory here. Follow Gloria's advice. Stop looking into this and forget about it."

She sat back. "But why?"

"Trust me, if you continue this line of inquiry, it will be career suicide. There's no good end in sight."

"I don't understand..." she began.

"Listen," he continued. "The gambling industry is one of the biggest industries in the world. We're talking multi-billions of dollars. There's a great deal of money in Washington D.C., and legions of people who are not afraid to use their power to protect that money. People love gambling. Politicians love gambling. Right now, we have several prominent senators who own casinos. You are up against some of the most powerful and influential people in the world."

Cara was quiet for a moment. She thought of her father, of Patrick, and all the other victims of this scourge. "My father was a gambling addict and died of suicide. My best friend growing up was a gambling addict and died of suicide just a few weeks ago. And, I had a boyfriend in college who died by suicide and may have been a gambling addict as well. At first, I wondered if it was a coincidence, and then, two weeks ago, I came across the title of your paper indicating a correlation. If there's a link and you've documented it, I want access to that. This is important information. We spend billions of dollars educating students about the dangers of drug and alcohol addiction and the connection to suicide. Why should gambling addiction be any different?"

"Look, Cara," said Ron quietly, locking his eyes on hers. "I'm sorry about your dad and your friend. I truly am. But there is nothing you or I can do to change that or stop this. Laws don't govern our country; greed and money do.

And the sooner you understand that and move on, the better."

Cara shook her head in denial. "I don't understand how gambling has stayed out of the public eye. Where's the education about it? There are so many programs for drug and alcohol abuse, but very few of them involve gambling addiction."

Ron continued staring at her for a long moment, his eyes boring into her as he considered what to say next. His stare totally unnerved her. "I'll tell you what. I have some information that will help you understand what you're up against. You need to see what a quagmire this is and why you should stop pursuing it."

She held her breath, waiting for him to continue, as he paused and stared into space. When he spoke, his voice was rough.

"I worked at the CDC with another colleague, Al Lawdly. We did some retrospective studies linking gambling addiction to suicide prior to the development of online gambling platforms, and then showed how the rise of online gambling correlated with a sharp increase in suicide among 20 to 25-year-olds."

Cara stared at him, openmouthed. *So there is a correlation,* she thought. It wasn't just a coincidence, and hearing him say it made it even more real. She leaned forward, hungering for more.

For a moment, he seemed lost in his memories. She noticed he gripped his coffee cup tighter as he continued. "We published some preliminary reports and intended to pursue this line of research, but within weeks of it going public, they shut us down. Apparently, the gambling lobbyists in D.C. bent the ears of some prominent senators, and they cut off all funding for our research."

He sat back with a half-laugh, letting go of the coffee cup. "I can still remember being summoned into Gloria's office with a 'pls see me' post-it note. She screamed at us: *'What the hell do you think you're doing? Who do you think pays your salaries?'*" Cara suppressed a laugh at his imitation of Gloria's voice.

"Since the government funds the CDC, they banned us from researching anything related to this, but not before Al uncovered some pretty damning evidence of a few illegal scams. Unfortunately, though, Al wouldn't share that evidence with anyone, not even me. He wasn't ready, he said, though he was certain that when the time was right, his disclosures would cripple the industry."

Cara's pulse quickened. Finally, she felt like she was getting some answers and had an ally.

"For reasons I could never understand, Al trusted Gloria far more than he should have. He had a habit of overestimating people's good intentions, or maybe it was underestimating their vices. He trusted Gloria enough to disclose some of what he knew, and the unfortunate result was he and I were both fired and given a hefty severance package, in return for our promise to drop this line of research completely."

"So... you caved," said Cara slowly.

"In a manner of speaking, yes," agreed Ron. "Though we had little choice."

"That's not true! What they did was criminal! It was blackmail!"

"Whoa, hold on a minute, Cara. There's more to this story." He paused again, gathering his thoughts. He ran his hand through his hair.

"Sorry," said Cara. "I didn't mean to jump all over you. I'm just angry they mistreated you."

"They did," Ron agreed, "and we weren't happy about it, but we were relieved to get away from there. We didn't completely cave. Yes, we accepted their deal, but we continued our research privately, figuring we could do it on our own. Once we left the CDC, we believed, mistakenly, we were off everyone's radar. That turned out to be a huge miscalculation on our part." He became quiet again.

"Al moved to California, and for a few months we corresponded by email. We were looking into online gambling specifically, trying to put together who the big players were. We were worried about a new online platform being developed by some of these companies."

Abruptly, he stopped and brought his hands to his face, fists against his mouth, closing his eyes. When he looked up a moment later, Cara saw tears had formed.

"I'm sorry," he said, his voice cracking. "It hurts to remember." He took a deep breath before continuing. "About six months into our work, I received an email from Al's wife, Jeanine." His voice caught again, and he cleared his throat. "Al was in a horrific car accident and hospitalized in critical condition. He survived another three weeks after that."

For a moment, his entire body shook. Cara sat in silence. She was familiar enough with grief in her own life to know when someone needed space. Finally, he found the strength to continue. "For much of that time, he was in a medically induced coma, but he had a few lucid moments at the end. He told Jeanine he thought someone had sabotaged his car, and he believed it was because of the work he and I were doing. There were documents he wanted me to have. She found some of them, but unfortunately, not all. He wanted me to know certain things, but he also told her to warn me to stay away from it."

"And did you stay away after that?"

Ron hesitated. "I did, for a while. I built a life here and attempted to stay out of view. What they did to Al was a warning to me. If I continued this line of research, my fate would be the same. I knew that."

"You're still working on this, aren't you?" Cara whispered.

Again Ron hesitated, then nodded. "It's a private project, one that I'm doing on my own time. Because of what happened to Al, I'm incredibly careful about how I gather information and have shown it to no one." His eyes drilled into her. "I repeat—no one. Sometimes, I'm not even sure why I'm still pursuing it. I know it's foolish. Likely it will go nowhere, but for Al's sake, I feel like I have to do something."

"I understand that," said Cara. "And I want to work with you. I told you, I've lost three people in my life to suicide, and I know at least two of them were gambling addicts. If there's a correlation, it needs to be investigated."

Ron cocked his head and looked at her. "I guess I didn't do a very good job of dissuading you," he said.

"Quite the contrary," she replied. "Now that I know the history, I want to work on it more than ever. Can you tell me a little of what you've found in the last few years?"

Ron shook his head. "I've told you as much as I can and more than I should have." His gaze hardened.

Cara glanced at her phone, realizing she needed to return to the symposium before her absence was noted. She didn't want to do anything that might draw the ire of her boss. She still held out hope of working with Ron, but recognized she couldn't push him right now.

"Well, you've given me lots to think about," she said.

Ron was suddenly all business. "We should leave separately in case anyone is watching. I don't know if the CDC still has me on their radar, but I can't take that chance. You go first and make sure no one is following you."

Cara stared at him. Hadn't her friend Em told her to be careful as well—that it sounded like people at the CDC didn't want her pursuing this? She felt nervous, yet gratified to be getting some answers. Added to that, she felt a personal pull toward Ron—a strong connection, the likes of which she hadn't felt with another person for a long time. *I wish I could see him again, even on a non-professional level.*

She had to give it one more chance. "Are you sure I can't see what you've uncovered in your research?"

He ran his hand through his shock of hair, once again fighting with himself. Turning away, he shook his head. "I can't drag anyone else into this."

But as she rose from the table, he turned back and looked straight at her with those piercing eyes. "Listen, I told you all this because I wanted you to recognize how dangerous it is. Al was murdered because he pursued it. But I can see you're not backing down. I need to think about this for a few days, but maybe I'll let you see some of my work. Once you're back in Atlanta, go to a post office there and sign up for a P.O. box. Buy a burner phone as well and send me a text with the P.O. box number." He took the napkin from under his coffee cup and scribbled a phone number on it.

"This is a phone I rarely use. Don't contact me in any other way. I don't know for sure if the CDC is still watching me, but I can't take any chances. If they discover I'm talking to a CDC employee, both of us could be in danger. I'm not kidding about this."

Cara smiled, pleased he was giving her an opening. "Now go," he commanded. "Before we both get into more trouble than you could imagine. My best advice is still to drop it all and forget about it."

Like hell I will, thought Cara as she stood up. *No way am I going to drop it.*

And that's exactly what she told Em when they got together for dinner that evening. With one more day left in the conference, Cara was now itching to get back to the CDC and try to uncover more information.

"The nerve of him, telling me to drop it and forget about it! This is personal for me. My dad and Patrick were victims, not statistics. I suspected a connection between online gambling and suicide when I learned the truth about both of them. And then, when Gloria reacted so strongly, I sensed a cover-up of some sort. Now that I have an inkling of what's gone on, I can't let it go. He's deep into this, and I'm sure he could use help."

Em already knew Ron had worked at the CDC, so Cara didn't see any reason to keep that a secret, and she thought Em should know about Al as well. Though Ron had asked her if the conversation was "off the record," she trusted Em not to betray any secrets.

Em peered at her friend. As roommates for four years, they had shared a lot together and had a deep connection. Cara was impulsive and stubborn, and once she got an idea in her head, it was tough to change her mind. Em knew what it was like to be ruled by passion in that way, yet she was aware of the danger it posed. She was also well-versed in the Washington D.C. political scene and worried Cara might not realize the enormity of what she was up against. She hesitated, knowing she needed to be careful with her words. How could she protect her friend without alienating her?

"It sounds like he's gathered a lot of information and he's being cautious," she began. "Maybe you should follow his lead. Let things settle for a few days before doing anything rash. I mean, you just started at this job, and if you charge full speed ahead trying to look up things against your boss's orders, you may very well end up out on your ass."

"I know you're right, but it pisses me off!" said Cara. "I took this job because I wanted to develop programs to educate kids about some of the triggers of suicide. The CDC has records documenting a correlation between online gambling and suicide, and they're hiding it. How can I go back there and not explore it further?"

"Think about it, Cara. If Ron includes you in his work, your position at the CDC might prove extremely valuable to him. Your job may be your key to pursuing this line of research, but first, you need to establish yourself as trustworthy. Be a model employee. Do your work and show Gloria you won't question her. In the meantime, I can do more background checking on this guy Ron and his partner Al. At least I can verify his story for you."

"You'll do that?" Cara asked.

Em nodded. "As long as you promise not to stir things up right now."

Though Cara felt a bit deflated, she thought she could play along for a short while. Em was right. Maybe this job could be an important tool. She looked at her friend, grateful for the help. Another ally, she thought. "Okay, but I am going to get a P.O. box and send the information to Ron. Maybe he won't respond, but at least I'll feel like I'm doing something."

Nine

BACK IN ATLANTA, AFTER a whirlwind couple of days at the conference, Cara reflected on what both Ron and Em said. Maybe she should bide her time for a few days and try to stay on Gloria's good side. As much as she didn't want to, it seemed the prudent thing to do. Sighing, she got into bed and glanced at her bedside table. The novel she purchased a few weeks ago but hadn't yet started was calling to her. She picked it up, hoping to get lost in a fictional romance, when her phone rang. Her mother calling. She debated not answering, but then decided it would be better to deal with whatever it was right away rather than put her mom off.

"Hi, Mom!" mustering as much cheer as she could.

"Oh, Cara! I'm so glad I caught you! I hope I'm not disturbing anything..."

Cara heard the tension in Sally's voice. "No, I was just sitting down with a new book. What's up? Is everything okay?"

"It's your brother. I'm so worried about him. I don't know what to do."

"What's going on with him now?"

"It's not him at the moment. Oh, this is so complicated! I hate to burden you with this, but I have no one else to turn to." Sally's voice cracked. Cara sensed she was on the verge of tears.

"Mom, slow down, and tell me what's going on," Cara said calmly.

Sally took a deep breath before plunging forward. "Well, you know Brady's 18th birthday is coming up next month, right?"

"Of course," answered Cara. "It's a big milestone."

"Yes, well today, I met with my accountant and the estate attorney to talk about Brady's trust fund. Your dad set it up to go directly to Brady, but as a surviving spouse, I hoped to have more control over it so Brady wouldn't be able to use it for gambling. Today, I found out it's all his, and there's nothing I can do about it." She was openly crying now.

"I *know* he's gambling—just a little right now, but I remember how it was with your father for years. This could destroy him, and I don't know how to talk to him about it! I'm so afraid of driving him away if I say the wrong thing. How can I get him to see that he may have a problem? I don't-"

"Mom, slow down a minute." Cara interrupted. She felt a heaviness in the pit of her stomach. She thought back to when she received all that money. For a brief time, she had entertained thoughts of using it for travel after graduation from college, but then she met with a financial advisor who showed her some sobering statistics. People who inherited a large amount of money at a young age often ended up destitute later in life. He recommended she get herself established with a career first and not touch the money for at least five years. She took his advice and invested it, figuring the time would come when she would know what to do with it. That was a year ago, and now, though she could access the money in an emergency, she felt proud to be supporting herself, and she considered that money off-limits unless she was desperate.

But Brady was different. He didn't view money the same way she did. Her mom was right. He might very well gamble a large lump sum of money and blow through it quickly. Even if he met with a financial advisor as she had, he probably wouldn't take that advice to heart. Brady needed more information about their dad's history.

"Mom, listen. I agree this could be a problem for Brady. We have to tell him the truth about Dad. He needs to understand he's at risk. You can't keep this secret from him any longer."

"I'm not sure, Cara. I'm so afraid of disappointing him. He idolized your father, and I don't want to destroy that."

"I idolized him as well, and I still think it's better to know the truth!" Cara exclaimed. "Eventually, Brady's going to find out. And he, of all people, needs to know—if only to keep him from going down the same path! Addiction is hereditary, Mom! Forewarned is forearmed. Brady needs the truth, and he needs it soon." Cara could hear her mom's muffled sobs.

"You may be right, but he and I are not communicating well right now and I can't tell him. Even if I could, he wouldn't believe me."

Annoyed, Cara spit back, "So, you want to dump this on me? Make me take the heat?"

"I didn't mean..." Sally cried openly now. "I don't know what to do! And I'm scared!"

Cara softened. "Look, Mom, I'll try. Last month, when I was home, Brady and I chatted a little about gambling. I'm overdue to call him. I'll see if he's free to talk over the weekend. As long as I have your permission to tell him everything. And I mean everything. No more secrecy, okay?"

"Okay, if you think it's best. I'm sorry to put you in the middle of this, but he'll listen to you more than me."

"Mom, it's all right. I want to help, and I know Brady will appreciate hearing the truth." *At least I hope so,* she thought as she hung up the phone. What could she say to him? He needed to know about their dad, and he needed to be aware of the dangers of compulsive gambling. It would help if she knew more about it as well. As far as she was concerned, knowledge and information were power, and if she knew more, she would be in a better position to help her brother. She could start by following up with Ron and getting a post office box and burner phone.

She again recalled her own experience receiving that money. It was a direct gift from her dad and felt sacred. She couldn't just spend it on anything. Surely Brady could understand that! She texted her brother, asking him if he had time for a video chat over the weekend, then noticed the book she had been about to start. That felt like ages ago, and there was no way now she could concentrate. For the first time in her life, she was truly angry at her dad. He deserted them and left a colossal mess for them to clean up. What was going through his head when he decided she and Brady should each get such a large sum of unrestricted money? Did the possibility of passing the "gambling gene" down to either of his children ever cross his mind?

RON WAS ANGRY. HOW could he have let his guard down so easily? When he returned to campus after meeting with Cara, he was summoned to the Dean's office.

"Where were you for the last hour?" Dean Richards asked.

Ron looked at the Dean in surprise. "I went to lunch with a friend. Is that not allowed here?"

"It depends on who that friend is. When she is an investigative reporter for the *Post*, that may indeed be a problem."

Ron's mouth dropped open. For a moment, he was stunned into silence. "You must be mistaken," he breathed once he found his voice. "Whatever gave you that idea?"

"Sue, our receptionist, was so excited to have met Libby Lewis that she couldn't wait to tell me. I'm warning you, Hynes—you may have been here a while, but we don't want any adverse publicity at this school. What you do on your own time is your business, but if this institution is mentioned in the *Post*, that becomes our business, and your job may be on the line. Understand?"

"Look, there must be some mistake..." Ron began.

"Do you understand?" Dean Richards repeated.

Ron nodded numbly as he backed out of the office, feeling betrayed, bewildered, and foolish. Who had he met with? Was it Cara Davenport, CDC statistician, or Libby Lewis, premier investigative reporter at the *Washington Post*? He needed to find out and had no way of contacting her. He decided to wait until she texted him, if indeed she would.

Did he say anything she could publish in the paper? If she were a reporter, would she publish a story without corroborating it? He didn't think so, but still, he worried, and as he recalled their meeting, his frustration grew. *Why had he opened up to her?* For the first time in four years, he had exposed some of his deepest secrets. He had allowed himself to trust another person, telling her things he had never admitted to anyone else, and now he wondered if that was a mistake.

For the next three days, he replayed their conversation in his mind. He tried to remember what he said to her, but couldn't recall anything specific. In his mind, all he saw was her face and the tears in her eyes when she talked of both her father and her best friend. He felt strangely drawn to the woman who called herself Cara and realized he didn't want to believe she betrayed him.

The following day, he received a text on his burner phone: "**3747**." *So, she was following up. That must be* *her P.O. box number.* It was time to verify her identity. Using his burner phone, he texted a coded message to his friend Gerry asking for a call back. Gerry worked in Human Resources at the CDC and had supplied him with a few snippets of key information since he had left the organization. He hated to involve former friends at the CDC, but he saw no other choice. He needed to find out who he had met with.

Although both he and Gerry had unregistered phones that were not connected to the internet, Ron felt only moderately secure. Gerry had an effervescent personality, and Ron worried his talkative manner might be a problem. It wouldn't surprise Ron if word got back to others that he and Gerry spoke. It was vital to keep this as casual as possible.

He was still planning his strategy when Gerry called. "It's good to hear from you, Ron!" said Gerry in his usual booming voice. "What can I do for you?"

Ron wished Gerry would be a little quieter and hoped he wasn't in earshot of anyone else. "Thanks for talking to me. I'm on a fact-finding mission for my niece. She's a recent college graduate looking for a job, and I told her I would check to see if anyone in my old department is hiring right now. She's interested in curriculum development, where I worked. Are there any openings there?"

"Your old stomping grounds?" Gerry asked. "Nah... not in that department. I can tell you right off the top of my head because those were our most recent new hires. Henry Ives and Cara Davenport. I remember Davenport specifically because soon after she started, she took a two-day unpaid leave break to go to a funeral in her hometown."

Ron's ears perked up. What had Cara said to him? *"My best friend growing up was a gambling addict and died by suicide just a few weeks ago."* This was proving to be easier than he had thought. There was no way Libby Lewis, an investigative reporter, would have made that up. Still, he had to wonder why Cara used that name. And Henry Ives sounded familiar. When had he heard that name?

It amazed Ron that Gerry was still at his job in Human Resources, with the way he casually dropped names and information. Ron reminded himself he needed to be careful not to reveal too much, but so far, he felt the conversation was above suspicion.

Gerry rambled on about how the direction of the agency had changed in the last few years, and how difficult it was to keep up with all the personnel issues that were popping up. "I've been at this agency for 25 years now, through four different administrations. Never has it been in as much turmoil as it is today. Even during the height of the pandemic, we had better leadership! You're lucky you got out when you did. Seems like every day a new project is being cut from the budget. We're laying off far more people than we're hiring, that's for sure. Tell your niece to look elsewhere."

"That's too bad. I'll let her know. Hopefully, things will smooth out soon for you."

"I hope so, too! Meanwhile, I just have to learn to live with the chaos. I sure miss our basketball games. Ever since you and Al left, it just hasn't been the same. And Carmen. I especially miss him."

"I miss those games, too," said Ron with a smile. He had fond memories of many intra-agency games, which had been one of Al's major contributions. Al and Carmen, the CDC librarian, had started the league to help develop better relations among the various departments, and it worked beautifully for a while. But then, Ron and Al were let go, Carmen retired, and the league apparently fell apart.

Better to keep the past buried. "I'd best be going now. Appreciate you talking to me. I'll let my niece know there's no job there for her right now. Thanks again." He clicked off the phone, feeling a little more confident of Cara Davenport's identity, but he still needed to be 100% sure. And the mention of Carmen gave him an idea.

♦♥♣♠

I LOVED YOU! YOU waited patiently for me to grow up, promised me the world. And I believed you. I couldn't wait to turn eighteen and play at a casino. Enough of this small-town shit. I was ready for the big leagues! Nothing was going to stop me!

Ten

Saturday morning, Cara prepared a cup of tea, taking a moment to get comfortable on her sofa before calling her brother. She feared this would be a tough conversation. Since their father passed, she and Brady rarely talked about him. It hurt too much. Today, however, she needed to confront that pain and hoped Brady could accept what she intended to tell him. Mustering her courage, she punched in his name on her phone. A moment later, she saw his face on the screen.

"Hi, Sis," he answered cheerily. He had a blue bandana tied around his chestnut hair, enhancing the tint of his eyes. Once again, she was struck by his resemblance to their father. She managed a quivery smile.

"What's the big occasion?" he asked. She had texted him saying she wanted to talk about something important, and told him to plan on it taking some time. Now she felt awkward and wondered if that had been the best strategy.

She wasn't ready to plunge into it yet. *Start with small talk*.

"Hey," she answered, dragging her fingers through her hair and rubbing the back of her neck. "We haven't spoken in a while, and I wanted to know how you're doing."

"I'm good," he replied. Cara was glad to see he looked upbeat. "You know, not much changes around here. I put in my college application and finished midterms at school, so that's a relief."

"Do you have any plans for your birthday?" she asked.

Brady hesitated. "Actually, I do, but you probably won't approve...."

No time like the present, thought Cara. Aloud, she said, "Let me guess—you're going to gamble at a casino since you'll finally be old enough."

"Busted!" said Brady with a big smile. "There's a new casino called 'Pair o' Dice' and I've heard it's awesome. Dad used to go there, back when it was named Nuggets. Some other company, Majority Rules, bought them out and rebranded it. A bunch of friends are taking me. Please don't tell Mom. She'd chain me to the bed if she knew."

"She would, and with good reason. That's sort of what I need to talk to you about," Cara said carefully, biting her lip.

"Cara, I don't need you to lecture me..." began Brady.

Cara cut him off. "I'm not planning on lecturing you. But there are some things you need to know. Family things. It may help you understand why Mom has been so controlling lately."

"Like what?"

She took a deep breath. "It concerns Dad. His... history. I learned a few things recently and I think you should know them, too. I'm not sure how to tell you all this...." She paused for a moment and pursed her lips. "Oh, hell, I may as well just dive in! Do you remember how Dad was with us when we were kids?"

"What do you mean?" asked Brady, narrowing his eyes defensively. He didn't particularly want to talk about their dad. The loss still felt raw.

"I mean, what he liked to do with us."

"Like playing games? Cards, that sort of thing?" he asked.

"Exactly! You mentioned that place, Nuggets. Do you recall him taking us there when you were really young?"

"Sure!" exclaimed Brady, glad to focus on a happy memory. "It was awesome! We walked in and it was like a different world, with lights flashing, bells ringing, and whistles blowing."

"What else do you remember about that trip?"

"Not much," Brady admitted. "I thought it was the coolest place."

"Think hard, Brady!" she commanded, wishing she could conjure up the memories for him. He *had* to remember. It was the only way she could think of to get him to pay attention to what she needed to tell him.

"I remember going for pizza and humongous ice cream sundaes after," Brady said slowly. "And I guess I remember him telling us to forget about it. I remember that because a few days later, I asked him something about it, and he got mad at me."

"Yes, that's it! Close your eyes for a moment. I want to fill in the blanks for you a bit." Brady did as she asked, squeezing his eyes closed while still keeping a smile on his face. Cara struggled to keep her voice even as she continued. "You were seven years old, and I was twelve. He took us to a casino one afternoon, and *he left us in the car* for three hours while he gambled. He *abandoned* us after saying that he'd be back in a flash. We had to go into the casino because you needed to pee. If that hadn't happened, Lord knows how long we would have waited in that car. And then he took us for ice cream and told us to keep quiet about it."

No longer smiling, he opened his eyes. "Okay, so? Yeah, I remember being in the car for a while, but I don't think it was three hours..."

"It was. I was wearing the new watch I had gotten for my birthday, and I kept checking it. You were seven years old and barely knew how to tell time! What he did was wrong on so many levels!"

"Maybe," Brady admitted, with a pained look on his face. "So, why are you telling me this?"

Cara took another breath and again ran her hands through her hair. "Dad was a gambling addict." The words tasted like acid on her tongue, but she pressed on. "He spent a lot of time in casinos when we were growing up. All those times when he disappeared for a couple days without telling us where he was going? Gambling. And according to mom, several years ago, he starting gambling online and that was what killed him."

"What are you talking about? Gambling can't kill you! He died of a heart attack!" Brady stared at her. His eyes, so like their dad's, felt like a dagger going straight into her heart. She hated what she had to say next.

"Well, that's part two of what I need to tell you. It wasn't a heart attack. That's why the insurance is tied up." She paused. "He actually died by suicide."

"He *what*?" Cara saw Brady almost drop the phone.

"You heard me. He took some drug to mimic a heart attack, but it was officially ruled a suicide."

"Why?" asked Brady incredulously as he juggled the phone back into position. "Why would he do that? He never seemed depressed."

"That's not true, and you know it as much as I do!" she shot back. "Remember the last two Christmases when he never came out of his room?" Brady's breath caught, and Cara watched his face sag as the memories took root.

She wiped the tears from her eyes. *This really sucks.* "Dad was a gambling addict and had massive debts he couldn't pay back. He took out a bunch of credit cards in his and Mom's names and maxed them all out, leaving Mom with a ton of debt. I imagine he felt embarrassed and trapped and saw no other way out." She waited a moment to let that sink in.

"*That's* why I told you to back off the gambling. That's why Mom has been so tight with money and pushing you to get a regular job. She didn't want to worry you, but I—well, both of us actually—felt it was better if you knew. Mom was afraid to tell you because she knew you worshiped him, and she didn't want to burst that bubble. But Brady, you need to know the truth. You need to know he had a disease, and it's often a hereditary disease." Cara stopped, wondering if she had gone too far.

Brady was silent. Cara saw the muscles of his face twitch as he struggled to absorb this information, much as she had done a few weeks ago. "I don't believe you!" he yelled. "How would you know? You're just making this up...."

"Mom knows. She knew for a long time and denied it while he was still alive. She tried to shield us from it as much as possible. But the credit card debts are real. She can manage if you both tighten up a bit, but we can't pretend our way out of this."

Brady turned off his video, leaving her staring at a black square. Cara stopped, listening to the silence at the other end of the line. "You still with me?" she asked gently. Faintly, she heard Brady sniffling.

"Yeah," he whispered. "I'm here. This is a lot to take in."

Cara steeled herself before continuing. "There's one more thing I need to talk to you about."

"What else? Haven't you dropped enough bombs for one day?" accused Brady as he turned the video back on.

"Just listen, okay. This is important." She paused once again, taking one more breath to collect her thoughts. "When you turn 18, you're scheduled to inherit a large sum of money from a trust Dad set up years ago."

Brady's ears perked up. "Seriously? So, what's the problem? I thought you said Mom has no money."

"The problem is the money is going directly to you and it's completely unrestricted. That means you can do whatever you want with it. On your 18th birthday, it's yours to save or to spend. You alone get to decide."

"Do you know how much it is?" asked Brady.

"$100,000," she answered.

Brady whistled as his eyes widened. "Are you sure?"

"I am, and that's why I'm talking to you right now. Mom worries you might go down a similar path to Dad and not manage it properly. She thinks it could be more of a curse to you than a blessing. She knows you've been playing lots of poker with friends, and she's concerned you'll gamble this money and end up with a full-blown addiction that will plague you for the rest of your life."

Brady was silent. Once again, Cara felt his struggle to process all this. "Wow. I had no idea. I don't understand, though. Where did this money come from? I thought you said he left Mom nothing."

"Dad set up two trusts a long time ago when he was on a winning streak—one for me and one for you—and he made them iron-clad so nothing could be changed. He did it all without consulting Mom, so she never knew about them until after he passed."

"So you got money as well? How come you never told me?"

"I was over 18 when Dad died and got mine immediately. At the time, I didn't tell you because I felt a little guilty. You still had to wait another year. Also, I wasn't sure what to do with it and was afraid if I told anyone, I'd get too many opinions about how to handle it."

"What *did* you do with it?" asked Brady.

"I met with a financial planner and invested it so I wouldn't be able to get to it easily in the short term."

"You mean you didn't spend any of it?"

"Not a penny. One day, I'll use it for something major—I don't know, maybe a down payment on a house, or to start a business. When the time is right, I'll know. But that time isn't now. The money came from Dad, and it's sacred to me." She paused, wondering if she was getting too preachy. She wanted Brady to be like her, she realized. But he wasn't. She reminded herself he didn't view money the same way she did. *What would her dad say to him right now?*

"The money is yours, but I doubt Dad intended you to blow it on gambling. Remember how withdrawn he was the last few years—the holidays when he stayed in his room for days on end? Would he have wanted you to end up like that? You're young enough to have some choices in your life. Don't make the same mistakes he made! At least put some of it aside."

Again, Brady turned off his video and was silent. Cara wondered if he was still on the line. She strained her ears and thought she could hear him crying softly. Finally, he mumbled, "Mom asked you to talk to me, right?"

"She did. She said the two of you barely speak to each other, and she felt uncomfortable telling you all this. I agreed to talk to you as long as there were no more secrets about Dad. Go easy on her, okay? She's doing the best she can. She wants what's best for you, even though it might not look like that right now. And keep me posted how things are going. Please?"

"Okay. I'll try. But you sure hit me with a lot all at once."

"I know. I wish it didn't have to be this way. Promise me you'll use your head?"

"Sure... whatever that means." Brady replied. He turned his video back on. Cara noticed his face was puffy.

"It means you won't take the money and spend it on a crazy gambling spree. It means you'll talk to Mom. And maybe it means you'll meet with my financial advisor. I'll text you his information."

"Sure, whatever," repeated Brady.

Cara wanted to say more, but realized her brother was pulling away. He needed time and space to sort it out. So much for not wanting to preach to him. She sighed. "Listen, I love you, little brother. I'm always here for you. Let's talk next week, okay?"

At least she had started the conversation. All she could do now was keep the lines of communication open and hope he wouldn't go into denial about it.

THE PHONE CALL DRAINED Cara almost to the point of numbness. *If only I could do more for Brady!* She sighed, realizing it was up to him to make his own choices.

Perhaps, though, there was something else useful she could do. She had told Ron that researching the connection between online gambling and suicide felt personal to her, and she wanted to learn more. Now seemed like a good time to follow that path. She picked up the go-phone she'd purchased after returning home from the conference. She'd only used it once to text Ron her post office box number. The post office would still be open long enough for her to walk there and check the box. Maybe he had sent her something. At the very least, the walk would help clear her head.

She felt a little foolish. Who purchased P.O. boxes and burner phones? Only people who were trying to avoid the law or hide things. That certainly wasn't her, though she had to admit she had done a few things lately that might put her in that category—sneaking around at work to get information, meeting Ron, and pursuing this investigation against the clear directive of her boss being on top of the list.

As she walked down the street, she wondered if Ron would respond. She hoped so. Given Gloria's attitude when she searched for a few papers at the library, she doubted she could learn much from the CDC archives without Ron's help. She needed to see what he had been doing since he left there. Added to that, he was pretty cute, and she wanted to see him again. She felt a brief flutter in her stomach at that thought, causing her to pause. If she was attracted to him, could she work with him on a professional level? The more she thought about it, the more confused she became. How much of her desire to pursue this research was because of her interest in learning more about online gambling, and how much was her personal attraction? She thought back to their meeting and felt certain he was drawn to her as well. But was that real, or just her imagination? *Why was this so complicated?*

The fresh air and walk to the post office helped her stop thinking about Brady, but now thoughts of Ron consumed her. She opened the mailbox, surprised to see a small white envelope with no return address. *What did you expect? A love letter?* Gingerly, she opened it to reveal a typewritten message. "Who the hell are you? If you value your life, call me as soon as you get this! And make sure it's a secure phone. We need to talk!"

Cara stared at the paper. It was certainly not an endearing message. *So much for him being attracted to me.* She looked again at the message. Why would he ask who she was? And what did he mean by "if you value your life?" It sounded like he was angry with her or trying to intimidate her. She recalled his initial reluctance to share information with her. It had not been easy for him, but she thought that by the end of the meeting, he had resolved that.

She sighed. Maybe she should tear up the note and forget this whole venture. But then again, he said to call him and that they needed to talk. At least she could give him the opportunity to explain.

After a few more moments of battling with herself, she decided she had to find out what was going on with him. She sat on a picnic bench overlooking the city and punched in his phone number. Predictably, she got his voice mail. Short and to the point. "Leave a message."

She debated texting him, but his note said call, so she left a brief message: "Ron, this is Cara. I have a new phone. Your note said to call. You can reach me at this number." That seemed innocent enough, she thought. The response was immediate as a text:

"r u alone?"

"Yes," she replied.

Her phone rang. "Hi," she said, trying to sound calm, though her pulse quickened.

"Tell me the truth," the voice on the other end demanded. "Who are you?"

"I told you, I'm Cara Davenport," she answered, unsure where his anger was coming from.

"Why the hell did you tell the receptionist at the school you were Libby Lewis?"

Shit! She had completely forgotten about that. How could she have been so stupid? No wonder he was upset.

Sheepishly, she said, "Oh... oops! I guess I screwed up. I wasn't sure if you had left the CDC on bad terms, and I was afraid you wouldn't talk to me if she announced me to you. I got flustered, so I said the first thing that came to mind."

"But why her?" he demanded again. "You know she's a reporter with an enormous nose, don't you?"

"I do," Cara said slowly, wondering how much she should reveal. Em didn't want anyone to know about her dual identities. Libby was a pen name. This could get messy fast if she wasn't careful. "Look, Libby Lewis was a casual friend of mine from college, and I had just read one of her articles in the *Post*. It was the first name I thought of. I didn't mean any harm by it."

"Well, the receptionist went straight to the Dean, and he gave me a huge dressing-down. He hates publicity, especially if it shows up in the column of an investigative reporter. And I have to tell you, I was pretty angry as well. How do I know who you really are? I trusted you with some extremely sensitive information. If you want to work with me, we can't have any lies between us. I need your word on that."

"You have my word," said Cara, silently hanging onto the phrase *if you want to work with me....* "I promise you, I am Cara Davenport, and your secrets are safe with me. I want to work with you more than anything. It's personal for me. When we first met, I told you three people in my life died by suicide in the past three years. Two were gambling addicts for sure, and I suspect the other may have been as well. I have a younger brother at risk, and I worry he might become another statistic. Kids need information so they can make better choices. I want to provide that and change the way this entire industry operates, and from what you've told me, you do too."

"Cara, what I told you is you're being naïve if you think you can make a difference. You really should just hang up and forget about it." Cara blinked. She pictured him running his hands through his dark hair.

"I can't do that," she said, with measured deliberateness. "One way or another, I'm going to follow through with this. And to do that, I need information. Information you've spent the last five years collecting. At least let me see that."

Ron was quiet. "Okay," he said finally. "But before we go any further, I need to know with 100% certainty that you are who you say you are. I'm going to ask you a question that only a researcher at the CDC could answer: What's on the hallway wall outside the library?"

Cara laughed. How could she forget that? "You mean the creepy yellow graffiti? Carmen was here: 1994!" She was about to ask him if he knew who Carmen was, but then thought better of it. She could save that question for a future conversation.

"Okay, Ms. Davenport, I believe you. I'm trusting you're on my side and hope I'm not being naïve about this. Check your mailbox in a few days and make sure you're not being followed. I'll do my best to put out the fire you started here with the Dean."

"Thank you, and I promise—no more secrets." She clicked her burner phone off.

Eleven

THOUGH SHE WAS IMPATIENT, Cara forced herself to wait several days before returning to the post office. She grabbed the note saying she had received a package and fidgeted at the counter as the postal clerk retrieved it. The size of the box surprised her.

For a moment, she felt giddy, like a teenager opening a letter from her current crush. She tore open the box and found a metal safe with a combination lock and a post-it note stuck on top: *"Make sure you're alone and then text me for combo."* A bit deflated, she trudged the mile back to her apartment, cursing Ron as she lugged the heavy parcel.

Now, late at night and nestled alone in her apartment, she eagerly opened the safe. Inside was the report, along with a warning to keep it locked up whenever she wasn't reading it. This promised to be far better than the romance she had attempted to start last week. *He's trusting me with something he poured his heart and soul into*, she thought. She vowed not to take that trust lightly; she would absolutely keep the report locked in the safe unless she was reading it.

Despite the size of the box, the report was just twenty pages long. She flipped through it, then settled back with a yawn and started at page one, hoping his writing would be lively enough to keep her awake, and wondering what secrets it would reveal.

CONFIDENTIAL
Online Gambling:
Growth history and dangers of current practices
Prepared by R. C. Hynes
with posthumous contributions from A. J. Lawdly

History and Overview
1994: Birth of the industry

The Free Trade and Processing Act passed in Antigua and Barbuda granted licenses to companies wanting to start online casinos.

The same year I was born, thought Cara. *Same year Patrick was born. And Ben....*

She sat upright, no longer sleepy. Reading through this was better than drinking coffee. She pored over the description of how the ability to send and receive money through the internet allowed online gambling to evolve from simple amusement to multi-player games, themed slot machines, progressive jackpots, and live dealers in a very short span of time.

She gasped as she read that the estimated current value of the online gambling industry was over $50 billion, up from $30 billion five years ago, making it one of the fastest growing financial industries in the world. *How was it possible for an industry to grow so big in such a short time?*

The next page of the report answered her question. Online platforms with little government regulation fueled much of the growth. Children using their parent's credit cards, people gambling while drunk or under the influence of other drugs, and people moving quickly from one loss to another merely by switching sites were all problems which this industry exploited.

She pictured her dad, holed up in his home office on Christmas Day with his stack of credit cards, clicking around from one gambling site to another rather than joining his family. Her mom made excuses for him—told them his work stressed him out and they shouldn't disturb him. For a moment, she buried her head in her hands, letting the frustration and rage in those memories wash over her. She realized now—he loved gambling more than he loved her. But was that his fault?

Lack of government oversight allowed the industry to engage in many illicit practices, and online platforms made this easier. Cara shuddered as she read: **These sites use mind-controlling techniques to feed addiction, preying on the weaknesses of ordinary individuals to boost their profits.**

Ron detailed many of these practices, starting with the use of electronic cash, which disguised the actual value of money being gambled. He described a variety of devious methods used to drive people to gambling sites even if they were looking for other types of entertainment, and to keep clients there once they arrived. These included pop-up ads and embedded meta-tags, as well as misleading payout rates for new players, which spurred customers to play more games once they were on the site. Companies routinely provided practice or "demo" modes with increased odds of winning.

She read about online client tracking, and how gambling sites collected data on people to boost client retention. Every time a targeted customer turned on their computer or checked their phone, pop-up ads invited them to take part in the next big game, the next promotion or loyalty program. Cara could see how this would be impossible for a compulsive gambler to avoid, making it disastrous for them.

She felt a flutter of foreboding as she read of the use of Virtual Reality (VR) in online gambling platforms. She had seen news articles about VR recently, but she wasn't familiar with how it worked. While the technology was still in its infancy and currently required the user to invest in expensive equipment, Ron considered it the most frightening aspect of internet gambling. In his words: **As VR technology becomes more sophisticated, one can envision easily accessible Virtual Casinos in which players may struggle to differentiate between fantasy and reality. Given the highly addictive nature of gambling, this is an extremely dangerous use of a technology designed to trick the mind into believing things that are not real. Potentially, this could have a tremendous impact on suicide rates, especially among an already vulnerable population.**

Cara put the manuscript aside as the enormity of what Ron was suggesting hit her. The sights and sounds of the casino had captivated her young brother when he was just seven years old. Though he had assured her he didn't gamble online at all, it wouldn't take much for him to become hooked on an online experience, particularly if it mimicked the feel of a real casino.

Picking up the report again, she considered the connection between online gambling and suicide. Ron laid out a clear correlation, citing multiple studies. Perhaps the inability to distinguish between fantasy and reality made some people more susceptible to suicidal thoughts. *Was that a factor in her dad's death? Did he get so deep into the online experience that he forgot about his family and his life in the real world?* She didn't know if she'd be able to forgive herself for having missed all these signs.

Shaking her head sadly, she forged ahead with reading, despite the late hour. She couldn't stop now. Ron turned the spotlight on the industry leaders: smart, ruthless entrepreneurs who recognized the upcoming boom and took advantage of technology in novel ways. Many were business majors in college or studied math and economics with a focus on statistics. In contrast to the typical mobsters or gangsters of old, they understood business, had clearly established business plans, and were not afraid to exploit new technology to its fullest.

They catapulted the industry to a whole new level, capturing the interest of Geraldine Major, owner of Majority Rules, and arguably the most influential business owner in the casino world. Ms. Major, originally from California and now living in Gibraltar, inherited several brick-and-mortar casinos with the brand "Pair o' Dice" from her father in 2012. Within

five years of her father's death, she acquired a few new casinos, then turned her attention to building her business online. However, she has kept several casinos to showcase her new Virtual Reality technology. She is currently using these physical spaces to draw more clients to her online platforms. Her newest Virtual Reality platform "Pairadice" is due to go live in six months.

Wasn't "Pair o' Dice" the name of the place Brady said he was going to for his birthday celebration? Had he gone already? Probably. His birthday was two days ago and, with a twinge of guilt, she realized she hadn't talked to him since. She made a mental note to check in with him first thing in the morning and turned her attention back to the report. There was one short section remaining:

The Gambling Industry Research Institute

This organization embodies the heart of the problem of online gambling. Established four years ago by a group of online casino owners led by Geraldine Major, it purportedly focuses on providing public education about gambling. In reality, it is a sham organization, modeled after the Tobacco Industry Research Committee of the 1950s. Their mission: to delude the public into believing gambling is a non-addictive, fun pastime that can—and should—be enjoyed to promote relaxation and ease stress in one's life. During the past four years, this institute has propagated hundreds of ads relating to the general health and well-being aspects of gam-

bling. The perpetrators of this misinformation have portrayed online gambling as equivalent to spending a relaxing day at the beach, or indulging oneself at a resort, and they have repeatedly touted it as "better than drinking alcohol." Their ad campaign espouses the health benefits of gambling while downplaying or completely ignoring the dangers, particularly the connection between online gambling and increased su icide rates.

Cara paused. Hadn't Gloria mentioned that group? She distinctly recalled Gloria telling her that gambling addiction was under the jurisdiction of the Gambling Industry Research Institute. She picked up the report and continued reading. The remainder implicated some of the highest-ranking government officials as complicit in these advertising campaigns. It was a scathing attack on the U.S. government and would devastate many officials if released. For sure, it was a huge political quagmire and could be career-ending for some. She now understood why the CDC might want her efforts blocked.

She slammed down the paper, letting the anger bubble up inside. For the first time since her dad had died, she allowed herself to weep openly. She pounded her pillow. It was all so senseless! Patrick's death, her father's, and countless others. She seethed at the thought that the right laws might have prevented these tragedies. Who benefitted from all this? She wished she could hunt down Geraldine Major and all her associates and strangle each one of them. Major corporations were making millions by deliberately preying on the weaknesses of others, and she wondered about the involvement of politicians. Perhaps they received kickbacks from the industry.

There was a clear link between online gambling and suicide, yet the CDC, the pre-eminent organization in the United States dedicated to public health, was ignoring it. Worse, it was blocking research into it. And to think she worked for this organization! She clenched her fists in rage. She didn't think it was possible to be angrier than she was right now.

Her whole body shook. She pulled her legs up tight against her body, wrapping herself in a hug. Finally, the shaking slowed enough for her to uncurl and sit upright. Despite the late hour, she wanted to text Ron. She reached for her burner phone, but before she could pick it up, her regular cell phone rang. Her mother calling. *What was she doing up at 4:00 am?* Thankfully, her mom hadn't called five minutes ago. Cara's voice, at least, was steady enough for her to answer the phone.

"Mom? What's wrong?"

"Cara—it's Brady!" She could hear her mom's sobs. "I'm worried he's going to hurt himself."

Uh-oh... I should have called him yesterday. Aloud, she asked, "What happened? Is he home now?"

"He just left the house. He went out with some friends for a few hours, and I thought he went straight to bed when he got back, but I just woke up to the sound of his car door slamming and the tires squealing as he backed out of the driveway. I'm sure all our neighbors woke up as well. I have a bad feeling about this. I don't know what to do!"

Cara looked at the clock again. *What could she do at this hour? What could either of them do? If Brady was speeding in his car, did it make sense to text or call him?* In the midst of her own turmoil, the best she could think of was to help her mom calm down. "Mom, it's the middle of the night. There's nothing we can do right now. He probably just wanted to go for a drive. Or he's gone to talk to a friend. Let's talk in the morning, okay?"

"I'm scared, Cara. What if something bad happens to him? I can't do this alone!"

"You're not alone, mom," Cara reassured her, though she too had a sinking feeling in the pit of her stomach. "I'm just a plane flight away. Try to get some sleep and not worry so much. Brady may call me, and I'll let you know the moment I hear from him." She still heard her mom's muffled sobs on the other end of the line.

"Cara, I'm sorry. I know it's the middle of the night and I shouldn't have woken you. I'm just so frightened."

"You didn't wake me—I was reading. I'm scared and don't know what to do either. We shouldn't text him if he's upset and driving. I promise I'll call him in a couple of hours."

"Call me if you hear anything at all!" said Sally, ending the call abruptly. Cara looked at her phone. How had it gotten to be so late? She was so wound up with worry that she didn't know if she'd be able to sleep at all, but she knew she had to try. She collapsed back on her bed and stared at the ceiling. Then she turned and buried her head in her pillow, praying for sleep to overtake her.

She was with her father. She saw him—no, felt him—tossing her high in the air. Was it a memory? She was three years old, and they were at the beach. Over and over, he threw her farther in the air until she reached the sky and grabbed hold of a cloud. Then she was flying, spinning around as she gripped a giant roulette wheel. Numbers and colors whizzed by. Where was her father? She trusted him to always be there for her, but now it looked like he abandoned her! She heard his voice. "It's the devil in disguise!" The wheel slowed, and she desperately wanted to get off, and then she saw Brady trapped in the middle. He called to her, but she couldn't reach him. She woke in a cold sweat and sat up, gasping for breath. Her father had called it "the wheel of destruction," but her nightmare made her think "wheel of terror" might be a better name.

Was her mom right about Brady? Had something bad happened to him? *Please don't let Brady be another suicide victim*, she thought, as she curled herself into a ball and sobbed once again.

I WAS FLYING—UNSTOPPABLE. SOARING in the space you created for me. Time no longer existed. There was only this moment. This bet. Anything was possible... until it wasn't.

♦♥♣♠

Twelve

BRADY SLAMMED HIS LAPTOP closed and threw it across the room. "Nooooo!" he cried. He hunched over in his bed, his head in his hands, wishing he could tear his hair out. How could he have been so stupid? He needed to get out of the house. He needed air. Grabbing his car keys, he ran downstairs, slamming the door as he left the house. It didn't matter who he woke up. Nothing mattered. He had just blown his entire inheritance from his dad in less than four hours. How was that even possible?

The past 12 hours were a blur. Despite Cara's warning, he went to a casino with his friends, Chris and Bobby, to celebrate his 18th birthday. As he walked in the door, he felt instantly at home. Years ago, his father had introduced him to this place, and unbeknownst to Cara or his mom, his dad had brought him there several other times during his teen years. They never stayed long, and he wasn't allowed to gamble, but the red-and-black-patterned carpeting, the blinking lights, and the constant whir of the slot machines fascinated him. He looked around now and breathed in the air. The distinctive sweet odor reminded him of his father. His pulse quickened.

He and his friends started with slot machines, but then they wandered to the blackjack tables. Brady had studied the statistics and was determined to win.

And win, he did. His friends drifted away, bored, to try other games, occasionally checking back with him as he continued to rake in the chips. He was unstoppable! After a short six hours, they dragged him away to cash out. "I'm just getting started!" he wailed.

Brady felt like a king, even though his friends looked around nervously as he stuffed wads of cash in his pockets. Neither of them had ever seen that amount of money.

In the car, Chris turned to him. "You know, I heard the other day that they build casinos to keep you captive."

"Maybe," said Brady. "But if that's the case, it's the sweetest jail in the world."

"No, seriously," said Chris. "You know they actually pump oxygen into the room to keep people energized?"

"So? What's the problem with that? Wouldn't you rather be awake when you're playing?"

"Yeah, but they do all these crazy things. Like no clocks anywhere on the premises, and no windows, so you can't see outside and lose track of time. And the sounds—all those bells and whistles that make it seem like someone is winning every 30 seconds. It's overkill, man!"

"You're just complaining because you lost," said Brady. "I think it's pretty awesome and can't wait to go back!"

Chris glanced at Bobby, but neither of them said anything. Brady didn't notice. He was still riding high on a buzz of adrenaline.

They dropped him off at his house, and he ran up to his room and turned on his laptop. Though he had told Cara he rarely gambled online, that wasn't quite true. He had recently set up an account and begun dabbling in it. The first three times he had played at this site, he'd won, and he thought that was a good omen. It wasn't quite the same as being at the casino in person, but he was so jazzed by adrenaline that it didn't matter. He was on a roll and figured he could keep it going.

Unfortunately, his luck didn't hold out, and soon, he was putting in far more money than he was winning. The site was confusing though, and he had no idea how much was going in or out. He was hooked. Four hours later, he was still so engrossed in the game that he didn't realize his account was nearly empty. An alert signaling he was down to his last $100.00 caused him to look up. It was then that he glanced at the clock, threw his laptop across the room, grabbed his car keys, and tore out of the house.

Tires squealing, he backed the car out of the driveway and gunned the motor. So what if neighbors woke up? He just needed to be in another place. Anywhere else. Blinded by tears, he simply drove. As he rounded a bend in the road, he saw something. It was just for an instant. Maybe it was his imagination, but he thought he saw a pair of eyes, an animal frozen in place, staring at him. On impulse, he cranked the steering wheel, swerving the car straight into a tree.

His entire body felt chilled to the bone, yet he was dimly aware of a warm pressure on his hand. Was someone squeezing it? He tried to respond but couldn't. Another squeeze, and he heard his sister's voice, as if from afar. "Brady, it's not your fault." He struggled to hear and understand the words, but the sound of the machine forcing air in and out of his lungs muffled them.

"Stay with us, Brady!" His mom and his sister both talking. What did they know? For a moment, he teetered on the razor edge of shame. If they knew what he had done, would they be talking to him? No way! They would never forgive him. He was an idiot.

How did this happen? Cara had warned him. She told him to be careful, and he ignored her. What would he say to her? He was a failure. He felt himself drifting away. It would be nice to be free—free from the bondage of addiction, free from shame.

Did anyone truly understand him? The loneliness in his life cut through him like a knife. Ever since his father died, he had felt an emptiness in his life. Cara was right—he had worshipped his father, and gambling was a way to connect with him. But he was stupid. He took the money his father gave him, and he threw it away.

He heard his sister sobbing. "Brady, I need you. We need you! We don't blame you for anything. You were caught in a web."

He struggled to understand. What did she mean, "caught in a web?" He thought he heard another voice. "Don't make the same mistakes I made!" For a fleeting instant, he was sure it was his father's voice. "You're stronger than I was, and you have a choice."

Did he have a choice? At what point could he have stopped? One minute he was on top of the world with $100,000 fucking dollars to his name and suddenly... nothing. Gone. For what? For a few hours of mind-numbing thrills? Where was the choice in that?

"Brady, please, you need to fight to live! Your life is worth something. It truly is. Don't throw it away. We love you no matter what you did. I promise I'll do everything in my power to fight for you, but you need to fight for you, too." He felt the hand loosen its grip as he drifted into deeper unconsciousness. No voices right now. Just a blissful unawareness. Was this what death would be like?

CARA FELT HER MOM's comforting hand on her shoulder as they listened to the continual beeping of the hospital monitors and the rhythmic sound of the machine pushing air into and out of Brady's lungs. "I can't believe this is really happening! He seemed in such good spirits a few weeks ago!"

"We need to be strong," Sally whispered. It relieved Cara to hear her say that. Just yesterday, Cara had flown in from Atlanta after hearing of Brady's accident. She went straight to the hospital and found her mother in a complete frenzy, wringing her hands and pacing up and down in the hospital's lobby while she waited to be allowed back into Brady's room.

"They let me in to see him for a few minutes, but then told me I had to leave and wait until visiting hours to come back. So much machinery attached to him! So many tubes! What if he doesn't wake up?"

Now, as they sat together at Brady's bedside, Sally seemed calmer, even though she had barely slept since she had called Cara in the middle of the night. "He's alive, and that's a good thing. At least you're here. He must feel that."

"He seems so far away right now. I tried to warn him. I wish he'd listened to me."

Sally stared at her hands. "Addiction is a powerful force," she said. "And so is denial. I could never help your father because he wouldn't admit he had a problem."

"So, how do you get someone to recognize they have a problem?" Cara blew out a breath through her clenched jaw. "With all the funding out there for drug and alcohol abuse programs, there's so little information for problem gamblers, and my bitch of a boss won't let me investigate it. It has to start with education, and if the CDC has its way, that education will never happen!"

"I should have pushed your father more. I should have done more, but I didn't know where to look. Maybe you're in a better position to do this—not just for Brady, but for others as well," said Sally.

"How? I've been told to focus on drugs and alcohol and leave gambling out completely! How do I go back to work now, knowing this is such an enormous problem? At first, I thought I could drop it, but I've been researching this since you told me about Dad. I have a friend, Ron, who has studied this and shown me some of his papers. After reading about the deliberate deceptive practices of these corporations and seeing Brady on the edge of death after a gambling spree, I have to pursue it. Yet if I do, I risk getting fired. What am I supposed to do?"

"Follow your heart, Cara. Don't let fear stop you from making a difference for others. Maybe you should think about working somewhere else, so you'd be free to follow these leads."

"What—quit my job at the CDC after a few months there? I don't think that will put me in a powerful position to get a new job. Ron told me chasing this would be career suicide. For the short term, at least, I have to keep my job."

Sally was silent for a moment. "Cara, your dad had some weaknesses, but he also had some enormous strengths. He was an entrepreneur and a tremendous businessperson. He built several businesses from the ground up. I'd like to think you've inherited some of those skills from him. If he wanted to accomplish something, nothing got in his way. I admit, there was some risk-taking involved in a lot of what he did, but if he couldn't find the perfect job, he'd create one. If resources for problem gamblers are scarce, perhaps you can provide them."

Cara looked at her mother and shook her head. Like her dad, her mom was full of pipe dreams. Her mom was right. He *had* built several businesses, and some of them were fairly successful. But he had never settled with any one thing. He was always looking for the next challenge, often leaving a job before seeing the company he was at realize its full potential. In many ways, her mom and dad were made for each other. Perhaps that was why her mom had always made excuses for him and defended him. She had said he was in denial, but in Cara's eyes, Sally was equally culpable. She had put her husband on a pedestal and refused to challenge him.

Cara considered herself much more of a realist. "You make it sound so simple," she said ruefully. "I wish I had his business skills, but I'm just a statistician. I deal with numbers and don't have a clue how to run a business—especially a business that would provide resources for gambling addicts. I know nothing about creating opportunities."

Turning her attention back to Brady, she closed her eyes and tuned into the beeps, clicks, and hisses that combined into a symphony keeping him alive. She squeezed his hand. It felt so cold. *Could he feel any warmth coming from her*? For an instant, she thought she felt a return squeeze, but she couldn't be sure. "No matter what happens, I will fight for you. I promise."

Thirteen

EXHAUSTED AFTER THREE DAYS in the hospital with Brady, Cara headed back to Atlanta. Thankfully, Gloria had granted her time off (unpaid, of course). Brady had suffered severe trauma, and his brain needed rest. He was in a medically induced coma, and his doctors intended to keep him that way for several weeks before assessing damage. While Cara felt enormous guilt about leaving her mom alone, both agreed they should return to their lives. Brady was stable for now, and they would deal with whatever decisions they needed to face when they had more information about his condition.

She stumbled out of the airport and hailed a taxi, looking forward to arriving home and settling into her own bed. Her racing mind and the uncomfortable hospital furniture had kept her from sleeping.

As Brady's life hung in the balance, she once again pledged to herself to fight for him. The culture of the world needed to change, and why couldn't she be part of that?

Cara lived on the first floor of a small apartment building. Yawning, she gathered her mail in the vestibule and strolled down the hallway. She unlocked her apartment. Something wasn't right. A breeze came from the kitchen, yet she was sure she had locked all the doors and windows before leaving to go to Brady's bedside. Her pulse quickened as she entered the kitchen and noticed the patio door was ajar. On closer inspection, she saw it was pulled off its hinges.

The hair on her arms lifted. *Had someone broken into her house?* She glanced around to see if anything was out of place. She opened the door to her bedroom and gasped. Her desk was in shambles, and the locked safe, which had held Ron's report, was gone. Thankfully, the report itself was buried deep in her bag, where she'd put it for her trip.

Papers were strewn everywhere. Whoever did this was looking for something, and Cara was certain what that something was. She plopped down on her bed, taking solace in the thought that all they got was a locked, empty safe.

Should she call the police? Maybe it would be better to do a thorough inventory and make sure nothing else was missing. With shaking hands, she sorted through the mess, hoping the activity might help calm her. It worked, and within a few minutes, her heartbeat slowed to a more normal rate. She straightened up the room, tossing things she no longer needed and re-filing important papers. As far as she could tell, nothing was missing aside from the safe. She walked through the rest of the house and saw no evidence of further damage. The only casualty was the back door. She scrutinized it closely. Whoever did this didn't bother to cover their tracks. That, and the obvious mess of her desk, made her wonder if they wanted to intimidate her. But who were "they"? Was it the same people who went after Ron's colleague, Al? She shivered. Her boss, Gloria, was the only one who knew what she was working on and that she would be away for a few days.

Still unsure if she should call the police, she reached for her burner phone in the drawer of her bedside table, but it wasn't there. *Uh-oh.* Whoever broke into her apartment took that phone. It was password-protected, but how secure was that? What if someone bypassed that security and linked her to Ron? She needed to warn him, but she worried he might be angry.

Trembling, she realized she needed a plan, and she needed it fast. There was only one other person she was comfortable enough to turn to. She slipped out the back door of her apartment and ran across the park to the small shopping mall to purchase a new phone, then walked as casually as she could to a bench overlooking her apartment building. She scanned the surrounding landscape, making 100% sure she was alone before placing her call.

Em didn't answer. *She probably thinks it's a spam call,* thought Cara. "Em, it's me, Cara. I got a new phone. Call me ASAP."

Her phone buzzed. "Hi Cara. What's up?"

At the sound of her friend's voice, exhaustion, coupled with the events of the last few days, came crashing down. With all the craziness in her life, she realized she hadn't even told Em about her phone calls with Ron since the conference ended, or about Brady. Barely holding back her terror, she began, "Em, I need your help..."

"What's going on?" asked her friend.

"I'm scared. I don't know what to do or who to turn to. My brother Brady is in the hospital, in a coma, and I just got home and..."

"Wait a minute," interrupted Em. "Back up a minute. Brady's in a coma? What happened?"

"He was in a terrible car accident a few days ago. I flew to New Hampshire and spent the last three days in the hospital with him. He's stable, but still in a coma. We won't know much more for a few weeks, so I came back here, to Atlanta, and when I walked into my apartment, I realized someone broke into it, but at first, I didn't see anything missing and..."

"Whoa... you're talking too fast again," said Em. "Did you say someone broke into your apartment and took nothing? Did you call the police?"

Cara babbled on. "That's just it... I didn't call the police because nothing was missing. At least, nothing obvious at first. But they ransacked my bedroom and completely emptied my desk. They were looking for some confidential documents that, thankfully, I had with me, and now I'm scared. No one knows I have these documents and..."

"Sorry to keep interrupting, but I'm still trying to follow you!" said Em. "Who's 'they'? And what documents are you talking about?"

Cara paused. How much should she tell Em about Ron's report? She needed help and had impulsively called her closest friend, but could she trust her? Ron had said this was for her ears only. Yet she needed to talk to someone, and Em was someone she could depend on. She bit her lip. "Okay—but this is off the record. Swear to me, this is just between us."

"You have my word," replied Em.

"Remember I talked to you about Ron Hynes?"

"Sure," said Em. "I've been meaning to call you. I did a little digging and his story checks out fully."

"Well, since leaving the CDC, he's compiled an extensive amount of information which he mailed to me in a locked safe. He made me promise to keep it completely confidential. That's why my house was ransacked. I'm sure of it. The only thing they stole was that safe, which was empty because I had the report with me. I can't go to the police—what would I tell them? That someone stole a locked empty safe, thinking it held a confidential document which I can't show them?"

"Wow!" said Em. "This is a lot to digest. I assume you talked to Ron about it?"

"Not yet," said Cara sheepishly. "I need to call him, but I'm afraid. He can be a little... prickly." She recalled how angry Ron was when he wasn't sure of her true identity. "He told me to buy a burner phone to communicate with him. When I saw someone trashed my desk, I wanted to call him but couldn't find the phone. Whoever went through my stuff took it. I panicked when I saw that, then ran out to buy a new phone and called you instead."

"You need to talk to him right away. At the very least, tell him you no longer have the phone in case someone tries to use it to reach him. Knowledgeable people can hack even password-protected phones."

"You're right. My mind was in such a jumble. I called you first because I felt like I was having a panic attack and was embarrassed to talk to him. He's going to be angry and probably blame me for not being careful enough to cover my tracks."

"It doesn't matter if he blames you. You still need to tell him. Call him now, and let me know what he says, okay? This phone number is safe to use any time you need to reach me."

"Thanks!" Cara replied, feeling a little better now. Em was right. Embarrassed or not, she needed to let Ron know the phone was gone. But she also needed to come clean with Em. "Um... there's something else I need to tell you. I probably should have said something the night we had dinner together, but I forgot." She hesitated. "Please don't be mad. I used your pen name when I first visited Ron."

"You what?"

"The receptionist at Ron's college asked me who I was, and I was afraid if I gave her my actual name, she'd tell Ron and he wouldn't talk to me. So, I said I was Libby Lewis. She was impressed, but it was a big mistake on my part because she told her boss, who was furious with Ron for talking to a reporter. And Ron was pretty angry with me as well."

"And rightly so!" exclaimed Em. "What were you thinking? I told you, I need to keep that identity a secret! Do me a favor, and never do that again, okay? Remember, you don't know Libby Lewis. No one does. My name is Emiline Jackson, and we were friends in college. Period."

"Em, I'm so sorry. Truly. I wasn't thinking clearly. I'll be more careful."

"Call me if anything changes with Brady. I always liked him. We'll talk again soon."

Em hung up, leaving Cara feeling bereft. She was glad she had unburdened herself to her friend, yet she still felt stupid. Crud. She just remembered she'd told Ron that "Libby Lewis" was a college friend of hers. *Why did I tell him that?*

HER MIND STILL IN a jumble, Cara punched Ron's number into her phone. She left him a brief voicemail saying she had a new phone. As she waited for him to call her back, she thought of the break-in to her apartment. The only person who could be behind this was Gloria. No one else knew she was away.

"I'm sure Gloria set this up to intimidate me," she told Ron. "But her plan backfired, because now I'm more committed than ever to see it through."

"Cara, I admire your tenacity. But you still don't understand what you're up against," Ron replied. "You're right—breaking into your house was likely meant to intimidate you. It was a warning, and you should pay attention to it."

"I'm not backing down," she snapped.

"And I'm not asking you to," Ron replied. "But we need a plan, and we need to be careful. These people are ruthless, though I'm not convinced Gloria is behind it. Don't jump to conclusions. Someone may have followed you to the Post Office and might suspect you received something important. That's all we know right now."

"Maybe..." she said. "But where do we go with all this?"

"I'm not sure," he answered. "That's a question I've been struggling with. I spent four years putting that report together. You came along right as I was wrapping it up. It's been hard to do in secret, but I didn't want to go public with it too soon. You're the one person who knows exactly what I have and how explosive it could be."

"Why not just publish it on some mainstream platform?" she asked.

"And risk the same fate that happened to Al? Besides, I already told you, my current boss hates all publicity. I'd lose my job in a heartbeat. No... we can't come out with this until we have a concrete plan."

Cara smiled at his use of the word "we." Ron seemed to want her input. "Well, we can't stop greedy entrepreneurs and politicians directly, but we can educate people, especially teens, who are so susceptible. With education, people might make better choices."

"You're right, and for a while now, I've been considering the most effective way to do that. It would be easy to be labeled as fake news, and then no one would listen. We need a massive media campaign, from a reputable source. You said the journalist, Libby Lewis, was a college friend of yours, right?"

Uh oh. She promised Em she would keep her secret. "No, I didn't really know her. I mean, she went to my college, but we weren't close friends. I'm not sure how to contact her, and I doubt she'd remember me if I called. We were just casual acquaintances."

"That's too bad," said Ron. "Because after reading her recent columns, I think she'd be a great connection. She's not afraid to speak her mind, and people are listening to her. You saw how the receptionist was so delighted to meet 'her'. What you didn't see, though, was my boss's reaction. His face was beet red as he pounded the table and told me to stay out of the limelight. There is no way I could set up any kind of meeting with her. But you might..."

"I don't know," Cara interrupted, casting about for a way to change the subject. "In the meantime, you need to get a new phone. I don't want them finding any way to connect us."

"I'll do that," he said, though Cara heard the disappointment in his voice. She wished she could help him, but she had made a promise to Em. She'd have to find another way to assist him. Right now, though, she needed his advice.

"I have to go to work tomorrow and face Gloria. Do I mention anything about my apartment being broken into while I was away? Or do I simply do my job and pretend nothing out of the ordinary happened?"

"Be a model worker and make Gloria trust you," he replied. "She values keeping work and personal experiences separate. It's best if you say nothing about it."

Cara winced. She knew he was right. Even though she suspected Gloria, it would be better if she had more evidence.

As if reading her thoughts, he added, "It'll be hard, but this is the best strategy for now. Stay calm. And I hope your brother comes through this. Keep me posted."

"Thank you," she whispered. As an afterthought, she added, "I wish I could see you." Her hand flew to her mouth. *Where had that come from?*

"That makes two of us," he replied. "Take care, Cara." And with that, he hung up.

She stared at the phone. She needed to keep her personal feelings at bay if she was going to work with Ron. What a mess this all was! Should she involve Libby Lewis? Given what Em had said earlier, she doubted it would work, but what else was there to do? Ron was right. They needed to take this outside the confines of the CDC, and they needed support to do that. Perhaps Em could help. After all, she was a rising star on the staff of the *Post*. She glanced at her phone again. It wouldn't hurt to at least ask Em.

"Cara, I told you to leave Libby out of this!" Cara would have bet money that her friend was pacing back and forth. Em's *modus operandi*, Cara thought. She recalled countless times in college, trying to sleep while her roommate paced back and forth in the room through much of the night. Em said it helped her focus.

"I didn't suggest this! Ron did!" Cara exclaimed. "I told him I barely knew you and you probably wouldn't remember me at all. And then he said, 'that's too bad because I thought Libby would be a great connection' or something like that. I didn't promise him anything."

"How does he think I can help?"

"My understanding is that he wants to publicize this in a big way, and he thinks you'd be the ideal person to do it. But why don't you meet with him and ask him? It wouldn't hurt just to talk to him, would it?"

"Cara, you have to understand the way I work and the steps I take to protect my identity. I have to be extremely careful about who I talk to. I already told you how angry my boss was because he thought I tried to talk to Ron. This guy has a lot of eyes on him already, and if I'm not careful, I could lose my job."

"The bigger the risk, the bigger the payout," Cara whispered. "I remember you telling me that once before."

"No fair throwing my words back at me! You may be right, but I don't know how deep I want to get involved in this. It's dangerous to be on the wrong side of some of these corporate lobbyists and politicians. I got lucky with one story, and I'm making a name for myself, but that doesn't mean I'm an expert at it. I still have a lot to learn."

"How about we do a 3-way phone conversation—a simple meet-up? Give him a chance to tell you what he has. After that, you can decide if it's something you want to pursue."

For a moment, Em was silent. "All right. One conversation. A phone call, not video. Tomorrow 7:00 pm. Make sure you are somewhere where no one can overhear you. Whoever broke into your apartment may have wired it. You're not in your apartment now, are you?"

"No, I'm sitting outside." She stood up and scanned the park. "I can see 360 degrees, and there is no one in sight."

"Good. Tomorrow, go somewhere else. Tell your friend I'll call you and we'll conference him in. And don't tell him my actual name. For the duration of the call, I am not Em. As far as your friend knows, I'm Libby, but the less you use my name, the better."

"Thanks, Em! You're the best!"

Fourteen

CARA RETURNED TO WORK the following morning, prepared for a grueling day. She expected Gloria would push her to make up the two days of missed work in one day. She entered the office, determined to act like nothing unusual had happened, and was surprised to see Henry lounging in his chair with his feet up on his desk.

"Where's Gloria?" she asked. It was not like her boss to come in late.

"She had a meeting this morning," said Henry. "Said she'd be in about 10:00 and you should get started on the three reports she emailed you."

When the cat's away.... She shook her head in amazement as she tried to focus on her work, but the sound of him clicking a pen in the oddly quiet office distracted her. *Where was everyone?* She realized how little she knew about her office-mate. He seemed to blend in with the furniture, though the constant click-click of his pen was grating on her.

He broke the silence. "How's your brother?" he asked. Startled, she looked up from her computer screen. Had Gloria said something to him about Brady? Gloria was the only one who knew about her brother, and she didn't seem like the type who would tell everyone else in the office. "Okay, I suppose," she said, not wanting to discuss her family with him. Besides, she needed to pay attention to the work in front of her, and being reminded of Brady made that much more difficult. Not wanting to be rude, she again focused on her computer monitor. "Listen, I need to work on these reports. I want to finish them before Gloria gets in."

Henry shrugged and rose to get a cup of coffee. He didn't seem too keen on working, but Cara tried to stop thinking about him. Today was her day to get on Gloria's good side.

At 10:00 am sharp, Gloria bustled in and motioned for Cara to take a seat in her office. Thankfully, aside from clicking the pen, Henry had remained quiet long enough for her to complete the three reports. *So far, so good*.

"How's your brother doing?" Gloria asked. Cara blinked, momentarily taken aback at this show of concern. This was not what she expected, given Gloria's previous behavior, when she had returned from Patrick's funeral.

"Honestly, I'm not sure," she began. "He's in a medically induced coma, and the doctors won't know the extent of damage for about two to three weeks."

"I'm sorry to hear that," Gloria replied gruffly. Then, in a softer tone, she added, "If there's anything you need, please ask." Once again, Cara felt totally confused by the friendliness. It must have showed on her face, because Gloria lowered her glasses and peered at her. "Look, I'm aware we've had our differences during the past month, but I am genuinely sorry you're going through this."

"I don't understand," said Cara, slowly shaking her head. "When I returned from my best friend's funeral, you told me to forget about him and get right back to work. And now, you're saying you're sorry my brother's in the hospital? I'm confused."

Gloria sighed. "You're right. I was hard on you after your last trip home. But you were brand new here, and you hadn't proven yourself yet. You've done a remarkable job in the last few weeks. The symposium was a tremendous success, and you impressed many people. And this is your brother. It's different." Cara still looked puzzled, as Gloria pressed on. "How old is he?"

"Eighteen," replied Cara. "He turned eighteen last week."

"I had a brother once," Gloria said, staring off into space. "Joey was eighteen when he died in Vietnam."

Cara's hand flew to her mouth. "I didn't know..." she began.

"Of course not," Gloria said sharply. "How would you know? It's not something I talk about. But I'm familiar with the feeling of caring for a younger sibling. I grew up in a military family and all Joey ever wanted was to go out and fight for his country. The army was his destiny from the time he was born."

"I'm sorry," mumbled Cara.

"It's nothing for you to be sorry about. I just wanted you to know I understand a little of what you're going

through. And now, we both need to get back to work."
She turned her attention back to her computer, signaling
to Cara she was dismissed.

"Thank you," Cara stammered, as she stumbled out the
office door. She was almost afraid Gloria might do something in that moment which would shatter the illusion of
decency. Returning to her desk, she sat down and rubbed
her temples. Gloria was an enigma.

"You look like you saw a ghost in there!" exclaimed
Henry. "Whatever did she say to you?"

"I don't understand that woman!" replied Cara.

"Well, that makes two of us," said Henry. "I, for one,
am glad you're back because she's been unbearable all
week. She's been going to some high-level meetings with
politicians, and they are really cracking down on what can
and can't be done here."

Cara considered asking Henry for more information
about those "high-level meetings" but then reminded
herself she needed to keep a low profile for the next
few days. It was best if she stayed focused on her work.
Yet Gloria's sudden change of attitude flustered her. She
made a mental note to ask Em to check into Gloria's
background. Did she really grow up in a military family
and have a brother who died in Vietnam? That should be
easy enough for Em to uncover.

During her lunch break, Cara sat outside on a bench
overlooking the park. She pulled out her burner cell
phone and her heart skipped a beat when she saw a new
message. Ron had sent her his new phone number. She
texted back that she had set up a conference call with
Libby Lewis for that evening. As an afterthought, she

wrote: **"Did you know Gloria had a younger brother who died in Vietnam?"** She dashed off a second text to Em, asking her if she could check into that.

Nervously, she rubbed the back of her neck, still berating herself for her impulsive impersonation of Libby Lewis. Hopefully, both Ron and Em would forgive her. Maybe, once they connected, they would find a way to work together. She imagined the three of them might make an excellent team.

The sound of someone approaching startled her. Without asking, Henry slumped down beside her, forcing her to slide to the edge of the bench. He had no sense of boundaries. She placed her bag between them, hoping he would get the hint.

"You playing a game on that phone?" he asked. Without answering, Cara turned away from him. She craved privacy, but Henry was in an exceptionally chatty mood and remained a little too close for comfort. "I've been struggling with this report for the last two days and Gloria keeps sending it back to me," he said. "She wants more clarification. More references. More statistics. My mind is numb from staring at a screen all morning. I need a break from it all. Does she do that to you, too? I really think she has it in for me..."

Cara listened to him drone on a few minutes longer, then got up to leave.

"You never talk to me about what you're working on," he whined, blinking rapidly.

"What?" she asked, startled. "Why should I? It's not like we're collaborating on anything."

"No... but as a co-worker, I would think maybe you'd want some advice or something," he mumbled.

Cara stared at him. "We share an office. That's all. I have a lot on my plate right now, and I need to work on stuff alone. I enjoy working alone. If I need your advice on anything, I'll ask for it, but don't count on it." Angrily, she shouldered her bag and walked away.

Fifteen

"IT ALL CHECKS OUT," said Em (aka Libby Lewis) as they began their three-way conference call that evening. Cara sat alone outside her apartment, picturing Ron and Em similarly situated at their houses. "Gloria Spiegelman did have a military upbringing. Her father was an ultra-conservative Republican, a renowned and outspoken commander, stalwart in his defense of both flag and nation. Interesting that he would name his daughter Gloria. Her family moved every year or two. She lived in several countries, including Germany and Sweden. Her younger brother, Joseph, died in Vietnam at age 18. She's been employed at the CDC for the past 35 years."

"That explains her general bossy attitude," said Cara. "She runs the department like a military base. I don't understand her sudden shift, though. She was so nice to me today. It could be because of her brother, but I'm not sure I trust her. And no one else knew I would be out of town for a few days."

"I dug up one interesting tidbit... today is the anniversary of her brother's death, so that may play a role. Are you sure no one else knew you were going away? Maybe Gloria told someone in Personnel."

Cara pondered that for a moment. "Wait, there is someone else. My office-mate, Henry. This morning he asked me how my brother was doing, which I thought odd because how would he have known? Gloria might have said something to him, but I doubt it. I had a creepy feeling about him today... like he was stalking me. It's not like he did anything out of the ordinary, but several times, I caught him looking at me strangely. And then, when I was sitting alone on a bench eating lunch, he came up to me and sat down without asking. Real close, you know. It made me so uncomfortable I had to put my bag between us."

Ron cleared his throat. "Cara, where is your bag now? The one that was next to you on the bench?" Cara opened her mouth to speak, but Ron interrupted before she made a sound. "Don't say anything out loud, but if it's nearby, can you put it somewhere out of earshot?"

Cara's hand flew to her mouth as she stared at the bag beside her. "Listen carefully now," Ron continued. "It's unlikely, but it's possible he dropped a listening device in it and he can hear everything you say, though he can't hear us on the phone. If he put a bug in there, you just alerted him you're suspicious, so you need to think on your feet and say something to distract him in case he's listening now. Make something up! Have a fake conversation with your mother for a minute and then put your bag away. We can wait."

"Okay, you're right!" said Cara brightly, standing up and casting about for a way out of this. What had she just said? She grabbed her bag and started walking toward the parking lot, while pretending to talk to her mom on the phone. "Honestly, it's not a big deal, Mom! I'm just sad about Brady, and that's making me edgy. Everything is magnified right now. Henry is fine. He was just trying to be nice, and I overreacted. I know you worry about me, but really, I'm fine!" She paused to catch her breath. If Henry *was* listening, he would think her mom was talking. "Yes, I know I complain about Gloria, but work is good for me right now. I'll check in with you tomorrow, okay?" Finally, she reached her car. "Bye, Mom!" she said, tossing the bag in the back seat.

Back on the bench overlooking the parking lot, she scrutinized the area. She was sure no one else was around, yet the hair on the back of her neck stood on end. What if she was being stalked? Would she even know? No, she would not let paranoia block her from doing what she needed to do. She turned her attention back to the phone.

"I put my bag in my car," she whispered. "Do you actually think he put a bug in it?"

"We need to cover all bases, Cara," said Ron. "I've been living like this since I left the CDC, so I may be more paranoid than necessary, but the more I find out, the more careful I've become. These people will stop at nothing to protect their interests. Are you both alone now?"

Cara looked around again. As far as she could tell, there was no one in earshot. "Yes, I'm alone here," she said.

"I am too," said Em. "I'll do a background check on Henry as well. But in the meantime, keep a close eye on him."

"I have a connection in the Personnel department at the agency," Ron chimed in. "Perhaps he can dig a little into Henry's history."

"I'm grateful to you both," said Cara. "Now I suppose we can get to the real purpose of this call."

"Sure," said Em. "Ron, I understand you asked Cara to set up this meeting with me. How can I help you?"

Ron cleared his throat again. "I'm not sure how much Cara told you," he began. "I'll start at the beginning. But first, I need your 100% guarantee that this is completely confidential until I tell you otherwise. This is a tremendous story, but I need total control of when this goes public, if it goes public at all. None of this can leak out prematurely. I'm serious about this."

"I understand," said Em. "You have my word. Cara didn't tell me much, so the more background you can give me, the better."

"Okay, so Cara, I apologize if this is repetitive, but you might hear it differently this time. This is a story about money and power.

"Before I began at the CDC eight years ago, there was a distinct uptick in suicide deaths in young adults, particularly boys between the ages of 18 and 25. My primary job, along with my colleague Al, was to figure out why this was happening. We looked at the usual suspects of drugs and alcohol, searching for any new drugs on the market (on the streets or otherwise) that might have been fueling this. To our surprise, we found drug use wasn't involved in many of these suicides at all. The deeper we dug, the more convinced we became that online gambling was contributing to this trend in a big way.

"We wrote several papers as internal CDC documents and were about to publicize this when the CDC halted all funding for further research into it. Our boss told us to stop this line of research and re-focus our efforts on drug and alcohol abuse only, and she buried our findings."

"Wow!" said Em. "I imagine that was frustrating for you."

"Right. Al and I were not happy, but we kept at it on our own time, as much as possible. At some point, higher-ups at the CDC discovered we were still looking into it, and they fired both of us from the agency. They gave us each a substantial severance package in return for our promise to stay quiet." Ron hesitated for a moment, remembering. It didn't get any easier, no matter how many times he talked about it.

"Did you sign a non-disclosure agreement?" asked Em.

"In a manner of speaking, yes," he continued. "We both agreed to leave without contesting the firing, and we signed a paper stating we would not 'seek employment which involved further research related to what we had been doing at the CDC.' Interestingly, they did not specifically spell out what that research was, most likely because they didn't want it in writing.

"Because of the way they worded the document, Al and I both decided it didn't legally prohibit us from doing some independent side research. After all, we weren't 'seeking employment.'

"Al moved to California, and a few months later, his wife emailed me to tell me he was in a horrible car accident." Ron's voice cracked slightly. "Before he died, he told his wife he thought someone had sabotaged his car because of the work we were doing, and he urged her to warn me."

The phone line went quiet for a moment, as all three participants sat with their own thoughts. As Ron recalled losing his closest friend, Em remembered her childhood friend, Libby, and Cara thought of Brady, her dad, and Patrick.

"Al may have wanted me to stop, but his death fueled my desire to continue. We were onto something major and I wanted to understand it. Much of the data I've gathered implicates some high-ranking officials. This could cost them their careers. I want to go public with this, but it's tricky. Given what happened to Al, my life—and the life of anyone who works with me—might be in danger. I need a strategy to stay anonymous and attack this industry from the inside out."

Em spoke. "There's a lot here! I'm sorry about your friend. I lost someone close to me as well, and I'm very familiar with the desire to want to fight for them and be their voice. It's why I went into journalism."

"I've read Ron's report," Cara said. "There's so much information in there. He's right... there are some highly connected politicians involved in this. A direct attack won't work. Yet the public needs to know that the government funds the CDC, and industrial giants are lobbying the government to block research. It seems like the only way out of this is to change the lobbying laws, though I don't see that happening anytime soon."

"Right, because politicians are all under the influence of the Gambling Industry Research Institute," said Ron.

"You describe that in your report, but I'm not sure I quite understand what it is," said Cara. "Gloria mentioned it as well a few weeks ago, when she told me to stop research into all this. Who are they?"

"I've heard a bit about them also," said Em. "It's a group of scientists investigating possible detrimental effects as well as benefits of online gambling. They've published quite a few articles in the past few years in mainstream media publications."

"Exactly," said Ron. "But what you don't know is that they're taking their cues from the Tobacco Industry to create confusion in the public mind."

"How so?" asked Cara.

"I'll give you a history lesson. If you look back about 60 years, you'll find many articles written by the Tobacco Industry Research Committee attempting to mislead people and make them think smoking was okay, even in the face of mounting scientific evidence to the contrary. Believe it or not, there are scientific reports going back as far as the 1920s about the health risks of smoking and the potential connection of smoking to cancer. During the 1950s and 60s, this committee paid hundreds of scientists to state there was no *actual evidence* that smoking caused cancer. Where was the proof? Their strategy was to undermine public faith in science and the scientific method by seizing control of the science and manipulating it to their ends. They wanted to create massive confusion.

"They hired industry 'experts' to do research for them and made sure those professionals agreed to produce results that fit their public message. Without ever directly denying the claims of health problems related to smoking, they distracted the public from knowing the truth by masking it in a confusing array of data and statistics. These 'renowned researchers' convinced the public that science, not cigarettes, was the enemy and kept open the question: was tobacco really harmful? They created a climate of scientific skepticism that still exists today."

"And it looks like the Gambling Industry has been quick to capitalize on that skepticism," said Cara. "I wonder where Gloria fits into all this. I find it hard to believe she would have any part of it."

"She may not be aware of the extent of it," said Ron.

"Or she may know a little, but choose to look the other way," chimed in Em. "Perhaps she's been told by whoever is above her to not ask questions. Her military upbringing would make her good at following orders and make her the perfect candidate for the position she's in."

"I'm going to talk to her about it," Cara announced. "I want to find out who controls her."

"Good luck with that," grunted Ron. "She is fickle. Just because she was friendly today doesn't guarantee she'll be nice tomorrow. She can't know of my involvement. You need to be careful what you share with her."

"I will," promised Cara. "But I feel like the work you did needs to continue and should be publicized, for the sake of my brother and everyone else afflicted by this addiction. If society's opinion of cigarettes could shift, then it can change regarding online gambling as well."

"Which begs the question," said Em. "How did public opinion of cigarettes change? What was the turning point?"

"I've been looking into that," said Ron. "It took over 40 years and a lot of hard work. A lot of laws were rewritten or enacted. It was an organic process, fueled by science and the media. Unfortunately, in today's climate of distrust of both those disciplines, we may have a harder time. It seems like the perpetrators of the tobacco scourge laid the foundation for industries which feed on addiction to thrive."

"So, we need a two-pronged approach," Em considered. "A massive public media campaign, along with a large and compelling body of scientific literature and the support of scientists worldwide. Hopefully, all that can spark interest in changing some laws which could take power away from those who are abusing it."

"Well, that's the crux right there," said Ron. "They found a legal way to do something illegal. The limited information I have implicates some of the highest-ranking officials in our government. I believe Al had more material, but I haven't yet been able to retrieve it. I'm still working on that, and I now know several people I'm investigating are stakeholders in the biggest corporations in this industry. They won't give up power willingly. We need a whistleblower, and we need to be very strategic in how we handle this."

"I'll try to get more information from Gloria," Cara repeated. "And yes, I will be careful," she added before Ron could jump in.

"I'll continue looking into the Tobacco Industry and how it unraveled. Given the Gambling Industry today has aligned itself with that paradigm, we may still discover some useful things there," said Ron.

"I can help you with some of that research as well," said Em.

"So... you're willing to work with us?" asked Ron. "I wasn't sure..."

"Hell yes!" Em exclaimed. "It may cost me my job, but at least I'll go out with a bang! My boss may not like it, so I'll have to work privately until I have enough information to convince him to go with it. For now, we should only communicate by secure phone calls."

"We all need to keep this quiet. I know from personal experience these people are ruthless and will stop at nothing to defend their empire. Cara, you, especially, need to be careful. There are eyes all over the CDC. You should get an emergency alert button—one of those medical bracelets you can wear. Program it with my phone and Libby's phone. If needed, you can press a button and we'll know immediately where you are and that you need help."

Cara rolled her eyes. She didn't think it necessary, but it felt good to have someone care a little. She sighed. "If you insist!" she said, laughing.

"I'm serious," said Ron. "Remember, Al may have been murdered over this. We are venturing into some extremely dangerous waters. And one more thing. Check your bag closely. See if there is anything in there out of the ordinary. If you see something, take a picture and send it to me."

AFTER THE CALL ENDED, Cara looked around. A breeze was stirring, and once again, she felt the hair rise on the back of her neck. She was both terrified and energized at the same time. Her thoughts turned once again to Brady as she retrieved her bag from the car. She said a quick prayer for him as she examined the bag. Could there be a bug in it? How would she even know?

Back in her apartment, she dumped the contents of the bag out on her bed. At first, she saw nothing unusual, but on closer inspection, she noticed a tiny metal disk on the bedspread. She picked it up and examined it. It looked like a small button battery. Her hands shook as she quickly put it down, photographed it, and sent the picture to Ron. He responded immediately. **"Nice work!"** he texted. **"That might even be a GPS tracker as well as a listening device. Keep it with you for now, but be aware it's there. If you're going anywhere and don't want to be tracked, just take it out of your bag. And get that alert bracelet!"**

Ron was right, she thought with a sigh. Now she really was feeling paranoid. Someone—Henry or someone he worked for—was stalking her. She needed to be extremely careful. Assuming her fake call with her mom worked, whoever it was didn't know she knew about the bug. Perhaps she could turn that to her advantage.

Sixteen

CARA SETTLED INTO A predictable routine at work. She welcomed the way Henry kept his distance. Perhaps he had listened in the other night and was trying not to appear suspicious. Or maybe someone he worked for had told him to leave her alone. Whatever the reason, he blended in with the background, allowing Cara to focus on her work. His habit of pen-clicking was annoying, but she could live with it. Gloria continued to be in a good mood, for which Cara was also grateful.

Cara took Ron's advice and researched alert bracelets, and this morning she sported a new piece of jewelry. She purchased a ring rather than a bracelet, figuring it might draw less attention. One push of a tiny button would alert both Ron and Em she was in trouble and give them her GPS coordinates. Given the discovery of the listening device in her bag the other night, she knew it was worth being a little wary.

She needed a plan. How might she get more information from Gloria without angering her? She and Gloria were meeting soon to review her most recent report. If Gloria was in a good mood, perhaps she could bring the conversation around.

As she stared at her computer monitor, another question nagged at her. How did Henry know about her brother? Was it possible he was listening to Gloria's conversations? If Henry could slip a tiny button-like device into her bag, how difficult would it be for him to leave something in Gloria's office? Easy, she acknowledged. She shivered as she thought of the break-in to her apartment. She had to find out who else Henry might be listening to. *"Think!"* she commanded herself silently. How could she find out if Henry bugged Gloria's office? A plan formed in her mind, and she rose to make a quick trip to the Personnel office, leaving her bag behind at her desk in case Henry was tracking her.

Returning to her office, she felt lighter. Maybe she could trick Henry. The buzz of a text on her phone startled her. *"Pls see me."* They weren't supposed to meet for several hours and she wondered what Gloria wanted.

Cara closed Gloria's office door without asking, and before she could change her mind, blurted out, "I need to ask you something. Did you tell Henry about my brother?"

Gloria's head shot up. "Goodness, no! Why would you think that?" she asked. "If there's one thing I respect in this world, it's the right to privacy when it comes to one's family."

Cara glanced through the window in Gloria's office, her eyes briefly resting on Henry, seated at his desk. He had been watching her through the glass but now looked away, acting engrossed in some papers. She had to find out if he was listening.

"Henry asked me about my brother, and I wondered how he knew about my trip home."

"Well, he didn't hear it from me."

"Well, somebody must have told him." Cara paused, pretending to be deep in thought. "Maybe it was Gerry in the Personnel office. I remember running into him on the day I left. I'll have to check with him about that...." Her voice trailed off as she turned back to look at Gloria. "At any rate, I'm glad you said nothing. I appreciate you keeping it quiet. Did you want to go over my last report? I finished a few more edits this morning."

"Yes, I do, but I called you in now because I need to reschedule. I have two important meetings today at our satellite facility across town. If you don't mind meeting me for lunch off-site, I'll have about an hour to review things with you. We can get lunch there and meet in one of the small conference rooms."

Cara couldn't believe her luck. If Henry did bug Gloria's office, this would solve that problem nicely. "Sure!" she said. "I don't mind meeting there at all."

HER SUSPICIONS OF HENRY confirmed, Cara sat in a private conference room with Gloria. She had brought her bag with the tiny battery-like device in it, but prior to walking into the room, she had removed the disk and left it in the hallway. If Henry was listening to her, he might wonder why she was silent for the afternoon, but she preferred that to him overhearing the conversation she intended to have with Gloria.

Cara had spent a lot of time perfecting her report, though she was certain Gloria would pick it apart. She hoped the process wouldn't take long because she had her own agenda for the conversation. It was not what she agreed to when talking with Ron and Em, but she had learned a few things that she felt Gloria should be aware of.

Gloria had few questions about the report, and after going over the details, it seemed their meeting was over.

"I appreciate how hard you've worked this week," Gloria said gruffly. "I hope you can keep it up."

Cara was quiet for a moment, searching for a way to bring the conversation around.

"It's been a hard week... and actually, there may be something you can do to help." She paused and looked directly at Gloria. "I keep thinking about my brother. He gambled online, and I suspect his car accident was an attempted suicide. This should never have happened to him. I want permission to look into the CDC archives for more information on gambling addiction and ties to suicide. I *know* there is information there."

Gloria peered out over her dark-rimmed glasses. "Didn't we go over this already? The answer remains no. I don't care if it's personal or not."

"But why?" pressed Cara. "Why won't the CDC investigate links between gambling and suicide?"

"Who do you think pays your salary?" Gloria asked, with a flat stare.

"The government?" Cara answered meekly.

"Okay—and who pays the government?"

"Uh… the taxpayers?"

"That's peanuts!" Gloria snorted, pounding the table. "For Lord's sake, wake up and smell the roses! Lobbyists! Lobbyists decide what does and doesn't get looked into. And if they don't want something examined, it gets buried. You can't fight this. It's too big. As long as lobbyists exist, the CDC is not free to carry out its mission."

Cara's mouth hung open. She knew Gloria had a temper but had never seen her this perturbed. "So, you're admitting a bunch of wealthy lobbyists, whose primary goal in life is to keep their fortunes growing, control this organization—the paramount public health institution in the United States. Is that what you're telling me?"

"Oh, it's way more complicated than that!"

"It seems pretty straightforward to me," said Cara bluntly.

"The relationships are what's complicated! This isn't about one person, or even one corporation. It pervades all of D.C. and is an incredibly tangled web with many powerful people in charge. If they don't want something made public, we don't question it. To survive here is to play that game!" She paused and blinked. Cara couldn't be sure, but she thought Gloria might be fighting back tears.

"Already, I've told you far more than I should have, but believe it or not, I'm worried for you. Your job is in jeopardy. You want to investigate something our sponsors don't want pursued, and they have tasked me with stopping you. I don't like it any more than you do, but that's where things stand. If you continue this line of research, they will stop you, one way or another. Beginning with firing you from this job."

"Unless I stop them first!" Cara shot back. "How dare you say you don't like it any more than me! My brother is lying in a coma because of their greed! During the past few years, I have lost three people to suicide. At least two of them were addicted to gambling and the third may have been as well. I'm sure I'm not the only person in the world in this position. This needs to stop. The public needs information. It's a crime to cover this up! You, of all people, should fight for what's right! What did your brother stand for? Did he give his life to defend a corrupt government?"

Gloria covered her face. Cara's words had hit their mark. When she looked up, Cara definitely saw tears. Gloria removed her glasses and placed them on the table. For the first time, Cara felt a twinge of compassion for her. Without that shield between them, Gloria seemed a lot more vulnerable.

"No," she whispered. "He thought better of the country. As did my father. I feel like I am doing some good here, trying to help the public, trying to do a noble job, though every day has been more difficult than the day before. But you have to understand, I have been at this job now for over 35 years. This is my life. I cannot risk losing this. There may be protection for whistleblowers, but I can't risk it."

"There *is* protection for whistleblowers! I've looked into this. The whistleblower protection act has been in place for 30 years. There are ways to fight this if you really want to," said Cara. This was more than she had dared hope for. "I intend to fight this, even if it means being an informant. But I have limited clout, as I've only been here a short time. I promise you, though, it will come out eventually. Join me in fighting for what is right, for what your brother fought for!" Gloria stared at her. Cara wondered if Ron was right, and this was career suicide.

She had one more card to play and hoped it would do the trick. Sitting back in her chair, she said, "By the way, Henry bugged your office."

"What?" Startled, Gloria looked back at her. "What are you talking about?"

"Henry has been listening to your conversations. I suspected it when I returned to work and he asked me how my brother was doing. You were the only person I'd talked to about Brady. Then this morning, I asked you, and you told me you didn't tell him. We were in your office, and I said it might have been the Personnel director."

"Yeah, Gerry's a pretty imposing fellow. It would be hard to forget talking to him," said Gloria.

"Well, I definitely did not see Gerry that morning. I set a trap and got Gerry to play along. Gerry texted me an hour ago to let me know Henry came by to ask if I spoke with him about my brother last week. Henry listened to our conversation this morning!"

Gloria blanched. "Are you sure about this?"

"I'm sure. Henry has bugged your office, though I have no clue who put him up to it. You need to be careful what you say there right now." Cara paused to let that information sink in.

Gloria seemed rattled. "Well, you've certainly given me a lot to consider, though I can't imagine why Henry would care what I say in my office. I understand your concern, but none of this changes my answer to your request. If you want to keep this job, do not continue to look into online gambling." She walked out of the conference room, leaving Cara wondering if she had gone too far and already jeopardized her job.

LOST IN MEMORY, GLORIA sat alone in her office. She removed her glasses and rubbed her temples. Four years ago, her two best researchers were fired because of her actions. *It wasn't her fault!* She had warned them not to continue their research into gambling, and they had ignored her. She did what she was told, and they did not. She pushed down a twinge of guilt, reminding herself they hadn't followed the rules. Gloria valued rules above all else.

With great clarity, she recalled her own emotional conflict at that time. What did one do when two sets of rules conflicted with one another? Her boss had explicitly told her to destroy all traces of the reports Hynes and Lawdly had compiled. Yet, CDC guidelines clearly stated: *"No CDC research should ever be destroyed."* Destruction of a CDC registered document was a federal offense. Documents could be transferred to microfilm, an organizational holdover from its founding, but the microfilm must remain accessible for future researchers. Once archived in the microfilm section of the library, the original could then be burned or shredded.

Destroy all traces or permanently archive? For Gloria, this had created uncomfortable conflict. Whose command should she follow? After much agony, she had finally decided that the organization's rule trumped her boss's order, and so she had hand-delivered the articles to the library to be microfilmed. No one would need to know they were there.

As she sat at her desk now, she remembered that day four years ago. When she arrived at the library, a new librarian was seated behind the counter. **ABIGAIL**, her nametag read. "Where's Carmen?" she had asked gruffly. Carmen had been caretaker of the library since before she arrived at the CDC and she trusted he would do as he was told with no questions asked.

"He retired a few weeks ago. I'm Abigail, the new librarian." Abigail held out her hand in greeting.

"Humph," said Gloria, ignoring the outstretched hand. "I would've thought they'd let us know he was leaving. After all, he'd been here forever."

"Well, I th-th-think it was a bit sudden," Abigail stuttered. Gloria seemed to make her nervous. "His wife was s-s-ssick. Is there s-something I can do for you?"

For a moment, Gloria had debated her plan, hesitant to put her trust in someone she didn't know. But what choice did she have? She placed the files on the counter. "I have these articles," she began. "They need to be stored on microfilm, but they are extremely sensitive documents, and no one can know where they end up. Not even me. I need you to hide them so if anyone comes searching for them in the usual manner—like with keywords—they will never find them. You are also to alert me if anyone ever asks for them. This is totally confidential." Peering over her glasses, she narrowed her eyes and looked straight at Abigail. "Can I trust you to do this?"

"C-certainly," said Abigail, grabbing the documents. "I can do this right away."

"I want the original documents destroyed once they're on microfilm. Can you do that as well?"

"We usually cremate papers once a month, but if you want this batch done separately, I can do it today," said Abigail. "Do you want to wait here for the ashes?"

"I will wait while you put them on microfilm, if you don't mind. I'd like to witness them being burned."

A half-hour later, after watching Abigail disappear into the stacks to hide the microfilms, Gloria had exited the library carrying a small can of ashes. The next day, she had presented it to her boss as proof of destruction of the documents.

She had thought this entire affair was behind her, but now, sitting in her office, she once again wondered if she did the right thing. The original documents were destroyed a long time ago, but the microfilms still existed. What if they surfaced now?

Seventeen

"Cara, are you crazy?" demanded Ron during their 3-way conference call that evening. "You basically signed your pink slip with the CDC. There's no way Gloria will keep you on after a conversation like that."

"She's changed, Ron," insisted Cara. "I honestly think she's considering being a whistleblower. She has so much information and could implicate so many people."

"Which is exactly why she won't do it," chimed in Em. "She knows who controls the purse strings better than anyone, and I'm sure she's aware of the risk to her job and possibly her life. She also plays by the rules and will follow the orders of her superiors. Remember her military upbringing. She won't go against authority. I agree with Ron. Expect to be fired when you walk in the door tomorrow. In fact, they may not even let you in the building."

"But I'm not backing down," said Cara. "I won't sign a non-disclosure if they fire me, even if they offer me a sweet financial deal. I will expose whoever I can, with or without Gloria's help. I owe it to my father and my friend Patrick."

"You still don't fully understand," Ron said. "We're talking about some highly unscrupulous people. Far more than your job is on the line here. They *murdered* my partner and made it appear to be an accident. We don't know who 'they' are, but I bet Gloria does."

"I'm being careful. I bought an alert ring, didn't I?"

"You did, and that's good, but it won't save you if someone ambushes you. You need to be more than careful; you need to be on high alert all the time. Especially now that you've told Gloria what you're after. She isn't trustworthy. I can't stress this enough, Cara."

Somewhat mollified, Cara replied, "I understand. I'm just so frustrated, and it felt good to share it with Gloria. What I said impacted her. She teared up! She may be fickle, but in my gut, I trust her not to betray me. At least not yet...."

"Al trusted her too, and look where it got him," said Ron.

"Just slow down a little, okay, Cara?" said Em. "We have time. Stay focused, and do the job they hired you to do. *If* you're not fired tomorrow."

Ron and Em were right. She had behaved recklessly. She needed to slow down and not let her impulsiveness get the better of her. "Fine," she muttered. "I'll behave myself at work as long as you two promise to keep working on this."

"I'm all in," said Ron. "Getting this information out is the best way I know of to avenge Al's death and I'm not about to stop now."

"I'm all in as well," said Em. "It's why I do the work I do. I promise to be there for you, but you have to promise to be careful and methodical. No more impulsive conversations!"

Cara wiped a tear from her eye. It was good to have friends who supported her. "How would I get through this without you both? Let's check in tomorrow."

CARA WAS BOTH SURPRISED and relieved to be allowed entry into the building the next day. Gloria barely acknowledged her, which gave her the opportunity to complete her work and let things unfold slowly. Day by day, she began to relax.

She was enjoying the quiet in the office. Gloria was at a meeting, and Henry had left to get a cup of coffee. He never worked when Gloria wasn't around. In fact, he rarely worked when Gloria was around, either. Cara wondered why Gloria didn't fire him. Actually, she wondered why Gloria didn't fire *her*.

An email from Abigail, the librarian, popped up on her screen. **"Gloria asked me to tell you the articles you requested are available. Please come get them as soon as possible."** Cara reread the email. *Seriously? Might Gloria be helping her, after all?* She grabbed her bag and started down the hall, but then thought better of it. Returning to her desk, she removed the tiny bug and placed it under her keyboard. She didn't want anyone tracking her to the library. That place was sinister enough, without the added worry of being followed. She walked down the hallway toward the elevator, trying to act as nonchalant as possible. She was glad no one could see her racing pulse. Her purse vibrated, indicating a text or call on her burner phone buried in the bag's bottom. She considered ignoring it, then decided to check it since Ron and Em were the only two people who had that phone number. Sure enough, there was a text from Ron: **"URGENT: Call me ASAP. And be alone!"**

Ducking into the women's restroom, she peeked under both stalls and called Ron. "What's up?" she asked brusquely. She wanted to keep this brief, since Abigail had said to come right away.

"You alone?" asked Ron.

"Yes, I'm in the women's restroom and I'm alone."

"I have information about your office-mate, Henry. I found his name in some of Al's old notes. His brother, James, was a gambling addict and died by suicide six years ago."

Stunned, Cara dropped her bag. This was the last thing she expected. "How...?" she began.

Ron interrupted her. "I can't go into all the details right now, except to tell you that Henry talked to Al before he died."

"Wait a second," said Cara, rubbing the back of her neck. "Henry's name was in Al's notes? How did they know each other?"

"As part of our work, Al interviewed people who lost family members to suicide. Henry's brother, James Ives, was on the list."

"Wow," said Cara slowly. "This really changes things. I thought Henry was on the side of the big corporations."

"Henry worked with Al on a report that I never saw. It's stored in the CDC library archives, and I suspect Henry wants it. He may have been plotting this for a long time. Also..."

Cara cut him off. She needed to get to the library before Abigail left. "Listen, Ron, can it wait until tonight? I'm in the middle of something important right now, and you should share this information with both me and Libby."

"Okay," Ron agreed. "There's a lot to talk about. But be careful around Henry. Given his erratic behavior, I suspect he's working alone. He may be on our side, as you say, but we can't be sure. Right now, he's unpredictable."

She debated telling Ron she was on her way to the library to get what might be the microfilm of that report, but decided she would tell him later. She didn't want to keep Abigail waiting.

As she exited the elevator in the building's basement, goosebumps formed on her bare arms. She shivered, wishing she'd worn a sweater. *Why was it always so chilly down here?* The dimly lit corridor didn't help the eerie mood. A few coats of paint and some better lighting would spruce up this place enormously, she thought. But, then again, few people came down here, so why waste money on redecorating?

She hugged herself, in part to keep out the cold, damp air and also to combat a disturbing feeling of isolation. A few short weeks ago, she had come down here for the first time and found it creepy, but now it seemed down-right sinister. The goosebumps on her arms had grown to the size of tiny peas. *Stop being paranoid!* Resolutely, she dropped her arms to her sides, stood up tall, and continued down the dark hallway, her heels clicking loudly on the cement floor. Reaching the library, she stared up at the dripping letters scrawled in yellow paint on the wall: **CARMEN WAS HERE: 1994**. *Who was Carmen? Did Ron know him?* She looked at the door. Last time she was here, there was a camera with a flashing red light in the hallway. The camera was still there, but the light was off. She waved at it a few times, wondering if it worked by motion detection, but the light remained off. Was it deactivated? *Stop being paranoid! It's probably just a dead battery.* All she needed to do was go in, pick up the papers, and leave.

She squared her shoulders and flashed her card at the high-tech card reader, once again marveling at how out-of-place it looked in this dungeon. The heavy door swung open with a groan, and Cara stepped inside. "Abigail?" she called out. "It's Cara Davenport. I'm here to pick up the reports." Her voice echoed in the small chamber. Peering around the metal desk, she could see the stacks where Abigail had retrieved papers for her a few weeks ago. The counter was empty now, save for a lone desktop monitor sitting in the corner. *Where was the librarian?* She should have been at her desk. "I'd better get out of here," she mumbled. "This doesn't feel right. There must be some mistake."

She turned to go, and behind her, heard a rustle. She froze in terror, her heart skipping a beat. "No. No mistake," Henry's voice rang out. "You surprised me, is all. You left your tracker upstairs, didn't you?" Cara slowly turned to see her office-mate staring icily at her, holding a box-cutting knife in his hand. Instinctively, she clasped her hands together, feeling the tiny button on her ring. *Should she press it?* She hesitated. If she pressed the button, Ron and Em would contact security. But given what she had just learned about Henry, was that the right approach? That might make things worse. *Think!*

"Come join my little party," Henry said, pointing with the cutter to nudge her along behind the counter and into the microfilm viewing room. Cara gasped as she entered the room. Seated on the floor, backs against the wall and eyes wide with terror, were Gloria and Abigail. Once again, her hands came together. *Now! Press it now!* said a voice in her head. And then Ron's voice: "*He's unpredictable!*" She pressed the button as Henry motioned her to the floor alongside the two women.

Henry was blinking wildly. Cara knew his tic was worse when he was agitated. He pointed the knife toward Abigail. "Tell me where the microfilms are. There is a report in there by Al Lawdly, and I want it."

Abigail was sobbing. "I t-t-t-told you! I don't know!"

"Henry, that film is lost..." Gloria began, her voice trembling.

"I don't believe you! It's here, and you're going to find it!" he roared.

Both Abigail and Gloria blanched. Abigail opened her mouth to speak, but Cara interrupted. "Henry, listen to me. I know how you feel..."

"STOP!" he roared again. "You have no idea how I feel." He waved his arms wildly in the air, the cutter still in his hand.

"Maybe I do," Cara whispered. Inwardly, she trembled, but she pressed on. "My father was a gambling addict, just like your brother. I understand the anguish of living with that."

Surprise registered across Henry's face. "I don't believe you! You can't know what it was like, living with that hell, day after day."

Her voice shook, but she kept on talking. "My father died by suicide."

Henry blinked rapidly and started pacing.

"Tell me about James," Cara encouraged. "What was it like, living with him, losing him?"

Henry paced faster, still blinking wildly. "It was horrible! My parents—they lived in despair for months. They tried to hide the worst of it from me, but I knew what was going on."

"Was he older than you?" Cara trembled, still trying to keep her voice level. *Why hadn't help come?* Ron and Em knew she was in trouble. Wouldn't they send someone from Security down here?

She thought back to her college psychology classes. One thing stuck in her mind—the power of listening. If she could keep him talking, he might calm down.

"We were twins. For years, we did everything together. We had no secrets from each other until he got hooked. He was 24 when he... when it ended." Henry sank to his knees, covering his face with his hands. "He would disappear for weeks, and when he returned, he pretended nothing was wrong. That hurt more than anything. Sometimes, he would act normally and I would think he was done with gambling and it was all just a bad dream. And then he would binge again."

She nodded. "I remember that feeling. It was easy to deny there were problems when life was good."

Henry blinked rapidly again and stood up. "My brother, he was smart. He wasn't into drugs or anything like that. He got obsessed with online gambling and couldn't break out of it. I saw the way they hooked him." He turned away, once again burying his face in his hands.

"After he died, I met Mr. Lawdly. He was interviewing family members of gambling addicts who died by suicide." Henry spoke more rapidly now. "Mr. Lawdly—he wanted to stop this. He wanted to hold these corporations accountable and dismantle them. He submitted a report and told me to be patient... and then he died." Henry looked directly at Cara now. "He had information, and he intended to use it to ruin the reputations of some of the biggest offenders. I helped him get it."

Gloria gasped and Abigail turned white as a sheet, leaving Cara wondering what they knew. Henry turned back toward them, glaring as he continued. "I intend to finish his work. I'm going after those monsters, and I need that report." He stared at Gloria and Abigail. "One or both of you knows where the microfilms are." Turning to Cara, he added, "You may know some things as well."

Gloria whispered, "The report is gone, Henry. We destroyed it four years ago. I watched Abigail burn it."

"Liar!" Henry screamed and pivoted toward her. Cara suspected the microfilm of the report still existed, as she saw a look pass between Abigail and Gloria. Henry hadn't noticed.

"Henry, let us go now, and we can work with you," Gloria said. "We can try to reconstruct what was in that report. I read some of it and know what that was. If you hurt us now, no good will come of this."

Henry crumpled to the floor, sobbing. "I want to hurt them, the way they hurt me. The way they hurt my family. It's not fair they get to go on making millions by preying on the weakness of others. It's so wrong!"

Cara pressed the button on her ring again. "I want the same thing. My family has been affected by this, too. I want to bring these industry leaders to justice." She paused and glanced again at Gloria, hoping she hadn't revealed too much. She still wasn't sure she could trust her. "Let us out of here peacefully. We can talk later."

Gloria shook her head. "This is a mess," she whispered. "You're right, Henry. That microfilm wasn't destroyed. It's here at the CDC, somewhere in the archives."

"I knew it!" Henry cried. "This is what I need -"

Gloria interrupted him. "You can't publicize it, though. If you do, and the Director finds out I didn't destroy it, I'm ruined. My job at the CDC is over."

She pursed her lips and continued. "That report was trouble! Al Lawdly recorded a meeting of gambling industry kingpins in which they laid out a plan to deceive the public in a variety of ways." Cara's mouth dropped open, though Gloria didn't seem to notice. She was looking straight ahead.

"He gave me a transcript of the meeting, and I worried it would cause great turmoil if it leaked out, but it wasn't my problem to handle. I took it to my boss, thinking he would support more research into it. But I didn't get the response I expected. The Director fired Al and his colleague, Ronald, and ordered me to forget the entire mess and obliterate the report." She buried her head in her hands.

"I didn't know what to do! Agency rules stated registered CDC documents should never be eradicated without first microfilming. I told the director I destroyed the report and even showed him the ashes of the burned document. But before I did that, I asked Abigail to put it on microfilm and hide it. She is the only one who knows where it is."

Cara stared in amazement. This was the evidence Ron was searching for. "If that recording is for real, it has to become public, can't you see? It's critical evidence. You did something truly courageous by not destroying it. Don't tell me now you're going to give in to them!"

Gloria looked up. "It wasn't courageous! All I wanted to do was keep my job and follow CDC regulations."

"There's the basis of a whistleblowing complaint," Cara pressed. "Your boss asked you to break the law by destroying all traces of an official CDC document. You have a pretty compelling complaint there. Personnel would back you for sure."

"Except that my boss is the director of the CDC. He is everyone's boss here, including the Personnel office. What a mess!" she repeated. She sighed, then turned to Abigail, who was still trembling. "Abigail, can you retrieve that microfilm?"

Abigail's big brown eyes overflowed with tears. She looked down and shook her head slowly. "I c-can't," she whispered.

"Why not? You did microfilm the report, correct?" demanded Gloria.

She shook her head more forcefully and looked up. "I... I did, but then I g-gave the film to Carmen," she stuttered.

Gloria's jaw dropped. "You what?"

"I g-g-gave it to Carmen," Abigail repeated. She hugged herself and looked down at the ground. "I was n-new at the job and d-didn't know where to put it, so I c-called C-carmen and asked for his advice." The tears flowed freely now.

"He was so h-helpful training me during my first week, and when he left, he t-told me to call him if I had any questions. He spoke so highly of you and said whatever you wanted sh-should happen. And he swore to me that the document would never end up in the wrong hands." She covered her face with her hands.

"Didn't it occur to you this was a confidential document which should stay on CDC grounds?" Gloria challenged.

Abigail rubbed her eyes. "You d-didn't say it had to remain on site. You told me to hide it away where no one would find it. Carmen assured me he could do that."

"Well," said Cara brightly. "This may be good news! All we need to do is find Carmen and get the report from him."

"Sure," snorted Gloria. "Except Carmen disappeared a few weeks after retiring. We wanted to hold a dinner in his honor, but there was no trace of him."

"I think he gave the report back to Mr. Lawdly." They all stared at Henry. He paced excitedly. "It's all clear to me now! Mr. Lawdly had enough rope to hang them all. He had the recording of that meeting. He just needed to release it at the right time."

Cara's mind went into overdrive. What had Ron told her? Prior to Al's death, he wanted Ron to know some things. Was this Al's "breakthrough" that Ron never got to see? A covert recording of some clandestine meeting? And what, exactly, was Henry's involvement?

"Okay," Cara said. "So, where does this leave us? As far as we know, the report is missing, and all our jobs are on the line right now."

She looked at them all. Gloria seemed defeated, though clearly still in the throes of her own inner battle. Where did her loyalty lie? Cara had to trust her to do the right thing. Abigail remained cowered in the corner of the room, terrified she had done something illegal by giving the microfilm away. To Cara's surprise, only Henry looked hopeful. She wondered if all he had needed was someone to listen to him and take him seriously.

She turned to Henry now. "Henry, you're not going to gain anything by keeping us here. I intend to work with you, and now that we know the truth, we can come up with a plan. I'm just not sure what that plan will be yet."

Without a word, Henry threw down the knife and ran out the door, leaving the three women staring after him.

"D-DO YOU REALLY THINK he's gone?" Abigail asked.

"Why would he stay? Once he realized the report wasn't here, he had no reason to keep us," said Gloria.

Cara breathed a sigh of relief, then looked down at her hands and noticed her ring. "We should have had some help. I have a panic alert button on my ring. I don't understand why it didn't work," she said.

"Magnetic interference," said Abigail. "Electronic devices can't transmit down here. I'm not sure, but I think it's because of all the metal in the walls and the ceiling."

"It's an intentional design," said Gloria. "Carmen once told me they don't want people copying things from here without clearance. Once something gets on the internet, it can be hard to contain."

Cara shivered. The CDC was so paranoid about things leaking out. It seemed the agency was more concerned about privacy than it was about researching and discovering new things. The more she learned about how things worked here, the more she questioned it.

"So, what do we do about Henry?" she asked.

"I'd say we do nothing for now," said Gloria. "As crazy as this sounds, I don't think he intended to harm us. He wanted something and thought we could get it for him, but now that it's clear we can't, he's no longer a threat to any of us. Let's just proceed with caution around him and see where this goes."

Cara stared at her. Gloria was changing, but Cara could see she needed time. They all did. They needed to process this recent turn of events, and Cara hoped Gloria would join with her to stop the corporate greed that controlled this organization.

Eighteen

THAT EVENING, CARA SAT outside her apartment building. What a day it had been! She wasn't sure how to begin to describe it to Ron and Em. Was it just this morning she had learned about Henry's brother?

Eagerly, she began the call. "You were right about Henry, Ron. You won't believe what happened today! Henry tried to trap me, Gloria, and Abigail, the librarian, in the library in order to get the microfilm of a report written by Al Lawdly. He lured me down there and ambushed me! Thank God you had told me about him before that! Knowing about his brother, I was able to calm him down and -"

Ron's reaction dampened her enthusiasm. "What were you thinking?" he said with exasperation. In her mind's eye, Cara pictured him running his hands through his shock of dark hair. "Why didn't you use your panic button to call for help?"

"I did! And I discovered something... the CDC is so worried about documents being stolen that they restrict internet access in the basement where the archives are. Electronic devices don't work down there."

Ron blew out a breath. "I knew that! I should have warned you about the library. It never occurred to me you'd be trapped down there."

"I was okay, though. There were three of us. We could have overpowered him if we had to."

"Seriously, Cara, you need to be more careful. He could have killed you!" Ron retorted.

"Hold on here," said Em. "Ron, you're right. Cara needs to be careful, especially given the people we're investigating. But let's put that aside for now so Cara can finish up everything she has to tell us."

"Okay," said Ron. "Though I have more information about Henry-"

"Henry is obsessed with finding that report Al wrote," Cara interrupted. "Do you have any idea what's in it?"

"I might. After Al and I published our initial paper, we learned Geraldine Major invited Senator Bly to a meeting in Gibraltar. We suspected she wanted to discuss how to deal with our revelations. Al wondered about the possibility of wiretapping Bly, but I never thought he could pull that off. If there was a recording of that meeting, it would be one hell of a story."

"Abigail said she gave the microfilm to Carmen. Who was he?" Cara asked. "I keep wondering that every time I go down to the library."

"Carmen was the CDC librarian for years. He and Al were close friends. All three of us were, actually. He retired shortly after they fired us out of solidarity with us. He and Al stayed in touch and he visited Al in California, then disappeared. I never heard from him after that. If he got the microfilm, of course he would have passed it on to Al. I'm sure of it. That must be the thing Al wanted me to know."

"If Carmen gave Al the microfilm, is it possible Al's wife still has it?" asked Em.

"I can check with her." Ron cleared his throat. "But there's something else a little unsettling you need to know about Henry Ives. When I heard his name, I thought it sounded familiar. This morning, I dug through Al's old notes and found a list of people he had met with who had relatives who died by suicide. I almost missed this connection because Henry's name was not on the list. However, James Ives was on the list. When I dug a little deeper, I discovered James had a brother, Henry, who died by suicide. Al interviewed James for his report."

"I'm not sure I'm following you," Cara said slowly. "Are you saying the Henry Ives who works with me isn't named Henry?"

"That's his brother's name. I'm sure of it. I kept some of those records when we left the CDC. James changed his name to Henry. He took on his brother's identity after his brother's suicide."

"Why would he do that?" asked Cara, intrigued.

"That's what I'm trying to work out."

"I'll look into the backgrounds of both Ives brothers," offered Em. "In the meantime, we need to figure out what our intentions are. What do we want to accomplish?"

"Believe me, I've spent a lot of time thinking about long-term goals," said Ron. "Unfortunately, online gambling is here to stay, and we can't change that. What we can change is public perception. I mean, cigarettes are still around, right? But most Americans recognize the dangers and stay away. It's gone from being a cool habit to a disgusting one, though it took decades to get to this point. The Gambling Industry Research Institute has poured money into glitzy advertising campaigns and false news. We have to give people basic information to refute that. It won't be easy to get our message out. Education is key."

"Legislation is key as well," said Cara. "The laws regulating the industry have to change. We need to change the way online sites operate permanently so this doesn't keep happening as other new companies pop up. Somehow, we have to get the lobbyists out of the way."

"That won't be easy," said Ron. "We're talking about some powerful people. Libby and I compiled a short list. At the top, we have Geraldine Major, an only child with both parents deceased. She was born in the U.S., currently lives in Gibraltar, and is arguably the most influential person in the entire online gambling industry. She is super smart and snaky and will do anything for money. Her company, Majority Rules, oversees brick-and-mortar casinos with the brand 'Pair o' Dice' as well as multiple online sites."

At the mention of Pair o' Dice and Majority Rules, Cara's stomach clenched. That was the casino Brady went to when he celebrated his 18th birthday. Silently, she cursed Geraldine Major.

"So, her company operates both online and in-person?" asked Cara.

"Yes, but my understanding is she's phasing out the brick-and-mortar casinos and only using them to drive traffic to her online sites. Based on the work she's done so far, I believe she is trying to develop a new technology for Virtual Reality—one that doesn't involve the use of any extraneous headgear. If so, this would revolutionize VR technology by making it far more accessible for the average user, and far more dangerous for the addict.

"In the past three years, MR's pre-tax profits increased 65-fold to almost $400 million. In the first three months of this year, it made $125 million. That works out to about $1.4 million per day, $58,000 an hour, or about $1,000 a minute." Ron paused to let that sink in.

"Taking Geraldine out of the picture would cripple the entire industry. She is the glue that holds it all together. Without her, there would still be online sites for sure, but they would be disconnected and have far less influence. However, taking her out would be next to impossible as she lives abroad and leads an extremely protected and secluded life. As far as I can tell, she never married and has no next of kin, though she doesn't seem to lack male companionship."

"I'm all for going after her," said Cara flatly. She recalled Brady's enthusiasm when he talked about going to the Majority Rules Casino for his birthday. "She seems to be the guiding force. Plus, Majority Rules owns the casino Brady went to just before his accident. Whatever we can do to weaken her organization would be good."

"Agreed," said Ron. "Though, if we're going to be successful in this, we have to take our personal feelings out of it. I want revenge as much as you do, Cara, but we have to stay focused on the big picture. And that big picture has other players besides Geraldine Major."

Cara clenched and unclenched her fists. She visualized Geraldine Major being brought to justice. Perhaps a car accident, like Al Lawdly? Ron was right. She wanted Geraldine Major to suffer. She wanted revenge. How was she supposed to take her personal feelings out of it? With an effort, she turned her attention back to the phone.

"Next on the list is Senator Richard Bly. I believe he was behind what happened to Al. He has a reputation as a conservative and upstanding family man. He married his high school sweetheart and they have two kids in their early 20s.

"Rumor has it he was a 'companion' to Geraldine for quite a while, though it seems to have cooled off lately. Whatever their social relationship, it's clear he's her right-hand man for lobbying efforts in the U.S. He is chairperson of the Senate Appropriations Committee, which controls the way the government spends money. That committee sets budgets for federal organizations."

"So, the CDC is under his financial control?" asked Em.

"Not exactly, but he has a major say in its funding. He doesn't overtly control the direction of research, but he can pressure the agency to focus on certain things and ignore others.

"There are a lot of other players out there, but those two are the foundation. Without them, the industry would be far more like the wild west—a bunch of greedy guys trying to skirt around laws. With an increase in public awareness and growing public pressure, those laws could be tightened. This really needs to be attacked on several fronts."

Cara thought for a moment. "What if we formed a non-profit corporation? An organization committed to providing public education and awareness of the dangers of online gambling, plus lobbying for better laws? Starting with programs for elementary school kids and working up from there?"

"That would be amazing, but takes money. Where would we get the funding for that?" asked Em. "This industry has an enormous amount of money to throw around."

The germ of an idea was forming in Cara's mind. It was a pipe dream, but might be something to aim for. At the moment, though, they had more pressing things to deal with.

"I'm going to talk to Henry, or James, or whoever he is. I wonder if he'll tell me of his identity change without me asking. Also, I think Gloria is close to melting. She may well be willing to go public about all this. Which reminds me... Ron, didn't you tell me you have a friend in Personnel? Is he someone we could trust to give Gloria advice if she chooses to be a whistleblower? She needs to understand her rights."

"I'll talk to my friend Gerry. He may be able to help. But it's risky. She needs to be prepared to go through some intense questioning, and it won't be pretty."

"We're getting close to all this now. I can feel it," said Em. "And now is the time when we need to be extra careful. It isn't just the three of us anymore. Now Gloria, Henry, and Abigail are also in on it, and potentially this guy in Personnel as well. The more people involved, the more risk there is of something leaking out at the wrong time. Given what happened to Ron's friend Al, we can't take any chances."

"Consider that a warning, Cara," said Ron. "I can see you rolling your eyes through the phone line, but you have to understand the danger. We know you're both smart and resourceful, but please, don't take anymore crazy risks, okay? You have a panic button for a reason. Stay away from the library and use it if you need to!"

Cara did indeed roll her eyes, though she felt touched. It was good to know there were people out there on her side. She closed her eyes, imagining a time when they could meet in person without fear once again.

Nineteen

CARA ARRIVED EARLY TO work, surprised to see Gloria's office empty and Henry already at his desk. "Can I talk to you privately?" he asked. Nervously, he averted his eyes, his face twitching.

"Sure," said Cara. "Go ahead."

"Er... can we walk somewhere? I think better when I'm moving."

"Okay," replied Cara. "Let's go outside. It's a beautiful morning."

Henry nodded and blinked a few times as they began walking. Cara tilted her head as she heard an odd rattling sound. It didn't quite sound like the pen he usually clicked.

"What's that noise?" she asked.

He blushed and pulled his hands from his pockets to reveal a handful of tiny magnets. "Sorry... I use them as worry beads. I always feel calmer when I rub them together." He looked away. "I can't believe I told you. How embarrassing."

Cara laughed. "I wish I had something like that right now!"

"Here—hold out your hand." Henry dropped two beads into Cara's hand. They felt warm and smooth as she rolled them around.

"Wow," she said. "These are amazing." She started to hand them back to him, but he stopped her.

"You can keep them. I have plenty more," he said as he resumed walking. He looked down again, then finally stole a glance at Cara and spoke. "I'm not sure where to begin." The rhythmic clicking continued as he fingered the magnets in his pockets. "I uh.... worked with Mr. Lawdly a bit. It was about four and a half years ago, two years after my brother died, and I was a Senator's aide in the government. Mr. Lawdly was interviewing relatives of people who died by suicide, and I found out about that through a friend. During the interview, Mr. Lawdly learned where I worked." Henry took the magnets out of his pocket and poured them from one hand to the other. "He asked me if I could get him some information."

Cara narrowed her eyes. "What kind of information? Where did you work?" she asked.

He pocketed the magnets. "I was an aide to Senator Richard Bly, who was on the Senate Appropriations Committee." Cara gasped as she realized the implications of that. Henry continued, "Mr. Lawdly suspected some high-ranking politicians wanted to de-regulate online gambling. When he discovered I worked in Bly's office, he asked me to watch for anything unusual. When the Senator traveled to Gibraltar, I went with him." Henry walked faster as the words tumbled out. Cara had to jog to keep up with him.

"I got a tiny recording device to slip into the Senator's pocket." He gave Cara a sideways glance. "It differed from the one I put in your bag. It was just a recorder, not a transmitter, because we feared a transmission might be intercepted. Ms. Major's office in Gibraltar is a primary hub and has transmissions going all over the place. After the trip, I took Bly's suit jacket to the dry-cleaner, retrieved the device, and gave it to Mr. Lawdly. Within a week, he and his partner were fired—because of information I gave him." Henry stopped and looked straight at Cara, unblinking for the first time in Cara's memory. His hands remained in his pockets, but the clicking ceased. Cara suspected he was clutching his hands tightly around the little metal balls.

"I heard Mr. Lawdly moved to California, and I wanted to find out what happened to the recording. After all, I had risked everything to get it. Even though I never listened to it, I was sure it was pretty damning if he got fired over it." The clicking resumed, and Henry started walking again, looking straight ahead.

"I visited him in California. He told me to be patient; he had enough information to go after some of the biggest leaders in the industry. He said the records were still at the CDC and he was trying to get them. I believed him, but now, looking back, I suspect he had the recording in his possession at that time." He paused again, blinking rapidly once again. "Two weeks after my visit, he was in a fatal car accident. I found out about it from his wife when I tried to call him a month later."

Cara stopped and waited for Henry to turn back toward her. For a moment, she couldn't speak. Finally, she found her voice. "Did anyone else know of the recording?"

"He told me he presented it to Gloria and she showed it to the Director, who told Senator Bly. I was working for Bly at the time and he was furious. For days, he stormed around the office, cursing at anyone who approached him. Everyone wondered what put him in such a foul mood. I knew the reason, though, and feared he'd discover what I had done. I wanted to quit right away, but Mr. Lawdly told me to wait. He said quitting would draw more attention to me." Henry resumed walking. The words came faster now, though his hands were quiet.

"Bly knew about the report. Even though he thought the recording was destroyed, he couldn't stand the idea that someone was aware of those meetings. Mr. Lawdly's mere existence was a threat to him, and I'm willing to bet he hired a hit man and had him killed. I had nightmares about that. What would he do to me if he knew of my involvement?" At this, Henry stopped and rolled his shoulders, trying to ease the tension from them.

"Wow," said Cara, squeezing her fingers around the two little magnets, just as Henry had done. The smooth balls soothed her nerves. "That's a lot to take in at once. Now I understand why you want that recording."

"I've been plotting to get it ever since I left Bly's office. But there's something else you should know, too." Henry looked away and rolled his shoulders again. He blinked and ran his hands through his scraggly hair. "When I left

Senator Bly's office, I was still afraid he might be a little suspicious of me, even though a year had gone by. I decided I needed to do something drastic to protect myself, so I changed my identity and went underground for a few months. My name isn't actually Henry. It's James." Cara let her mouth drop open, feigning surprise. She was glad he brought it up, but she wasn't sure she fully trusted him yet. She looked at him quizzically.

"Here," he said, digging in his pockets and bringing out 2 photographs. "This was me, when I worked for Senator Bly." Cara stared in amazement at the clean-cut man in the photos. Her gaze shifted from the pictures back to Henry's unkempt hair and unshaven face. *Could that be the same person?*

"It was actually Mr. Lawdly's idea," he added. "He advised me to keep the job for a year, then quit and take on Henry's identity in order to disappear. Since my brother and I were twins, it was an easy switch. Bly didn't know about my brother—Henry's suicide happened a year before I started working in Bly's office."

Henry seemed calmer now. The blinking had slowed, and he stood taller. He spoke clearly, with a sense of purpose. "By the time I quit, Mr. Lawdly was gone, and I understood how much Senator Bly was doing to promote online gambling. I wanted to stop him, and I wanted revenge. My brother died, and no one seemed to care." He looked straight at Cara once again.

"For what it's worth, I care," said Cara. "I wasn't kidding earlier in the library when I told you I know what it's like. I lost my best friend and my dad. And I worry about my brother. If there's a way to stop this, I'm going to find it."

"I want to get that recording, or at least the transcript of it. I thought it was still in the CDC archives. I waited a while, took a few classes, and got a job with the CDC so I could get into the library. I figured if I worked in Gloria's department, where Mr. Lawdly did his research, I'd have easier access to it."

Cara looked at him and realized she had underestimated him. She was glad he had confessed to the identity change and felt he could help their cause tremendously. If what he said was true, this was a bigger scandal than any of them ever imagined. And if they had that recording to prove it....

Just as she was about to invite him to listen in on her next conference call with Ron and Em, her phone buzzed. Her mom calling. She turned from Henry to take the call.

"Cara, it's Brady," her mom began. "He's waking up. Can you come home for a few days?"

I HATE YOU! You lured me in, and then you threw me out like I was a worthless piece of shit. How is it you have such a grip on me? I wish I could say we were done, but even now, I feel your pull. Why are you doing this to me?

Twenty

SHE SAT AT HIS bedside, holding his hand, watching his face twitch as he struggled to wake from the coma. She felt a weak squeeze of pressure on her hand. He opened his eyes.

"Hi, Sis," he whispered. Cara's heart fluttered with joy. He was awake and knew who she was! Relief flooded over her.

"Hi back," she said, clasping his hand. Brady shifted.

"I... sorry," he murmured. "Should've listened to you."

"Not now, Brady," Cara told him. "You have nothing to apologize for. I don't blame you. Your only job right now is to recover. We can talk later."

Tears formed in his eyes. She could see the effort it took for him to keep them open. If he could have turned away, he would have, but the collar around his neck made movement impossible. He was fading in and out of consciousness, each time lingering a few moments longer while

Cara and her mom took turns sitting with him, keeping the conversation light when he woke up.

He was in a semi-conscious state when the doctor came in to do her rounds.

"What's your name?" she asked him casually.

"Brady," he mumbled.

"Do you know where you are?"

"Hospital?" he asked. He couldn't move his head, but his eyes widened a little in anxiety.

"Right. You were in an accident and you're in the hospital. Your job right now is simply to rest, okay?"

"K," he murmured and drifted back to sleep again.

The doctor turned to Cara and Sally. "He'll be like this for a while. The most important thing for you to do when he wakes up is to keep him calm. Don't let him get anxious or agitated. He has a lot of healing to do."

"You think he can fully heal?" asked Sally tentatively.

"It's hard to tell. The good news is he's talking clearly, but unfortunately, he has no motor control in his arms and legs. We still don't know the extent of his injuries. It's hard to get decent images with so much swelling." She motioned for them to join her in the hallway, then whispered.

"He may seem like he's asleep, but it's possible he's hearing every word, so be careful what you say around him. For sure, walking will be difficult for a long time. It's possible he may never walk at all. We don't want to tell him this yet, but you need to prepare, just in case...."

"I want to be with him when you break this news to him. How long before you'll know more?" Cara asked.

"I can't say right now. It might be weeks before we're sure, and until that time, we don't want to worry him unnecessarily."

Cara sighed. She had only wrangled two full days off from work. That would have to be enough for now.

She spent those two days sitting quietly with him, holding his hand, sometimes along with her mom, and sometimes unaccompanied.

On her last afternoon with him, Brady opened his eyes once again. Every time he surfaced, he was more lucid. His eyes no longer had a foggy look to them. Now he almost managed a smile. "How much longer can you stay?" he asked.

"I'm leaving in a few hours. My boss has been nice enough to give me this much time, but I don't want to push it."

"You mean your boss, the witch?" he asked, startling her. So, he remembered at least part of that conversation. Perhaps he remembered more. She smiled as he shifted in his bed. She didn't want to agitate him, though she wondered what he remembered, especially about their father. That was a conversation she didn't want to repeat.

"Yes, my boss, the witch," she responded. "But she's not all bad. She monitors me closely, but lately, she's been a bit nicer. When Patrick died, she was nasty to me, but with you in the hospital, she's been a little more forgiving."

"Yeah, I was thinking of Patrick a little and about things you told me," he began. Once again, the memory surprised her. She wondered if it was okay to let him keep talking. Would this stir him up? She wanted to slow him down, but he was bent on continuing. "You warned me, but at the time, I couldn't listen. I fell into this deep, deep hole, and there was no way out. No—that's not even it. I didn't *want* to get out, and I'm still not sure I want to be out now. In there, I didn't care about the world, or my school grades, or relationships, or anything! Plus, I felt connected to Dad."

His voice was rising. *Keep him calm.* Cara took hold of his hand and looked straight at him. "I understand, Brady. But we don't need to talk about this right now…"

He cut her off. "I do! I'm more upset not to talk about it! Can't you see? It's running through my head, and I need to tell someone. This is important to me. Please, just listen!"

"Okay, but first you need to take a few breaths. The doctor told us to keep you calm."

"When I'm gambling, time is suspended. Part of me wants to stay in that mindless state forever. But I know I can't. It's not real. And that's hard to accept. Why can't I play just a little? All my friends can! They're able to stop appropriately, but I can't."

He stopped and closed his eyes. He was so still that for a moment, Cara thought he was asleep. She waited in silence, holding his hand, hoping her presence was enough. It was the best she could offer him right now. Slowly, his eyes opened again. "What you told me about Dad terrified me. I didn't want to believe it. I thought I could gamble and stop whenever I wanted, and if I could do that, it would prove you wrong. But I was the one who was wrong. For a while, I was in an alternate reality—a place where nothing mattered in the world except the next roll, the next play. Then it was over. I came crashing down, and somehow, I had gambled away *everything*. All of it. Every penny I had."

Cara wiped the tears from his face with a cloth. "For a while, I didn't care if I lived or died. No, that's not true either. I wanted to die. Death would have been so much easier than facing the reality of what I did and having to fight against it. I love poker. I love betting! I love the thrill of it and don't want to give that up. I AM SO STUPID!"

"You're not-" Cara began, but Brady cut her off.

"I am, though. Only a stupid person would do that. I should have known better, especially after you talked to me. I should have been able to stop." He squeezed his face, as if in pain. "There's more...." He moved his mouth, and a tiny sound came out. Cara leaned in to hear him better. In the barest whisper, he breathed, "For a moment, I heard Dad."

"You what?" exclaimed Cara.

He opened his eyes, his voice stronger now. "Dad spoke to me. He said, 'Don't make the same mistakes I made,' just like you told me he would."

Exhausted, Brady closed his eyes once again. "I want to quit. But the truth is, it wasn't under my control and it's still not. Even now, there's this voice inside saying, 'come back.' I'm afraid to open my laptop because I know what will greet me. I don't have the strength to say no."

"You're not stupid!" Cara repeated. "And you're not weak! You are incredibly smart, and you did a stupid thing when you weren't thinking clearly. That happens to all of us. Do you think I never do stupid things? Guess again! But that doesn't define me, and it doesn't need to define you either." She paused to let that sink in. Brady's eyes were closed now, but he fluttered them open to show he was listening.

"There's a big difference between stupidity and addiction. You have an addiction, and unfortunately, there are people in the world who discovered they can make money off it, and they will do everything in their power to get you to continue. *Your* power lies in recognizing that. It's your ticket out. Addiction sucks! But there are ways to treat it, and with help, you can beat it. Being aware of it and being willing to get help are the first steps."

Cara bit her lip. "I'm thinking of using dad's money to set up a new business—a non-profit company with a mission to educate the public about the dangers of online gambling. Maybe someday, when you're feeling stronger, you can work with me on this." Her own words surprised her. Though she'd been thinking of it for a while, it was the first time she had verbalized it aloud to anyone.

Brady stared at her, his eyes wide open now.

"You're crazy to take that on," he whispered. "There's no way you can win."

"We'll see," replied Cara, "but you never know...."

Twenty one

"Cara, you don't understand," said Gloria sharply. "I can't go public with this information. I'll lose my job."

They sat on a wooden bench outside the CDC building, overlooking a duck pond. Eight tiny ducklings followed their mother as she circled the pond. Cara marveled at the way they stayed in a perfectly straight row. Gloria was like one of those ducklings, she mused—terrified to step out of line.

"What about the Whistleblower Protection Act?" she asked. "The whole point of that is to prevent you from being fired."

"Who can I complain to? The Director is the problem, and no one will defy him. The only person above him is Senator Bly, and nobody will go against him either!"

Perhaps Gloria was right, but there had to be a way around this. "What about Henry?" she asked. "He gave Al the recording. Maybe he could come forward and say he has a copy."

"He doesn't have a copy, though. Would you ask him to lie under oath and testify that he has one? We can't. Plus, Senator Bly would say Henry obtained that recording illegally."

Cara watched one duckling turn and move out of the line. The project that had been percolating in her mind was taking shape. "What if you quit?" she asked.

"What?" Gloria looked at her in shock. "I can't leave! This is the only job I've ever had! I worked damn hard to get where I am in this organization, and I'm not about to walk out now! And whatever would I do?"

"Well," said Cara slowly. "I have an idea. Just listen, okay?" She shifted her body on the bench so she could face Gloria directly. "When my father died, he left me a lot of money in a trust fund. I wasn't aware of how he got it all, and honestly, I didn't care. It came from him, and I didn't want to squander it, so I invested it. It's now grown—substantially—and I've been wondering what to do with it." She looked straight at Gloria. "That money came from gambling. Gambling that led my father to take his own life and sent my friend Patrick down that same path. Online gambling needs to be regulated, and I want to use the money to help do that."

"You're crazy! You have no clue what you're getting yourself into. There's no way you can win," Gloria said.

Cara stood. Both Ron and Brady had told her the same thing, but she disagreed. "I'm not crazy! I know more than you realize. The Gambling Industry Research Institute used advertising to assure the public that online gambling is a wonderful thing, with absolutely no downsides. Those ads convinced people they could become millionaires overnight by clicking a mouse in the privacy of their own homes. And for the end user, it was all free to sign up!" Gloria nodded. None of this information was new to her.

Cara continued, "So far, it has worked. Industry profits have soared over the last four years. But no longer, because I intend to stop them." She glared at Gloria, daring her to argue.

"How?" asked Gloria.

"I have money set aside and I'm going to create an organization to counter those ads. You can help me! I'm forming a non-profit corporation and I want you to be the Director. We'll develop activities for kids and educate adults as well. We'll *show* people they're being deceived and manipulated. I have the seed money for this and can do some fundraising. Think what we could do together to bring this industry into line."

"You're offering me a job?" asked Gloria incredulously.

Cara smiled and sat back down. "I suppose I am. It would be hard work, and there might be pushback from the CDC eventually, but if you retire now, no one will suspect you of any nefarious motives. You can say you're leaving for health reasons, or that you're looking to make some changes in your life. And then you can quietly disappear. They don't need to know where you go from here. And you can finally be free to do what you know is right. You can make your father and your brother proud." Gloria sat back with a faraway look in her eyes. Cara bit her lip, wondering if her words made a difference.

"We don't have to reveal the recording at all," she continued. "No one needs to know it still exists, but that doesn't stop us from using the information in it. Think about it. Aside from Al Lawdly's 'accident', there's been no fallout from that recording. Senator Bly has probably forgotten all about it."

"I doubt that," said Gloria. "He doesn't forget much. Still... I might consider your offer. But I'll need a staff of people to work for me if I do this. As much as Henry scared the daylights out of me the other day, I think the man deserves a break and this might be an excellent opportunity for him." Cara looked at Gloria with shock. This was the last thing she expected to hear.

"If you must know," Gloria continued, "I've talked with him a lot over the past few days, and it's clear he had a hard life. I guess I've developed a bit of a soft spot for him."

He lost a brother too, Cara mused. It made sense that Gloria would side with him. She looked at the duck pond and saw two of the ducklings had separated from the line. They now glided along, side-by-side, on their own path. Maybe shared tragedy brought people together in unexpected ways.

Twenty two

CARA ARRIVED AT WORK, surprised to see the CDC Director sitting behind Gloria's desk. He beckoned her in, motioning for her to close the door. A balding, beefy man with broad shoulders and an even broader smile that never seemed to reach his eyes, he stood and held out his hand. Cara had met him only once before and wasn't sure she trusted that smile. Timidly, she shook his hand.

"Congratulations!" he said in a gravelly voice. "You are the CDC's new Acting Deputy Director of Public Health, Science, and Surveillance."

Stunned, Cara dropped her hand to her side and stared at him. She opened her mouth to speak, but no words came out.

"Gloria resigned. She has some health issues that need immediate attention, and she recommended you for promotion. She has full confidence in your ability to carry on the responsibilities of this department." Though the words flattered Cara, she heard the skepticism in his voice.

"I'm not sure what to say..." she stammered. "I mean, I'm just a junior statistician..."

The director cleared his throat. "Of course, we'll be looking for someone more qualified to fill the position permanently, but Gloria felt you could handle the immediate responsibilities."

"I'll do my best, sir," she said, wincing inwardly at how lame that sounded. If only Gloria had given her warning! Though perhaps it was better this way, she thought. At least she didn't have to pretend to be shocked.

"Good! So, you can settle in here. This will be your office now. Gloria is sending me a detailed list of the critical things you need to know. We'll meet later today to go over details." He bustled out, brushing past Henry, who was just arriving.

Henry blinked rapidly as he watched the Director go. "What was that all about?" he asked.

She waved him into the office. *Gloria's* office. She wasn't ready, yet, to think of it as her own office. Even sitting behind Gloria's desk didn't feel right. Instead, she stood with her back to the desk and motioned for Henry to sit in a chair.

"What's going on?" he asked.

Cara covered her face with her hands. "You won't believe this," she said, peeking through her fingers. "Gloria resigned suddenly, and they've appointed me Acting Director of the department!"

"Seriously?" said Henry, his face breaking into a wide smile. "That's awesome!"

"Is it?" she asked. "Because I don't know what the hell I'm doing! I've barely been here four months! How am I supposed to do this job? I don't even know the job description!"

Henry pulled out his phone and scrolled through it. "Here it is, straight off the CDC website: 'You are responsible for a wide array of services including facilitating programs and policies to identify and respond to public health threats both domestically and internationally'."

"Right!" said Cara. "As if...!"

"Wait, there's more," said Henry. He laughed. "You'll like this. Ironically, the mission of this department is to put science into action. No wonder Gloria quit!"

Cara groaned. Six months ago, it would have been a dream job for her, one she could barely contemplate qualifying for with her limited experience. But it was all a show. She was merely a puppet in a corrupt agency. Gloria had told her it all came down to money. Top government officials dictated which projects got attention and which ones were off limits, with online gambling being first on that list. And she was charged with keeping that narrative going.

"I wish I could quit now," she said glumly. "But the agency would likely track my every move."

"Think of it this way," said Henry. "You can set up your new non-profit right under their noses!"

"How do you know about that?" she asked, her eyes narrowing.

Henry looked down. "Er... Gloria told me about it," he stammered. "We've been talking a lot, and she said she thought I could work with her..." He brushed his fingers through his unkempt hair.

"Listen, Henry," she said firmly. "No one here can know that! And I mean NO ONE. My friends Ron and Libby are getting it going, and it looks like they'll have Gloria's help, but you and I should have nothing to do with this while we're here. You're right—this is an excellent cover for me, which is why I'm staying. I'll be 'Acting Director' here for a few months until they find someone more qualified, and at that point, we can both quit. But for now, I need you to keep a low profile. Understood?" Henry nodded, looking crestfallen.

The outer door to their office opened and the CDC Director walked in, accompanied by two distinguished-looking gentlemen. Henry stood up and blinked rapidly, then blanched. Without a word, he scurried out of the office past the incoming trio and disappeared into the hallway. As Cara welcomed the visitors in, she noticed one of them gazing after Henry's retreating figure.

"Cara," the Director said in his raspy voice. "I want to introduce you to Senator Tedesco and Senator Bly, both of whom work with the CDC to establish policies."

"Pleased to meet you," said Cara, trying to keep her voice neutral. She had seen the panic on Henry's face when the men walked in. He surely recognized Senator Bly. *Did Bly recognize Henry?* Given the photos Henry had shown her of his former self, she doubted it, but apparently Henry wasn't so sure. Perhaps he worried his facial tic might give him away. Bly shook her hand and eyed her keenly. "So, we hear you are Gloria's replacement." Cara nodded, not quite trusting her voice yet. Finally, she managed a weak smile, saying, "At least temporarily. Gloria left so fast, and it completely caught me off guard. I have a lot to learn. Hopefully, I can keep things afloat here."

The Director nodded with approval, his eyes darting back and forth between Cara and Senator Bly. "Gloria assured me Cara will do an excellent job, though, of course, we'll start a national search for the position. We'll see what happens."

"Tell me," said Bly, motioning toward the door. "Who was that gentleman who ran out just as we came in? There was something familiar about him..."

"Oh, that's Henry," said Cara, deliberately leaving out his last name. She hoped the Senator would forget about it. "He's a junior researcher." Bly shook his head, as if trying to remember something.

The Director gave a small cough. "Henry will, of course, continue working with you. The less disruption right now, the better." He glanced at the two senators for affirmation. "We want to get a sense of how much Gloria told you and what your priorities are."

"Um... I just found out this morning that I'm taking over this job," said Cara. "All I can tell you is Gloria was the most well-organized person I've ever met, and she had everything cataloged. When Henry and I first started working here, she showed us her detailed one-year plan, so we're aware of what she intended for the short term. I'm sure we'll stick to her agenda." She glanced at the Director, who nodded his encouragement. "We're focusing on the public health aspects of drug and alcohol addiction, as I'm sure you know. The newest venture she wanted to address was vaping, but she told us to wait on that until we had the go-ahead from you." Again, the Director nodded approvingly. "I'm sure there's lots more, but that's about all I can report on right now."

"Did she ever talk to you about other addictions, like gambling, for instance?" Senator Bly asked.

"Only in passing," Cara replied, realizing she was treading on dangerous turf. "When I was preparing for the Symposium on addiction last month, I saw a few vague references to online gambling, and I asked her if she wanted me to pursue them. She told me not to bother, so I dropped it." She hesitated, then continued. "I hope that was okay?" she asked timidly, looking from Bly to the Director.

Bly's lips curled in a small smile, and the Director cleared his throat once again. "Yes, certainly that is fine. We like to keep close tabs on how we spend our research money and make sure there is no crossover between different departments. We'll leave you to your work right now. You know how to reach me if you have any questions at all."

Cara pasted her best smile on her face as they turned to leave. She watched Bly closely. He seemed distracted, constantly peering out the window. *Was he still wondering about Henry?* She wished she could conjure up a way to throw him off track, but nothing came to mind. She hoped he would forget about it, but that hope was dashed in the next moment when she overheard him say to the Director, "Can we take a detour down to the Personnel Office?"

A few minutes later, Henry gingerly poked his head into Cara's office. "Are they gone?" he asked, looking around. Cara heard the familiar clicking of his worry beads in his pocket.

"Yes, but Bly suspects something. He asked who you were."

"What did you tell him?" asked Henry with alarm.

"What do you think I told him? I said your name was Henry, and we were co-workers. He didn't pursue it, but as they left, he asked to go to Personnel. Maybe he wanted to look up your full name."

"Shit!" said Henry. "The last thing I want is for him to realize I'm still around. If he realizes I'm James, my life is over. He'll arrange an accident, just like he did to Mr. Lawdly!"

"Do you really think he could recognize you? You showed me the picture of yourself four years ago, and you look totally different. I find it hard to believe he would put it together."

"Are you kidding? All he has to do is look at the personnel record and see the name Ives. Believe me, it won't take him long to connect the dots. Why did I keep my last name?" he lamented. "I should quit now and disappear again!" Cara saw the fear in his eyes.

"Are you sure?" Cara asked. "You may draw more attention to yourself, as Al Lawdly warned you four years ago. Bly will realize you're trying to hide from him. He has the resources to find you and he'll fund a massive manhunt. Maybe you should stay in plain sight. Act normal. Just do your job here and pretend nothing has changed."

"I can't," said Henry. "He terrifies me. You don't know him the way I do. He'll go to any lengths to keep his reputation intact."

Cara nodded slowly. She understood his frustration. "I wish you could stay a little longer, but I can't force you," she told him. "Just be careful. If you're on your own, you'll be an easier target."

"I won't be alone. I'm going to disappear for a few weeks and then get in touch with Gloria. I'll be fine. After all, I did this before and went undetected for almost four years! If there's one thing I'm an expert at, it's how to vanish!"

"I sure hope so," said Cara, taking his hand. "I'm counting on you to help me once I quit. In the meantime, what story do I give for you leaving? I'm sure the Director will want a reason."

"Tell him you have no clue," Henry replied. "Just say you and I were never close."

SENATOR BLY STARED AT his phone. He dreaded making this call. Geraldine was going to be angry, but he had to inform her.

The sight of Henry in the CDC office had rattled him. Something about Henry's demeanor had caught his attention, and when he looked at the Personnel records and saw the name "Ives," his hair stood on end.

James Ives had been his aide when he attended Geraldine's conference in Gibraltar. Had James changed his identity? Bly could think of only one reason for him to do that: to avoid detection. Everything clicked into place, as Bly realized "Henry" was actually James, and he was the one who had recorded the meeting in Gibraltar.

James was clever, but not quite clever enough. Bly itched to handle this, but first, he needed to let Geraldine know. He hated talking about this with her. It was the one colossal failure in his life. After Geraldine learned of the existence of the recording, their relationship became tainted forever. With a little trepidation, he punched "call".

"Well, well! If it isn't the big Senator!" she said. "I assume you have something important to tell me. Are you sure this line is secure?"

Bly flinched. "There's been a... development. This morning, I discovered who was responsible for the security breach at our meeting."

"You told me you already dealt with that," she answered curtly.

"I did! I took care of the man who tried to publicize it, but I never found out who actually made the recording. This morning, though, I discovered who it was."

"Who is that?" Geraldine asked.

"His name is James Ives, and he was my aide at the time of that meeting."

"Ah, yes, young James! I remember him!" she said. "A very good-looking, clean-cut man, but he seemed a bit off. He was always blinking, as I recall."

"Yes! Exactly!" said Bly. "That's how I recognized him! I saw him today working at the CDC. He looked totally different, but that facial tic caught my attention."

"He's working at the CDC now? I thought he still worked for you. What happened?" she asked with alarm.

"He worked for me for a year after that meeting, and then quit. I was a little suspicious of him, so after he left, I hired an investigator to follow him, but I was too late. He completely dropped out of sight. Every attempt to locate him ended up in a dead end. James Ives no longer existed."

"Why didn't you tell me this before?" she demanded.

"There was nothing to tell! I couldn't locate him, but I had no proof he was behind the recording. Today, however, I noticed an employee at the CDC. Something about the way he moved made me look twice. I checked with the Personnel office and discovered his name is Henry Ives, and the CDC hired him a few months ago. He is working in the same office as the man who wrote that report."

Geraldine pondered this. "If what you are saying is true, then he may have a copy of that recording...."

"I doubt it. If he did, he wouldn't have waited this long. He may think it's at the CDC, which is why he's taken a job there. But if he tries to get it from the archives, he won't get far, because we destroyed it."

"If he knows what was on that recording, we have a serious problem. You need to stay on top of this. Let's track him," she said matter-of-factly. "Find out everything about him—who he interacts with, where he eats, where he pees. I mean *everything!* And make sure he suspects nothing. We may need some leverage over him in the future. As long as you destroyed the recording, he'll eventually discover that, and we'll have nothing to worry about."

Senator Bly clicked off his phone with a smug smile. He had a trusted friend who was a master internet hacker. He hired the man to infiltrate all Henry's online accounts and follow his every move, as Geraldine requested. Every move Henry made, every keystroke made on his computer, and every conversation on his phone would be recorded.

James Ives had crossed him once before, humiliated him, and cost him dearly. Because of James, he would never be the same in Geraldine's eyes. Geraldine worried about her business, but for Bly, it was far more personal. He wanted revenge and began to formulate a plan.

Bly intended to steal Henry's identity. When the time was right, he would pounce. Eventually, the man would learn—no one made a fool of Senator Richard Bly and got away with it.

Twenty three

As the months dragged on, Cara worked diligently, staying with the agenda Gloria had created before she left. She filed reports on suicides related to drug and alcohol use, and refrained from research into online gambling. The one indulgence she allowed herself was a weekly, carefully secured conference call with Ron, Em, Gloria, and Henry. Using her seed money, they had set up a non-profit corporation to counter the propaganda being put out by Geraldine Major and her colleagues.

She listened with excitement as Ron told her he received the recording of the Gibraltar meeting from Al's wife, Jeanine. Now, they knew the exact origin and mission of the Gambling Industry Research Institute. However, both Gloria and Henry were adamant the recording stay secret for a little longer. Even though they were both in hiding, they remained terrified of Senator Bly and feared for their lives if the report went public.

Cara itched to leave the CDC and work with them full time, but she didn't dare quit, as she worried Senator Bly might follow her. All she could do was check in periodically. She was fuming over this when the door to her office opened and the Director strode in. She crossed her fingers behind her back, hoping he was there to tell her the CDC had hired her replacement. That would give her a good excuse to leave.

He flashed her his half-smile. "Ms. Davenport! It's good to see you!" he said, extending his hand. This time, she felt less timid about taking it.

"Hello," she said, rising from her chair. "What can I do for you?"

"Please, sit!" he encouraged. He pulled a chair up to her desk and cleared his throat. "I have some news for you. After a nationwide search, we've selected the perfect person to run this department—Angus Probelli."

Cara nodded and struggled to keep her face neutral. The selection did not surprise her. She knew what the agency was looking for and had interviewed many of the candidates. Angus was a well-known research scientist specializing in addiction and had written over 50 articles during the past 10 years, none of which mentioned gambling addiction. She was sure Senator Bly had pushed the appointment through.

The Director cleared his throat again. "I want you to know how much we appreciate how you have kept this department going, single-handedly, for the past few months. You've done a terrific job, and we sincerely hope you will continue working here, especially since your colleague Henry has gone."

Cara gazed around the office, smiling inwardly. Then she looked directly at him and spoke with a steady voice. "Thank you. I appreciate that. I've certainly learned a lot here." She hesitated. "I suppose this is as good a time as any to tell you. I'll be moving back to New Hampshire to work with my brother. He's slowly recovering, but life has been a struggle for him since the accident. He may never walk again. Brady needs me, and I want to be closer to him."

The Director blinked. Cara sensed he wasn't used to being turned down. "Are you sure?" he asked.

"Yes, I am. My brother wants to buy a franchise and open a fitness studio. He can't do it alone. He asked me to help him get this new business off the ground. I'm sure you can understand."

Brady had already set up his business as a cover for what she really planned to work on. She hoped it would satisfy the Director enough so he wouldn't monitor her actions closely.

"Well, I'm very sorry to hear that," he said, as he stood to leave. "Of course, if you need any references in the future, we will be glad to provide that."

"Thank you," she said, standing along with him and ushering him out the door. "I'll keep that in mind."

WHILE CARA DID NOTHING to draw attention to her interest in learning more about gambling addiction, it didn't take long for Senator Bly to discover what her friends were doing. From the moment he saw Henry, Bly was obsessed with following him. When Henry quit, Bly feared he might once again disappear. Henry stayed out of sight for several weeks, but during that time, Bly's expert tracker hacked into enough of his accounts that vanishing completely became impossible. By the time Henry began communicating with Gloria, Senator Bly was monitoring everything he did.

Bly hankered to bring Henry down. He wanted revenge. Geraldine, however, stayed his hand. "If we continue following him, we can find out what he's up to," she said. "He may have told others about the recording. If you get rid of him now, wouldn't that raise suspicions? We need to find out what he's planning now that he's left the CDC."

As impatient as Bly was, he realized she was right. They tracked Henry's actions, and it didn't take long to learn he had connected with a corporation dedicated to curtailing online gambling. Through Henry, they identified each employee and recognized the names of both Gloria Spiegelman and Ron Hynes.

"We should eliminate them all," Bly told Geraldine. He spoke with her daily now, as they watched Henry's every move.

"Not yet," she countered. "Look at how much we're learning about their operation! Information is power! I want to know everything about them. Plus, the more we know about Henry, the more control we can have over him in the future. I like your idea of stealing his identity."

Bly preened at the compliment. Geraldine doled those out so infrequently. Yet he worried she didn't understand how serious the situation was. "By tracking Henry, I can see their activity has ramped up considerably," he told her. "It looks like they might be planning a massive cyber-attack to take down the servers of many of the biggest gaming corporations simultaneously. If they succeed, it will be disastrous for the industry!" He struggled to control the panic in his voice.

"Seriously, Bly, I don't think we need to worry about that yet. An attack of this scope will take months to organize. Plus, it's illegal. I don't think they would risk it."

Bly practically growled into the phone. "Since when has the law ever stopped dedicated hackers?" he demanded. "You know as well as I do that laws governing cyber-security are worthless. There are all sorts of loopholes they can use to avoid penalties. We need to block it before it can get started. Why do you insist on waiting? The longer we wait, the more sophisticated their attack will get! Already, they're gaining publicity and changing public opinion. Why let them get so strong?"

"Come on, Bly, where's your sense of adventure and risk?" she asked playfully. "For sure, we could stop them now, but where's the fun in that? We have information on each of them and we're getting more each day."

She sensed Bly's exasperation when the call ended, but she didn't care. This was a game to her, and nobody was going to spoil it. After all, she rarely got to play games in her life. She had learned from an early age that gambling was a business, and she had to distance herself from the fun of it. But now... perhaps she could indulge in a bit of entertainment.

People were so stupid when you got right down to it, she thought. "Like hamsters," her father once told her. She smiled at the thought of her father as a younger man. Though time had dimmed the memories, certain things he said stuck with her. She closed her eyes for a moment, recalling the first time her father brought her to his workplace.

"Casinos aren't built by luck. They're built by understanding and exploiting the weaknesses of other people...."

She shook her head at the memory. If there was one thing Geraldine understood, it was addiction. She knew how to reel people in and keep them hooked, and she was hell bent on capitalizing on that knowledge. It had made her father wealthy and allowed her to expand his empire beyond her wildest dreams. No one could damage her, especially now, as she was embarking on developing new technology to make her virtual casino sites even more addictive. Virtual Reality was the wave of the future and she fully intended to stay ahead of that wave.

WILL I EVER BE free of you? I go for months without you, and I'm happy—and then, in a moment of weakness, I'm pulled back in. You hijack my brain, blocking out all other worries or thoughts. I become trapped in a mindless place, and your promise of another win keeps me stuck there. It feels like paradise—until I come back to reality.

♦♥♣♠

Twenty four

ALONE IN HIS ROOM, Brady stared at his laptop screen. Once again, he had acted stupidly. How did this happen? He had been so sure of his plan! Now he needed to tell Cara that he took the money she gave him to get his new business off the ground and gambled it, hoping to turn it into more.

He replayed the evening in his mind. At first, he had doubled her investment. He should have stopped then, but of course, he didn't. Now he was down to his last few hundred dollars. He smacked himself in the head. All he needed was one big win... just one to get him back even, and then he could quit. Was that so much to ask for? He *had* to win this time! There was no way he could face Cara and tell her what he had done.

If I can win, just this once, I promise I will never gamble again. But even as he had the thought, he knew it was a lie. Who was he kidding? He needed money, and the only way he knew to get it fast was through gambling. *Just one win*, he thought again. *I've won so much in the past. Why not now?*

CARA WAS GLAD TO be free of the constraints of her job. She was eager to move in with Em and work with her friends, but her first stop was her childhood home. She wanted to see her mom and help Brady launch his new business, and hoped to accomplish that in a few short days.

Her mind filled with plans for the future, she walked into her mom's house and froze. Everything looked different. All the carpeting was gone, doors were wider, and there was a wheelchair carrier running the length of the stairway. Her heart sank as she saw the full impact of Brady's accident on the lives of her mom and brother.

She had been blind to this. Hearing about it on the phone and seeing it were two completely different things. Suddenly, it was real.

She found her mom in the kitchen, standing in front of the refrigerator. When Sally turned toward her, Cara saw she had been crying. Cara dropped her bags, ran across the room, and pulled her into a hug. The two of them stood there, Sally quietly crying into Cara's shoulder. Cara led her to the sofa, where they sat for a few moments in silence.

Sally finally found her voice. "I'm sorry, Cara. We planned a wonderful greeting for you. It wasn't supposed to be like this." Cara bit her lip and waited for her mom to continue. She dreaded what might come next.

"He's been doing so much better!" Sally blurted out. "I thought we were through the worst of it. He was so excited for you to be coming home. But then last night—I don't know what started it—he gambled again."

Cara looked at her mom anxiously. "Where's Brady now? He didn't hurt himself, did he?"

Sally wiped her eyes. "He tried. He overdosed on sleeping pills, but then may have changed his mind. I heard him throwing things around the room. By the time I got to his room, he was passed out on the floor. He's in the hospital now. I'm not even sure which one. They may have transferred him somewhere, but until he gives permission, I can't get any more information. The only thing they could tell me is that he's stable. These damn privacy laws!"

Cara took a deep breath, knowing she needed to be calm for her mom. "Okay, Mom, we may not know all the details, but at least he's alive and I'm here now. I'm not going anywhere for a while. This has been a lot for you to handle on your own."

"It has, but I truly believed the worst was behind us and he was done with gambling! I thought he had hit rock bottom! Why did he go back to it after everything that's happened?"

Cara's anger threatened to overwhelm her. The deceptive ways these gambling companies lured in vulnerable people infuriated her.

"It's not his fault, Mom! You, of all people, should know that. Relapse happens with addiction, and there are forces out there pulling him back in. We have no control over that."

"I can't do this!" sobbed Sally. "I don't have it in me. I feel so guilty. After your father died, I felt grief, but I also had such a sense of relief. No more worrying about what was going to happen next. And now... I'm right back where I was, constantly expecting the worst!"

"It's different with Brady. We can talk to him in ways we couldn't talk to Dad. Brady's a smart kid. He'll come through this." *He has to*, she thought to herself. "You'll see," she said aloud.

Sally shook her head. "You sound so hopeful, like I used to be. This is not different. It's worse. That Brady would do this now, after all he's been through...." Her voice trailed off.

"Mom, he relapsed. It happens to every addict. Brady needs to learn that and learn how to manage it. He can do it as long as we help him."

"I wish I had your optimism, Cara, but right now, I feel like a failure."

"You're not a failure! You've done so much. Look at what you've done to make this house accommodate him!" She gazed around the room, once again taking in all the changes. "How did you ever afford all this?"

"It was our neighbors and friends," said Sally. "We set up a local fundraising campaign and had a 'barn-raising' party. People from the community have been coming by for the past month to donate time, money, and expertise.

It was Brady's idea to surprise you. He wanted to see your face when you walked in the door."

"Wow," said Cara. "He never ceases to amaze me."

"You and me both," said Sally. "That's what makes this so hard. He was so excited yesterday about you coming home. It makes no sense to me!"

"Nothing about addiction makes sense, Mom. It's a lousy disease." She paused as a new thought dawned on her. "I have an idea, though. There may be a way we can help him," she said. Sally looked at her questioningly.

"It's a new business venture I'm involved in." She looked at her mom with hesitation. "I'm working with a few friends to combat online gambling. We're building a huge ad campaign to counter all the false information that's out there."

Sally gave her a weak smile. "Didn't I tell you to quit the CDC and focus your time on really making a difference?"

"You did, and that's exactly what we're doing. I'm using the money Dad gave me to fund it."

"No wonder you're so optimistic. But how does Brady fit into this?"

"I'm not sure, but this idea just occurred to me. We want to provide more education, beginning with high school and middle school. If Brady would be willing to give some presentations to school-age kids, it might help him in his own recovery. I don't know—he may not be interested, but I can suggest it to him."

"That's not a bad idea," said Sally slowly. "Talking about his struggles might help him. But first, he has to talk to us."

"He will, Mom. Wait and see. We'll get through this and we'll all be stronger for it."

CARA SIGHED. SHE WISHED she felt as confident as she sounded. How much support would Brady need when he got discharged from the hospital? Would he even be interested in her idea? With a sinking heart, she realized this meant her plan to go to Washington and work with her friends would have to stay on hold for a while longer.

She had a conference call scheduled with Ron, Em, and Gloria, and was eager to get the latest updates. Now that she had left the CDC, she felt a little freer to talk on the phone, though she was still cautious.

Months ago, when she first started this venture, she had charged her small group of colleagues with building a foundation for their work.

"People want fun and instant gratification," she had declared. "That's why they're drawn to these online sites. Somehow, we have to convince them those temporary pleasures only bring pain in the end. We have to show them the downsides to it—the loss of relationships and morals, and the link to depression and suicide."

At the time, she had no idea how to do that. She simply knew she was going to work like hell to make that happen.

They were making progress. Besides Libby Lewis's articles, they had placed strategic ads laying out the risks of online gambling. They were changing public awareness, trying to counter all the lies and misinformation put forth by the Gambling Industry Research Institute. Em was spearheading these efforts.

As the call began, Cara decided to wait to tell them about Brady. She wanted to get their news first. "Libby, your column is awesome!" she said as soon as her friend came on the line.

Em's creation, "The Unlucky Gambler," was a multitude of stories about ruined lives. It contained links to their new website where viewers could find key information on gambling addiction, including how to recognize problem gambling, as well as detailed descriptions of how online sites used personal information to take advantage of vulnerable people.

"Thanks! We're getting lots of great feedback. It's helping people navigate the jungle of debt they often find themselves in. Here's a quote from one of our readers: '*It's good to see I am not alone, and this isn't my fault. Just that little bit of knowledge gives me hope for a brighter future.*'"

Cara smiled into the phone. She wished she could see Em's face, as she imagined her friend was smiling too.

"Things are changing, albeit slowly," Em continued. "Public awareness is building. People are realizing online gambling is a threat. Next week, there's a Senate hearing scheduled on the use of Persuasive Technology, and there are some new laws on the agenda. It's unclear if any will pass, but at least Congress is looking at it. There are some key elections coming up soon, and a lot of senators are paying attention to what their constituents are saying."

Cara was glad to hear this. She turned her attention to Gloria. "How's the fundraising going?" she asked. Though Cara's seed money covered much of the initial expenses, they needed a large infusion of cash to keep things going, especially considering the size of the ad campaign they wanted to run.

"We're in great shape! We're on track to raise over a million dollars from grass roots donations alone by the end of this year!" Cara heard the pride in Gloria's voice. "As a result of Libby's media blitz and a video game Henry created, many people are donating money to our cause instead of gambling. Henry has a talent for this. He's fantastic at digital game creation!"

"That's amazing!" said Cara. "I love the idea of replacing the gambling habit with something creative. If we're asking people to give up something they perceive as fun, we need to replace it with something equally fun. That makes so much sense. If we can get enough people to spend money on our mission—money that would otherwise have gone to casinos—then profits in the gambling industry might go down. It might be a drop in the bucket, but at least it's something."

"It's more than something," said Ron. "We're seeing their profits decline far more than I would have predicted. We're ready to move ahead with a full-scale attack on some online sites."

"Already?" asked Cara. "I thought we were months away from that."

"Now that we've laid our foundation, we can plan it." Cara heard the excitement in his voice. "It's not as complicated as I originally thought. Henry's been a tremendous help with this as well. We've targeted 10 of the largest corporations, and our plan is to overwhelm their servers and force the sites to shut down for at least three days, and perhaps longer."

"Wow!" said Cara. "That would be an enormous loss of revenue!"

"It would! Added to that, anyone who tries to log in during that time will see a message saying their devices might have been corrupted, and they should avoid these sites for the foreseeable future. This will cripple these companies for a long time, especially if we set up that message to occur weekly for the following 12 weeks. If you couple that with the massive amount of anti-online gambling ads Libby is creating, people may turn their attention to other things and company values will plummet."

"Aren't cyber-attacks illegal? What if we get caught?"

"They are, and that's where Henry comes in. He's a programming expert. He insists he can make it all untraceable—and if it gets traced, it will go back to him alone, and he will be the one to take the heat. I think he feels guilty about how he treated you all in the library, and he wants to atone for that. He desperately wants to do this, and my impression is he's going to do it with or without our help."

Gloria chimed in. "Henry is committed to destroying Senator Bly. He knows what's at stake and he's willing to take the risk. Ron's right. He's going to do it with or without our support, but without our support, he'll have a much lower chance of success. Technically, yes, it may be illegal, but there are lots of loopholes, and look at what we're fighting. This may be a situation where we have to consider if the end justifies the means."

Cara looked askance at her phone. Was that "play-by-the-rules" Gloria talking? Aloud, she asked, "Do you really think this can work?"

"I do," Ron answered. "I've been working on this too long for it to fail. We're close to seeing some big changes in how this industry operates."

"I want to be there with you all when this happens!" said Cara.

"Aren't you coming here next week?" asked Em. "My guest room is waiting for you!"

"I was planning to, but we have a problem here," said Cara. With a twinge of guilt, she realized she had forgotten about Brady for a short time. Talking with her friends kept her sane. She needed them now more than ever.

"Brady relapsed," she said slowly. "He gambled last night and then overdosed on pills. He's in the hospital now. I need to stay here until he's home and my mom is comfortable managing him alone."

For a moment, there was silence on the phone. "Well, I suppose that makes our mission even more urgent," said Gloria.

"I suppose it does," said Cara with a wan smile. This was certainly not the Gloria she used to know. She shook her head, marveling at the way people could change if given a chance. "I had this crazy idea when talking to my mom this afternoon. One thing we haven't yet addressed is programs for school-age kids. I'm considering enlisting Brady's help with this. It's a long shot, but I thought if he can take this on as a cause, it might help him. But I don't know... it'd have to be something he really wants to do."

Gloria cleared her throat. "Well, that's something else I wanted to talk to you about. Abigail quit the CDC and moved back to her hometown. She's been working with me on developing seminars for high schoolers. Don't worry... we're keeping it all secure and private. She's quite good at this. What she's done so far sounds great, but trying to organize this all by phone has been challenging. It would be better to meet with her in person. She lives near you in New Hampshire. The two of you could get together and she can show you what she has. And if Brady's there, maybe he could sit in on it."

"That's a good idea," Cara replied. "There's only so much we can do over the phone. But I'm not sure about her meeting with Brady. We'll have to take that one step at a time."

"Okay, I'll let her know and she'll contact you. Let's hope Brady gets home soon. I'm going to say good night now," said Gloria.

"I'm signing off as well," said Em, stifling a yawn. "I'll say a prayer for Brady. Hang in there. We'll keep things going and I look forward to seeing you as soon as you can get here!"

"That may be awhile. I imagine I'll be here at least a few months. I don't want to leave until Brady's stable."

"Understood," said Em. "Let's do another call in two days. Now that you're no longer at the CDC, you can be more involved. Bye."

"Bye, Libby," said Cara.

The line was silent. Cara waited a beat before asking, "Ron, are you still there?"

"I am," he replied. "I'm sorry you're going through this with Brady. All I can say is, based on my research, gambling doesn't always lead to suicide. Yes, there's a link, but statistics aren't ironclad. With support, he can beat this. Wish I could be more help to you than that...." His voice trailed off.

Just hearing your voice helps, she thought. "Yeah, well, addiction sucks. There isn't much anyone can do to help. I just appreciate all you guys are doing to keep this going."

"Cara, we each have our reasons for doing this. Every one of us. Remember, you're not alone. You have my phone number and can call any time. You don't have to wait for our conference calls. I mean it."

"Thanks, Ron. That means a lot. I haven't called you for the last few months because, well, working at the CDC and all...."

"I know. It's actually good you didn't call. It's likely you were being watched more than you might think." He paused. "I'm looking forward to seeing you in person—whenever that is."

Cara stared at the phone. How should she respond to that? She remembered back to the day she first realized the depth of her attraction to him, the day she went to check her post office box for the first time. Not much had changed since then. Except now, she no longer worked for the CDC.

"Same goes," she replied. "I hope it will be soon."

"Good night, Cara," he said.

"Good night," she whispered.

GET OUT OF MY life and stay out! I'm through with you! You destroyed my life! You don't own me. You are scum and I hope you rot in hell...

Twenty five

AFTER SEVERAL FAMILY THERAPY sessions in which Brady promised to reform his ways, the hospital discharged him. While Cara was glad to have him home, she wondered about his future. Ron had said Brady could beat this with support, but where would that come from? Unfortunately, since compulsive online gambling wasn't considered a major problem in the public eye, there weren't a lot of programs to help with it. The hospital encouraged him to join a local Gamblers' Anonymous group, but the nearest one met two hours from their home. There was no way he would do that regularly. They then suggested a local Alcoholics' Anonymous group, but Brady refused. He didn't see himself fitting in with that at all.

"I'm fine," he insisted. "I know what happened. All I need to do is avoid these sites. I let my guard down by responding to one ad and ended up at a site I should have blocked. It won't happen again, I promise."

Was it that easy? Cara wondered. If he didn't gamble, would everything be okay? He certainly seemed to think so, yet she feared he wasn't addressing some bigger issues. Since she didn't trust the changes in him, she chose to stay for a while so she could keep an eye on him. She couldn't force him to get support, but at least she could be there for him if he needed her.

A week later, Abigail arrived. Cara hadn't broached the subject of him working with her company yet, but when Abigail showed up and Cara introduced them, Brady seemed genuinely interested in talking to her. Privately, Cara wondered if Brady was attracted to her. He sat with them as Abigail outlined the program she wanted to present.

"When you first told me you had this idea to form this corporation, I thought you were crazy," he told Cara.

"I remember that," she said.

"But now, I'm not so sure. I mean, I still think you're crazy, but I also think you're right. I've realized how hard it is to avoid. Every time I pick up my phone or turn on my laptop, I see ads. I've purged my accounts of anything tying me to gambling, but short of completely changing my online identity, I can't stay away from it. All it takes is one pop-up ad and I'm right back in."

Abigail spoke up. "Brady, if you tell your story, it may empower you. Would you be willing to work with me? At least one trial? If it flops, you won't have to do more, but it's possible you'll find some meaning by doing this."

To Cara's amazement, Brady agreed, and Cara now found herself in the back of the high school auditorium as Brady wheeled himself onto the stage for his pilot performance. The room was filled with students, many of them former friends of Brady's.

Brady stared at the crowd. "My name is Brady Davenport," he began. "Some of you know me—I graduated from this school last year. But you may not recognize me, because last year, I could walk. I had hopes and dreams for my life. In my wildest dreams, I never imagined I would be giving this talk." He paused for a moment and looked around. The room was dead silent.

"I'm here to talk to you about addiction. But not drug and alcohol addiction. Believe me, I know how much you've heard about that in the last few years. There's another type of addiction that gets very little attention, and it's about as dangerous as drugs or alcohol. Can anyone tell me what it is?"

"Cigarettes!" yelled a boy from the crowd.

Brady nodded. "Yes, cigarettes are addictive, but you all know about that, right? That gets a fair amount of attention in your Health classes. At least it did in mine." He saw some students nod. "What else? Anyone have a guess?"

"Food?" asked a girl timidly. "Like sugar, maybe?"

"Very good," said Brady. "You're absolutely right. Food, especially sugar, can be highly addictive. But you learn a lot about that in Health class as well. I remember learning about healthy eating. I have something else in mind...."

"Video games!" called out another boy. Everyone in the audience nodded.

"Oh... you're getting closer. Video games are super addictive, and they're related to what I'm here to discuss."

Brady scanned the room. Though the students sat in rapt attention, no one ventured another guess.

"How many of you play poker with friends?" he asked. A smattering of students, mostly boys, raised their hands.

"Do you play for money?"

The boys all nodded. "Not much, though," said one boy.

"Have any of you ever played online poker?"

At this, most students were silent, but a few boys raised hands defiantly.

"Yeah, what of it? Our parents let us play."

"That's true," said Brady. "Gambling has been around for years, but online gambling is relatively new, and your parents may not be aware of the dangers. I used to think, just like many of you do, that drugs and alcohol were bad. I got the same information in Health class that you all are getting. But I can't remember ever being told not to gamble. Have any of you been told that?"

Collectively, the students shook their heads.

"Well, guess what? I'm living proof that gambling is a dangerous addiction. I became addicted to gambling last year, and once I got going with online sites, I couldn't stop. Online gambling is like quicksand. Once you step into it, there is no getting out."

Brady looked around the room. His eyes landed on Cara and she nodded encouragement. *"You can do this,"* she mouthed. Gathering his thoughts, he continued. "Some of you may be wondering how I ended up in a wheelchair. Last year when I turned 18, I inherited a lot of money—and I mean, a lot. Think about it... what would you do if someone gave you $100,000? Most of you might spend a little right away on some material things, but certainly not all of it. A normal person would take some time to figure out what to spend it on. But a gambling addict around money is not a normal person. The instant I had that money, I knew exactly what to do with it. I was already hooked. I had sampled gambling and seen with my own eyes how a little money could turn into a lot of money. Given that, I imagined what a LOT of money could turn into.

"I went to a casino with some friends, and they stopped me after a few hours. At that point, I was winning. I had thousands of dollars and wanted to keep playing. Winning, for me, was a high like I had never experienced before. When I got home, I logged into an online betting site, and in the privacy of my bedroom, I blew through all the money in less than four hours." Brady paused again and looked at the sea of faces watching him. He hoped they understood his message.

"I knew I was losing money, but I couldn't stop. I kept making bigger bets. When the money ran out, I was so ashamed. How could I have been so stupid? And how could I face my family and tell them what I did? I wanted to be anywhere else but here on earth, so I got in a car and drove it into a tree. Truly, I hoped to die that night. I should have died that night. Instead, I spent two months in the hospital and now have to accept that I will never walk again." Once again, the room was silent.

"What I want to tell you all is that I've also had to accept that I am still addicted to online gambling. I *know* it's wrong, but if the opportunity comes to me to gamble online, I will. I've already done that since the accident.

Even though I know it may ruin me and my family, I can't stay away from it. Once the internet knows you're a gambling addict, you become a target of a marketing campaign that is impossible to avoid. *That* is the danger of online gambling. Do yourselves a favor and don't start with it!

"If you take nothing else from this evening, remember this: your mind is your greatest asset. Gambling can poison it, just like drugs or alcohol or cigarettes or unhealthy food can poison your body. People say you can't overdose on gambling, but you can. Gambling scrambles your brain, so reality doesn't matter anymore. One moment you feel you're in paradise, on top of the world, and the next, you are lower than the lowest creature that crawls on the earth and you're stuck there. Many, many gambling addicts turn to suicide as a way out. *That's* what happens when you overdose on gambling. You may think it can never happen to you, but that's a lie. Don't go down the same path I did."

Twenty six

BRADY REMAINED IN GOOD spirits, and Cara felt ready
to move to D.C. She and her mom shared a last breakfast
before she left.

"I know it's the right thing for you, but I still wish you
could be closer," Sally said.

"I'm just a phone call away, Mom! You'll be fine."

"I wish I had your optimism," Sally lamented. "I can't
help wondering when everything will turn sour again."

Cara nodded. "I get it, Mom. I really do. But you can't
live the rest of your life waiting for the next bad thing
to happen. There's a reason the AA organization has the
slogan 'one day at a time.' "

"You're right. I just worry so much about Brady, no
matter how well he seems."

"Give him a chance. He has a purpose now, and it's
helping him. Besides, he won't be here much. He and
Abigail are taking their presentation on the road to other
schools soon. She's good for him." Brady and Abigail

seemed to have a natural rapport together, and Cara was grateful for that. She was proud of her brother, and it fueled her desire to pursue her work as well.

Sally sighed. "I hope you're right. Just stay in touch, okay? Brady may still relapse...."

"I know he may relapse!" Cara said. "It's the reason for the work I'm doing. Of course I'll stay in touch, but I'm not going to stop until there are so many laws and protections in place for gambling addicts that these corporations give up and shut down!"

"If only it were that easy," said Sally. "I told you to fight this, but you also need to be realistic about it. Remember, you can't save the world."

"I know," Cara laughed. "I don't intend to save the world. But if I can do something tangible to help Brady avoid gambling, and help thousands of others as well, that's worthwhile, isn't it?"

Cara arrived in Washington to find Em had a room ready and waiting for her. "I can't believe I'm finally here!" she exclaimed, giving Em a long hug. "Thanks for taking me in!"

"Of course!" said Em. "Once a roommate, always a roommate, right? It's so great to see you in person!"

"Agreed. I can't wait to see everyone else as well."

Em lifted her eyebrows. "Everyone, or ONE particular one?"

Cara blushed. "Come on, Em! I barely know Ron! Sure, we've talked on the phone, but I've only seen him once. And that was months ago!"

Em laughed. "I can tell a budding romance when I spot one. He's interested in something more with you. I hear it on every phone call. Why do you suppose he invited you to his house right away? He and I have yet to meet in person."

"Well, that's your choice. You set it up that way so he wouldn't learn your true identity."

"Not exactly my choice, but you're right," Em said wistfully. "I wish I didn't have to be so careful about that. At any rate, the two of you should have a good day together." She gave Cara a knowing look.

"We have a lot to talk about!" Cara said, still blushing. "I mean, phones are great, but it's different being face-to-face with someone."

"Okay, well, maybe. But my advice, for what it's worth: be careful around him! It may not be wise to get involved romantically. That could complicate things for all of us."

"I'll be fine," said Cara. "In the meantime, I'm looking forward to a nice hot shower, a good meal, and a good night's sleep!"

That dream again. It always started with her father tossing her high in the air. Up, up she went, until she reached the sky and grabbed a cloud. She gripped a giant roulette wheel, holding on for dear life as she flew and spun around. But this time was different. It wasn't numbers and colors whizzing by. It was faces... her father, Patrick, Ben, Brady... and then Ron. She woke with a start, her heartbeat racing out of control. It was pitch-dark outside, and the room was silent.

SHE WAS A BUNDLE of nerves as she drove to Ron's house. Though she had told Em she'd be fine, now she wasn't so sure. What she had not disclosed to Em was that she and Ron had been talking privately on the phone for the past few weeks. He was so easy to talk to! As their conversations had deepened, the personal and flirty nature of them made it clear to her Ron wanted something more, but what did she want? Was Em right? Would it complicate things if they had a fling? What was the harm in enjoying some pleasure in her life?

He stood in his doorway as she drove up, a lazy smile on his face. Those eyes! How had she forgotten about them? Eyes so blue, she could swim in them. She took a deep breath before getting out of the car. *Act casual*.

"Hi," he said. "It's good to see you."

Cara nodded, not sure she could trust her voice. He motioned for her to come inside. She followed him in, taking in the spectacular design of the house. From the outside, it looked like a quaint cabin with a beautiful wrap-around porch, yet the spaciousness inside amazed her. She stared at the forest in the back of the house through three enormous floor-to-ceiling windows.

"Al and I bought this house together before he married Jeanine," he said, in answer to her unasked questions. "After they moved to California, I bought out their share and stayed."

She laughed. "I pictured you in a small, sparse bachelor apartment. I had no idea you lived like this."

There was so much she didn't know about him. She needed to slow down and take it all in.

"Yeah, well, it's more space than I need, and it's an hour commute into work, but it's worth it. Once I got settled here, I didn't see any point in moving."

They walked out onto the porch and she stood looking out at the small yard bordered by a vast forest. A few deer romped through the woods in the distance, while closer to the house, a family of squirrels raced around a large maple tree.

"It's so beautiful! I can't believe you live here," she whispered.

He stood next to her, leaning on the railing. She looked into his eyes. Not swim in them, she thought. Drown in them. He pulled her close and breathed in her scent. For a moment, time stood still. As he bent down to kiss her, she pulled away.

"I... I'm not sure about this," she said, holding him at arm's length. "I need time." She looked at him, hoping he would understand. But how could he when she wasn't telling him the truth? "No, that's not it!" she stammered, shaking her head. "The truth is, my best friend growing up died by suicide. My last boyfriend died by suicide. My father... I'm a jinx, can't you see? Everyone close to me is cursed! It's not a safe bet to be with me!"

Ron took hold of her shoulders. "What if I don't like safe bets?" he asked. She shook her head slowly.

He stared at her. "I'm crazy about you, Cara. You must know that by now."

Cara blushed. "I just want to be sure," she said. "And I'm not yet. We haven't exactly had a traditional start to a romantic relationship."

Ron nodded. "I can give you time if you promise not to lump me in with all your past men," he said. "I'm not a gambling addict, and I have no intention of killing myself."

"I can't help it. Last night, I had a dream, and you were in it, along with all of them. I can't shake the idea that I'm the one connecting piece to all these suicides."

"First, they're not all suicides. Brady is still very much alive, as am I. And second, what makes you think you're the only connection? You and I both know addiction is a disease. It's not your fault you got involved with people who had this disease. It doesn't mean everyone in your life is an addict."

She nodded, feeling her shoulders relax. Perhaps he was right, but she still wasn't ready to dive in.

"I have an idea," he said, taking her hand and leading her inside. He stood by the door of a small, empty room with a vast picture window and a filing cabinet against one wall. "This may seem fast, but I've been thinking about it for a while. This is a spare room right now. That filing cabinet is where I've stored all my research papers for the last several years. You might want to go through some of them. There's a lot of information in there about the link between gambling and suicide." He looked at her with those piercing eyes. "Some of that might help you understand Brady a little more."

He listens to me. He knows exactly what I need.

"This room would make a great headquarters for your new company," he continued. "How about we set it up as an office, and you can work here during the week? I'll be out of the house most of the time teaching, so you'd have the place to yourself, but at least we could see each other each day. Usually, I get home mid-afternoon, and then we can work on the business together. What do you think?"

Cara looked at the room with its beautiful view, then looked at Ron. She felt as if she was about to dive into the ocean. Taking a deep breath, she said, "Okay—we'll try it." For a moment, the two of them stood in silence. Then she turned to him and gave him a hug. "Thank you!" she whispered.

Twenty seven

CARA SAT ON RON'S porch, enjoying the late afternoon sun. She never tired of the view. She smiled as Ron strolled in, thinking she never tired of looking at him, either. *I could definitely get used to this life*. Things were working exactly as Ron had described. He left the house each morning before she arrived, giving her a few quiet hours to work. Though she had read his summary report, the papers he had collected helped her solidify her own business plan. When he returned in the afternoon, the two of them did more strategizing about the business. She had yet to stay for dinner, though, and Em chided her for that.

"What are you waiting for?" Em asked.

"You were the one who said not to mix business and pleasure," replied Cara.

"Yeah, well, that was before I realized how smitten you were. You talk about nothing else. You need to push him a little, Cara."

Cara looked at Ron now, stretched out on the chair beside her. Perhaps Em was right. But deep down, she knew it wasn't Ron who needed pushing. It was herself.

"Everything's on track for the launch of our program. A few more days and we'll be ready. I just hope it works," he said.

"It'll work," said Cara confidently. "We've laid so much groundwork for it. After our attack, the online gambling industry will have a hard time picking up the pieces."

He looked at her sideways. "It'll be great, as long as you don't leave me in pieces when it's all over," he said.

She stared at him. "What do you mean?" she asked.

"Come on, Cara. You keep pushing me away."

"You're stronger than me," she replied, hoping to change the subject.

"How so?"

"I can't imagine you ever going to pieces. You don't need me. You've been living alone, working on this alone, for years. You're willing to go slow, to do the research. I know it hasn't been easy, but you stuck with it, even when you didn't know where it would all go."

"You're right, it hasn't been easy," he replied. She tried to look away, but he held her captive with his eyes. "Since Al died, my life has been a lesson in patience. But you're wrong about me not needing you. You came along right as I was about to give up. I wouldn't have kept going if it wasn't for you."

"But you tried to push me away at first..." she stammered.

"I pushed you away from the work because I was afraid. I lived in constant fear of being discovered, and I couldn't bring anyone else into that—especially someone I was starting to care about."

How did he keep turning the conversation back to her? Everything he said tugged at her.

"Well, we didn't get discovered, and now, after dancing around this for the last six months, our long-term strategy is about to pay off," she said.

Ron sat up slowly and faced her. "We've been dancing around something else as well," he said, taking a strand of her hair and placing it behind her ear. He pulled her closer, his eyes boring into her.

One kiss, she thought. *What was the harm in that?* But then she heard another voice in her head. Was it Brady's? Or maybe her father's? *"Once you start, you'll never be able to stop."*

She knew, beyond any doubt, that it could never be one kiss with him. She was all in—or nothing.

"I can't..." she said. "It's just... I'm not..."

He backed off. "You're not ready. I get it. But a guy's gotta try, right?"

She turned away. He asked so little of her, yet what he wanted now seemed impossible for her to give. She stood up and paced the floor. He undeniably attracted her... so what was the problem? What was holding her back?

"Let's go for a walk," he said, standing up and taking her hand. "It'll help clear the air for both of us."

They walked in companionable silence through the forest. She loved the feeling of his hand in hers. It felt so... natural. He was right. Being out among the trees helped clear the air. For a brief time, words were unnecessary.

Hand in hand, they emerged from the forest a few minutes later and looked across the yard at Ron's house. A strange car was parked in the driveway, and a tall, glamorous woman stood beside it. "What the...?" whispered Ron.

Cara stood, frozen, as Ron dropped her hand and raced across the yard. He caught the woman in a huge embrace.

"What are you doing here?" he exclaimed.

"I had to be in D.C. for business and thought I'd surprise you. I'm only here for one day and couldn't resist seeing what you've done with this place."

The woman looked around and spotted Cara standing at the edge of the yard. Then she turned back to Ron. "Oh... I didn't realize you had company. You were always such a recluse!"

"Cara, come meet Jeanine!" Ron called out. Turning to Jeanine, he said, "Cara and I are working together on a project. She's using the spare room as an office during the day. Cara, this is Jeanine Lawdly."

"Hi," said Cara shyly, holding out her hand. Inwardly, she cringed. Ron and Jeanine had some history together. She wondered if it was more than Ron had told her.

"Well, good to see you're not alone out here! I hope I'm not interrupting anything," Jeanine said, looking at Ron. "I was hoping we could have dinner together and get caught up a bit."

There was an awkward silence as Cara looked at the two of them. Finally, she stammered. "I was just leaving. We've finished work for today."

Ron looked at her closely. "Why don't you stay for dinner as well, Cara? The two of you could get to know each other."

Cara looked at Jeanine again. The woman had long dark hair, glowing skin, and a willowy figure accented by a tight-fitting pants suit. In contrast, Cara wore a loose t-shirt and jeans. For a moment, she thought of staying, but then decided she'd end up spending the entire evening comparing herself to this woman. And Jeanine used to *own* this house. Suddenly, Cara felt she didn't belong there.

"Thanks, but I'm going to head out. Maybe some other time. I'll see you tomorrow afternoon," she said to Ron, as she got into her car.

She drove off and glanced in the rearview mirror, watching as Jeanine took hold of Ron's arm and they walked into the house together.

"I SHOULD HAVE STAYED!" she exclaimed to Em an hour later, as they sat at dinner. "But I just felt so... small around her."

Em shook her head. "Why are you so hard on yourself? She's an old friend of his! The man's allowed to have old friends, isn't he?"

"Yeah, but there was more to it than that. The way he greeted her... it wasn't just as an old friend. I could tell. She lived with him in that house! I can't compete with that!"

"What do you mean?" asked Em. "It doesn't sound at all like a competition to me. You're making this all up. The man is crazy about you. It's obvious, but you keep putting him off. And now you're accusing him of being interested in someone else who he knew long ago? That doesn't sound very fair to me."

"I don't know what I want!" Cara cried. "Why is this so complicated?"

"Oh... you know what you want," replied Em. "But you're scared. Look, I recall how thrown you were when Ben died. You may not remember, but I do. You blamed yourself! I tried to convince you otherwise, but you felt you caused him to kill himself. Nothing we said helped. But you didn't cause it." Cara opened her mouth to speak, but all that came out was a sob. Em hugged her close. "Listen, Cara, I know I told you earlier to be careful, but I think this is important for you. You light up when you talk about him. You need to give this relationship a chance!"

"Maybe you're right, Em, but I can't shake the feeling that Ron isn't for real. That he's just flirting with me and as soon as I give him what he wants, he'll abandon me. Hell, he's probably gone already!"

Em sighed with exasperation. "That doesn't sound like Ron at all! Trust him, Cara!"

WHEN CARA ARRIVED AT Ron's house at her usual time the next morning, she knew he'd be out of the house. She walked into the kitchen and froze. Next to the sink were two empty coffee mugs. Had Jeanine spent the night? With a twinge of guilt, she searched the house for any other signs of that, but realized she wouldn't be able to tell. The only parts of the house she had spent time in were her office, the porch, and the kitchen.

All day long, she fought with herself. She fumed at the thought of what might have gone on last night. Yet was that fair? Did she even have a right to be jealous? Ron owed her nothing, but that didn't make her any less angry. By the time Ron arrived home late in the afternoon, she had worked herself into quite a snit.

She heard him come in and pretended to be engrossed in her work. "Hi," he said, leaning on the wall by the doorway.

"I'm busy," she said curtly.

"I can see," he said. He came up behind her and placed his hands lightly on her shoulders. Immediately, she tightened up.

"Why so tense?" he asked.

She turned toward him, her face pinched with anger. "Really? You really don't know?" He looked at her with confusion.

"Did Jeanine spend the night?" she blurted out.

"What? No... of course not! Why would you even think that?"

"There were two coffee cups by the sink this morning..." Cara faltered.

Ron stepped back, his clear blue eyes turning steely. "I need a minute," he said. "I'll be on the porch if you want to talk about this." He turned and walked out.

Uh-oh, she thought. *Had she read too much into the situation?* But she needed to know what was going on. After a few moments, she summoned her courage and joined him on the porch.

"Another walk?" she asked, hoping that might help calm her jangling nerves. He nodded, and they started walking, though this time, he kept his hands to himself.

"Look, Cara, there's a lot you don't know about me, but one thing I can promise you is I will never lie to you. First, I didn't lie to you. Jeanine and I went out to dinner, then she returned to her hotel. She came by early this morning to see me before I went to work. I swear, that's the truth." He kept walking, looking straight ahead.

"She completely caught me off guard yesterday. I haven't talked with her in months and had no idea she'd simply show up." He walked in silence for a few more minutes, his hands deep in his pockets. "I told you I bought this house with her and Al, and they married a short time later. What I didn't tell you is that Jeanine met Al through me. She and I briefly dated before the two of them met. We had... I guess you'd call it a one-night stand. Then, the two of them got together, and it was love at first sight. They wrote me out of the script, so to speak. It was clear from the beginning they were meant for each other."

"That's pretty noble of you," she said tartly.

He looked at Cara sideways. "Actually, it wasn't. Al was head over heels in love with her in a way I knew I would never be. For me, it was a fun night, but I could see he was in it for far more." He continued walking, looking straight ahead now as they circled back toward the house.

"She certainly seemed friendly with you yesterday," said Cara.

"I'll admit, last night, she came on to me a bit. She asked about you, and I told her I hoped things would grow between us. She wanted another one-night thing, but I put her off."

Cara couldn't look at him. Guilt and confusion threatened to overwhelm her. Her stomach clenched. *Was she just looking for an opportunity to make him a villain?* Maybe Em was right, and she was just plain scared to get involved.

"Here's the thing, Cara." They were back at the house now, standing by the door. He stopped and turned her toward him. "I'm a really patient guy. You even said that yesterday. You told me you admired my patience. Nothing happened with Jeanine last night, but that patience is running thin. Jeanine pointed out to me you don't own me. My choices are my own, and I didn't want to do anything last night to jeopardize what you and I might have together. But you need to make a choice as well. Either you're in or you're out. I can't put my life on hold forever." Once again, his eyes were the color of steel.

Cara looked away. He was right, she realized. He had every reason to be angry with her. As Em said, she wasn't being fair to him. But that didn't change the fact she wasn't ready to jump in.

"I can't give you what you want right now," she said, looking back at him with pleading eyes.

"Fine, then you can't be angry with me for living my life however I wish," he shot back. "You can't have it both ways, Cara." With that, he strode into the house, leaving her alone.

Twenty eight

SENATOR BLY WAS RUNNING out of patience. His investigator had been tracking everything Henry did for months. Bly knew a massive cyber-attack was coming and who was behind it. The Gambling Industry Research Institute had a counterattack planned, but needed Geraldine's okay to launch it. If they didn't start counter measures soon, the financial consequences for the industry would be disastrous.

Bly knew little about Geraldine's strategy, beyond that she was developing a new Virtual Reality platform and she intended to use that technology for their counterattack.

"I want to lure Brady into one of my new sites," she'd told Bly. "Our test run showed it won't be hard to attract him and keep him there. We'll use Brady as bait to bring Cara into the site so she can watch him in action. Cara will do anything to keep Brady from gambling. We simply need Brady to continue gambling until Cara agrees to our demands and drops her campaign against us."

Bly didn't like that she was targeting Brady and Cara—it seemed too personal, like she'd forgotten the money they all stood to lose, but she insisted Cara held the power to stop the cyber-attack. Once Cara did that, they could turn their attention to the other individuals involved. Ronald Hynes, Gloria Spiegelman, that pesky journalist Libby Lewis, and especially James (Henry) Ives. They were all his enemies, and he wanted to destroy each of them.

His first target was Henry. With access to all of Henry's financial information, Bly was poised to steal Henry's online identity. What better way to get revenge than to ruin him financially? Perhaps Henry would spend the rest of his life in jail.

Bly had already begun a trial run by maxing out one of Henry's credit cards, using multiple charges to some sham betting sites. After logging in to the account and seeing it was at its limit, he called the credit card company and closed the account. Then he sat back and smiled. Henry was in for a big surprise the next time he used his credit card.

Henry was engrossed in his work when he got a text alert. The message on his phone puzzled him. An automatic payment for one of his bills hadn't gone through. He'd deal with it later. With the launch of their cyber-attack tomorrow, he had more important things to worry about.

He stood up and stretched. After staring at a screen for three straight hours, he needed a break and some fresh air. He dashed out of his temporary rental office to the coffee shop across the street. He was surprised when the payment on his credit card was denied. Luckily, he had just enough cash in his wallet to cover the coffee, though not enough for a tip. With a look of embarrassment, he exited the coffee shop and ran back to his office.

Once there, he logged into his credit card account and froze. He stared at the balance of $50,000—his current credit limit. He blinked, but the number remained. *How was this even possible?* Since leaving the CDC, Henry had been compulsive about managing his bank accounts and protecting his online identity. He found it hard to believe his security was breached, yet there it was, on the screen in plain view. Someone had hacked into his credit card account.

If someone hacked his bank account, what else might they have compromised? He fished around in the office for his emergency burner phone. Since he joined with their group, Ron had insisted he get a separate phone for business-related calls. He purchased a new phone every few months and kept it off the internet. When Gloria didn't answer, he called Cara.

"What's up, Henry?" she asked.

"My bank account got hacked." He knew Cara could hear the panic in his voice. "Someone ran up $50,000 in charges. All to these weird establishments. These are all sham gambling sites. I'm sure of it. Someone is onto what we're doing."

"But how?" asked Cara with alarm. "Everyone's been so careful." They had done everything possible to keep the cyber-attack a secret.

"I'm not sure how. I took as many precautions as I could." Henry replied. "If someone got into my bank account, they may have gotten other information as well—about me and everyone I've been in contact with. They may be expecting our attack. But what do I do about a $50,000 credit card bill?" His voice rose to a high pitch. Cara pictured him blinking uncontrollably.

"Listen, you can handle this," she said. If she was going to help Henry stay calm, she, too, needed to remain level-headed. "Did you call the credit card company to report fraudulent activity on your account?"

"Not yet," he admitted. "I need to do that."

"Right. Do it and call me back."

Henry gritted his teeth as he called the credit card company and was routed through a maze of virtual options. He paced the room, screaming "agent" and "representative" into the phone, desperately trying to connect with a real person. He was about to give up when a woman's voice came on the line. "I'm sorry, sir, but that account has been closed," she said in a sweet, syrupy voice.

"Closed by who?" asked Henry, perplexed.

"The account holder."

"What are you talking about?" asked Henry, still pacing in his kitchen, his hand on his head. "I didn't make any of those charges, and I didn't call this morning to cancel the card. And now you're telling me I'm liable for $50,000? That's crazy!"

"We have on record that you did call. Unfortunately, we cannot undo those charges now. You needed to arrange that before cancellation."

"So, what am I supposed to do?" he yelled into the phone.

"I'm sorry, but we cannot reverse any charges once the account is closed," she repeated. "Is there anything else I can do for you today, Sir?"

"Oh, for Christ's sake!" Henry threw the phone across the room. He needed a lawyer. Or perhaps he needed to change identities once again.

Henry knew Senator Bly was behind the hack, and he knew what the Senator was capable of. He trembled as he thought of Al Lawdly's car accident. He had worked hard to conceal himself from Bly, but apparently he hadn't been careful enough. If Bly could get into his credit card account, then he could also find out where he lived and worked. He needed to disappear once again before some freak accident took his life.

He picked up his burner phone and called Cara back. "I'm going underground for a while," he told her. "Tell the others not to contact me. I'll be in touch when I think it's safe." Cara heard the fear in his voice.

"But why...?"

"I don't have time to explain. The cyber-attack will launch tomorrow afternoon. Go ahead with it. They may know it's coming, but they don't know the exact timing. I set that secretly today, and I'll put out a decoy command right now to confuse anyone who might be monitoring things. You have all the information you need. Just beware—it's possible everything I've done for you has been tracked. I have no clue how, but I can guess who. Be careful, Cara. You are dealing with some criminal masterminds."

With that, he hung up, leaving Cara staring at her phone. This wasn't the Henry she'd once worked with at the CDC. Unassertive, she had thought at the time... like he could almost blend in with the furniture. Perhaps his greatest strength lay in not having a strong identity, so it was easy for him to become a completely new person.

Should she call Ron? Given his frosty demeanor the day before, she wasn't sure she wanted to talk to him. She texted: **Henry away for a few days... worried identity stolen. He said go ahead w/ plan but don't contact him.**

SENATOR BLY SMILED AS he imagined Henry's reaction once he realized how much money he owed. *Let him sweat a little. Serves him right for making a fool of me.* He had no doubt Henry would know who was behind the hack. It didn't matter to him in the least. It was more important that Henry experience genuine fear. This was far more satisfying than simply exterminating him. What Bly didn't realize was that Henry had already slipped away overnight with quite different plans.

The ringing of his phone broke his reverie. Geraldine calling.

"Game on..." she said.

Hey... I hear you have a cool new site. I know I cut you off, but sometimes I wish you'd contact me. Others get to enjoy you... why can't I? One little visit... I won't stay long. What would be the harm?

Twenty nine

BRADY RUBBED HIS EYES as he stared at the computer screen in his office. A familiar icon flashed in the corner. *This can't be happening.* He had abstained from gambling by blocking all the triggers from his internet feed. He had removed all gambling and gaming pop-up ads, notifications, and autosuggestions from his computer and phone. He had also blocked himself from accessing certain predatory websites and receiving multiple offers for new credit cards. Without those constant reminders, he could avoid being drawn back in. It was getting easier, but he still had to be vigilant.

He did a double take as he looked at the icon on his monitor. Why was it showing up now? It was an ad for a Virtual Reality casino. VR was the latest thing in online gambling, and he was sorely tempted to test it out. He shook his head and rubbed his eyes again, thinking of Abigail. She had told him to call her whenever he felt an urge to gamble, and this was one of those times. He called her and she didn't answer. "I need to talk!" he said to her voicemail.

He was tired and knew he should avoid it, but what would be the harm in checking it out? On impulse, he clicked on the link and stared in awe. This was unlike any gambling site he'd ever seen.

His pulse quickened as he stared at the virtual space. He felt himself rise from his chair and *walk* toward the casino, all rational thought immediately banished from his mind. After six months of sitting in a wheelchair, he couldn't believe the freedom he felt.

In his mind, he climbed a small flight of stairs and peered inside the building, but his view was blocked. Above the door, he noticed a large sign: "Pairadice", but as he tried to enter, a tall, stern woman blocked his way. "Look at how much fun everyone is having! Do you want to join?" she asked.

"Hell, yeah!" exclaimed Brady, stepping forward, but the woman stood her ground.

"There is a price for you to enter." Brady instinctively reached for his wallet. "Not a monetary price. Even as we speak, this place is in danger. You need to help us convince your sister to stop her cyber-attack."

He knew about Cara's plan to attack online gambling sites and overload the servers. What would she say about this place? He could almost hear her voice. "Brady, it isn't real!" But when he looked at the woman in front of him, she seemed undeniably real. "What does Cara have to do with this?" he asked. "She would just tell me this isn't real."

"Absolutely!" the security woman beamed. "That's exactly what she would say! But it is real, isn't it? You can see it. Here, come closer... you can hear it, right? Now look inside and take a deep breath. You can even smell it!" Brady breathed in the sweaty scent of a room filled with gamblers and fast food, and underneath it, a distinct, sweet odor he knew to be unique to casinos. And the sounds! Cards shuffling, slot machines clanging, tokens spewing out at an alarming rate. It was all, unmistakably, real.

He turned his attention back to the woman. "What is this place?" he whispered.

"It's our new Virtual Reality Gambling platform! Our state-of-the-art technology allows you to have the experience of being in an actual casino without ever having to leave the comfort of your home. We are in the last stages of testing it, and as one of our premier users, we are inviting you for a special pre-launch experience. It has everything a brick-and-mortar casino would have, though it's all in your mind."

"How can I get in?" he asked.

She smiled. "You must bring your sister here. She will want to fight it. She will say it's evil and we are controlling people's minds. But you know better! You know how much fun it is. We need you to convince her of the value of what we are doing. But you have to do it here, where she can see exactly what you are talking about. And you have to do it right away before she destroys what we have created."

Brady looked past her. All he wanted was to get into the casino and play. He would do whatever it took to get there. If it meant convincing Cara to stop her attack on their gambling sites, then he could do that. Once Cara saw this, she would give up her fight. Of course she would! After all, so many people in there were enjoying themselves. Brady could see it in action, and he desperately wanted to be part of it. "How do I bring her here?" he asked.

"Close your eyes, and when you open them, there'll be a flashing icon in the corner of your computer screen. Click there, and a link will pop up. Send the link to your sister. Tell her it's urgent that she check it out right away. Make it convincing! Then click on the link yourself to re-enter and wait for her. Once she's here, I'll let you in, and your job will be to show her just how real it is."

Brady closed his eyes, feeling the surrounding air quivering. When he opened his eyes, he was staring at his computer screen. As promised, an icon flashed in the corner. For a moment, he sat there paralyzed. What just happened? Should he send the link to Cara? What if it was some weird computer virus? But then he recalled the feeling of *standing* at the door of the casino, and how much he wanted to enter and play in there. The only way to gain entry was to get Cara there, too, so he emailed the link to his sister with a note. *"Check this out now!"* he wrote. *"I'll explain later."* He hoped it would be enough to get her attention. Then he clicked on the link to return to the casino. Immediately, he was back at the entrance with the security woman in front of him. He peered around her and once again saw people, even as a little voice in his head said, "It's not real!" In the distance, he heard Cara's voice. "Brady, where are you?" He turned and saw her running toward him.

"What happened? I clicked on the link in your email, and my screen went blank. What is this place?"

"Hi, Sis," he said with a smile. "It's a new Virtual Reality casino! It's awesome! Come check it out." Cara approached cautiously and peered inside. "Brady, it isn't real!" she whispered. "None of this is real! We need to get out of here, fast."

Brady frowned as he looked at her. "Just one game? Come on, it'll be fun!" He started toward the door, but the woman was still there, blocking the way.

"You told me you would let me in if I got her here!" Brady exclaimed.

The woman stood there stone-faced. "She needs to enter with you."

Brady turned to Cara and tried to drag her in, but she pulled away from him and he crumpled to the floor. "He can only walk if he enters the casino, and he can only enter if you go with him," said the woman. "Sorry... house rules." She shrugged.

Brady looked at Cara. "Can't we just go in and check it out? I want to go in there and feel like I'm walking."

"It's not real, though!" said Cara. "They're toying with your mind to control what you do. They want you gambling again, so they'll make more money!"

"I just want to stand and look," pleaded Brady. "I won't gamble in there... I promise." He glanced at the security guard, who nodded. "*Please* come in with me. We don't have to stay long..."

Against her better judgment, Cara capitulated. "Alright," she said. "We can go in and look around, but you are to stay right by my side the entire time. Absolutely no gambling!"

Brady stood up, and the woman stepped aside, allowing them to enter. Together, Cara and Brady entered the casino. Cara couldn't believe her eyes and ears. How was this even possible? Everything looked so real. Yet she knew it wasn't. It was a lure to get people to gamble more. The next generation of tricks in the online gambling industry. Clearly, someone wanted her to see this. Did they know of her company's planned cyber-attack?

Another woman approached them, this one quite seductive in contrast to the guard at the door. "Welcome to Pairadice!" she said, flashing a broad smile. "We wish to give you the VIP tour! Follow me!" Brady and Cara followed the woman onto the main floor, staring at the myriad of card tables and slot machines. There were customers at every machine, and most tables were full of either blackjack or poker players. Cara blinked hard, trying to discern some subtle clues showing the people were not real. She thought she could tell if she looked closely enough, but it took a lot of effort. It was far easier to accept it all as real.

"What you are seeing here at Pairadice is the latest platform from Majority Rules. It is launching next week and we are currently beta testing. Want to join a game?" the woman asked Brady. "There's a chair here, just for you." She pointed to an empty spot at one of the poker tables. Brady hesitated, looking at Cara.

"No!" exclaimed Cara, pulling Brady aside. Her phone rang, jolting her out of her reverie. She looked at it. Mom calling. She heard her mother's frantic voice.

"Cara, thank God you picked up!" she cried. "I'm scared! I got a call from someone who claims Dad owed him a lot of money, and he wants me to pay up. There's no way I can afford it. He said you have to let Brady play, whatever that means."

Cara stared at her phone. *This can't be real,* she thought. When she looked up, both Brady and the woman were watching her. She turned back to her phone, but her mom had hung up. "One game, Cara," Brady was saying. "One game and then we can leave." Numbly, she nodded, with a sinking feeling in the pit of her stomach. If this was Majority Rules' newest platform, then there was no way to stop them. People would flock to this like lambs to slaughter.

She watched as Brady started playing. The woman sitting near him stood and walked toward her, as if to talk to her. Suddenly, Brady looked up, fell to the floor, and vanished. Cara gasped.

Where had he gone? Her phone rang again. She stared at it. This time, it was Ron.

"Cara, we have a problem," he blurted. "I just got a text from Jeanine. She's being threatened by someone and said something bizarre about you letting Brady play. If you don't, her life could be in danger."

This can't be happening, she thought again, staring at her phone. *It isn't real.* But as she looked up from her phone and gazed around, she questioned that. The longer she remained in here, the more real it seemed.

Panicking, she held the phone to her mouth. "Ron, I got pulled into some sort of Virtual Reality with Brady. It's a virtual casino!"

She glanced at her phone. It was dead. She tried to call Ron back, but the phone was completely out of charge. What was going on? She looked up. The beautiful woman escorting Brady had also disappeared.

She looked around, thinking she should be worried, but somehow she felt calm. The atmosphere of the casino drew her further in, pushing any uneasiness aside. Unable to contact anyone, she began exploring on her own. She wandered the rooms of the casino, in awe of what she saw. Though a piece of her brain told her it wasn't real, it seemed so authentic. She gazed at all the people. Were they people? She was almost certain they were all bots, yet they all had *personalities*. There was the elderly woman at the slot machine, pulling the lever over and over with abandon, pausing now and then to stuff the tokens into her oversized bag. She turned her attention to the drunken black-jack player, clearly getting more and more agitated as the dealer kept raking in the winnings.

Against her better judgment, she began to explore as the technology pulled her in deeper and deeper, banishing all thoughts of the outside world from her mind.

Thirty

GERALDINE FROWNED. SHE WAS monitoring Cara's actions and didn't like what she saw. Cara was drifting about, watching the various activities of the bots. Of all the simulations her team had run, this was one they hadn't planned for. Cara was the one who should have left, while Brady kept playing and remained hostage.

When Brady sat down to play, a cascade of events should have occurred. They had programmed a bot to talk to Cara once Brady became engrossed in gambling. The bot had a script, which included their demands plus instructions for Cara to get out. Unfortunately, Brady's disappearance interrupted the script. With Brady gone, the program no longer worked, and the bot wandered off, leaving Cara trapped there.

They needed to get Cara out before she learned too much. But with Brady gone, if they pulled her out now, they had no way to force her to stop the cyber-attack. It was time to get Bly to put pressure on Henry Ives.

STILL IRRITATED WITH CARA, Ron paced in his office at school. Her cryptic text last evening about Henry hadn't helped. The woman was maddening, that was for sure. How much longer was he supposed to wait for her? He was preparing for class when he received a strange text from Jeanine.

"I'm back in CA. Someone visited me this morning and told me to deliver this message to you: 'Call Cara and tell her to let Brady play.' Please—for my sake... do this now! — J."

Baffled, he called Cara, hoping for an explanation. He repeated the message as soon as she answered, but then the connection was lost. Still bewildered, he called Jeanine, but was interrupted by another incoming call.

"Ron, Abigail here. I'm with Cara's brother, Brady, and you need to talk to him. Something weird just happened that involves Cara. I can't figure out what he's talking about. I'm putting him on the phone now."

Brady's words tumbled out so fast that Ron had difficulty following.

"Cara's in trouble. She's caught in a Virtual Reality and I'm not sure she can get out. You need to cancel the cyber-attack! Stop everything now, or they'll keep her trapped in there."

"Wait, slow down a minute. Take a breath! What are you talking about?" asked Ron, now totally confused.

Brady tried again. "I was working on my computer this morning and clicked on a link that popped up on my screen. It brought me to a Virtual Reality gambling site, one run by Majority Rules. It was so realistic that for a few moments, I felt like I was in an actual casino. I couldn't believe it."

"Hold on a minute. A Virtual Reality gambling site? Wouldn't you need a headset for that to work?" Ron asked.

"Apparently not," Brady replied. "They've developed a Virtual Reality platform that doesn't require any external hardware beyond your personal computer or phone. It's brand new, and they invited me in for a pre-launch experience."

"More like lured you in," muttered Ron, "but go on."

"They convinced me to bring Cara in as well so they could show her how real it was. Stupidly, I fell for their trap and sent Cara a link."

"Wait... who's 'they?' Did people actually talk to you?" Ron asked.

"Yes! They talked to me! In the casino! And I talked to Cara! She wanted me to stop playing, but I didn't listen to her and played anyway. I wasn't aware of anything else until I felt someone grab my arm and push me to the floor. Everything around me dissolved, and when I looked up, Abigail was standing over me in my office, with my computer turned off."

Ron ran his fingers through his hair as he paced back and forth. "Put Abigail back on the phone," he ordered. "I want to hear her version."

Abigail took the phone. "It was a gambling site. Brady promised me he wouldn't visit those anymore." She shot Brady a scathing look. "Anyhow, as soon as I saw what was going on, I grabbed his arm and flipped off the monitor. Then I pushed him away, and he fell out of his chair. He looked up at me and started crying out for Cara."

Brady grabbed the phone back. "Cara's trapped, don't you understand?" He sounded frantic again. "We have to get her out of there. The longer she stays, the more real it will seem, and the harder it will be for her to come out. We have to do as they say and stop the cyber-attack!"

Ron paced faster as he ran his fingers through his hair. He needed to get to Cara, fast. Canceling the cyber-attack was not an option. The sole way to cancel at this point was with a special code, and only two people had access to that code—Cara and Henry. Since Henry had disappeared the night before, that left Cara, and apparently she was trapped somewhere in cyberspace, whatever that meant. Ron shivered at the thought of that. What was happening to her now?

He dashed off to his class and canceled it, telling the students he had a family emergency. Then he headed to his car for the hourlong drive home.

♦♥♣♠

HENRY SLIPPED IN AND out of the shadows, following her. Something wasn't right. He had noticed the commotion earlier at the poker table and was stunned to see one of the patrons at the table vanish. That rarely happened. And then he saw Cara. What was she doing in here? He doubted she was here voluntarily. Someone must have tricked her into entering. If that was the case, Geraldine and Bly probably knew what their group was up to and were trying to block the cyber-attack.

Henry worried Cara might be in imminent danger, but he couldn't confront her directly. That would blow his cover and put them both at even greater risk. He closed his eyes and covered his ears, trying to formulate a plan through the haze of dim lighting and background noise of rolling dice and shuffling cards. More than anything, he needed to remain invisible to the site builders. He was simply a beta tester, and he needed to perform those duties without drawing extra attention to himself.

Beta testers monitored the bots and watched for inappropriate behavior—anything that didn't fit the scene or might pull people out of the Virtual Reality experience. They were also expected to spend a specified amount of money at various tables and keep meticulous track of all winnings and losings. Visits were limited to four hours at a stretch. The testers' agreement clearly stated: "prolonged periods of time within the application may cause an inability to differentiate virtual reality from true reality." Each time he exited, he had to submit to a battery of psychological tests before re-entering. Initially, he had found even brief trips messed with his mind. It had taken him weeks to work up to handling a four-hour session.

Periodically, beta testers were told to leave when the system went into maintenance mode for updating. Henry thought they might also put it in maintenance mode during the cyber-attack, and he was curious what would happen if he stayed. He thought if he was inside the application when the animation shut down, he could gain a better understanding of how it worked. It was risky, but since he had been in here many times, he figured he could handle it. If he became trapped, so be it. He was prepared to stay for a while. But Cara was a different story. She had no idea what this was, and he feared being stuck in here for a long time might do severe damage to her mind. Cara needed to exit the platform prior to the planned cyber-attack. It was vital he get her out without drawing attention to both of them.

As a beta tester, Henry could move around freely, but he was certain Cara was being closely watched. He needed to get a message to her and avoid notice. He found a pen at the reception desk and scribbled on a paper napkin. *"I'm not a bot—I'm a beta tester with red hair. The bots all have a tiny button on their right earlobe. You are in danger. Follow me. PRETEND YOU DON'T KNOW ME! Henry"*

He trailed Cara as she observed a blackjack table. When she turned and headed his way, he put out his foot to trip her. He grabbed her hand to stop her from falling, firmly planting the balled-up note in her palm. Then he turned and walked away. Luckily for Henry, Geraldine had looked away from her screen for a moment. Her attention was elsewhere as Cara stood up, brushed herself off, and realized the napkin had writing on it. She quickly scanned it. Henry, a beta tester? She shook her head, wondering how long he had been doing this without telling them. He was certainly full of surprises!

The brief connection with the outside world caused a shift in her mind. While wandering around, she felt dazed and not fully present—almost emotionless. Part of her wanted to stay in and explore, but perhaps he was right. She felt a twinge of fear. She had seen enough, and maybe it was time to leave. But how? She looked around for someone with red hair and spotted him readily. Was that really Henry with short red hair and a goatee? She wasn't sure what was real anymore. The man nodded imperceptibly and walked down a hallway. Cara's pulse sped up as she followed a discreet distance behind.

GERALDINE COULD NOT BELIEVE Brady had beaten her system. Clearly, she had underestimated him. He should have kept playing, but something had pulled him out. Moments after she watched Brady leave, Bly called her.

"It looks like your plan has failed," he said. "We have the wrong person in there and no way to block the attack on our primary system."

"How did this happen?" she demanded.

"I think someone switched off Brady's monitor," Bly replied.

A small slip-up, but an important one, she realized. Given the stage of development of the platform, they had warned current beta testers to use the app only when alone and not at risk of being interrupted. Brady wouldn't have known that. Geraldine had been so intent on using this platform today that she cut a few corners. Perhaps she should have waited before bringing Brady in.

"She's been in there for a while watching the tables and may already know a few things that shouldn't be made public. We can't let this continue!" she said. "This platform is the future of our industry! If she discloses too much, it will destroy us. I'm putting the app into maintenance mode for a little while. That will keep her from learning more. She won't know how to exit, and that will keep her in limbo and confuse her."

Bly was silent for a moment. "You want to trap her mind in there indefinitely?" he asked. "That seems risky to me. The few beta testers who have stayed in there longer than four hours had difficulty coming back to reality, and that was with the app fully functioning. If she's in there alone with no animation, it could drive her crazy."

"She may have some confusion initially, but there shouldn't be any long-term damage."

"Are you sure?" he asked.

"Damn it, Bly, can't you see we don't have a choice? I don't intend to keep her there long. But every moment she's in there with the animation on, she's learning more and more of our secrets. We need her to go a little crazy. We have to make sure that by the time someone discovers her and breaks her out of this, she will have forgotten everything she saw earlier."

Bly thought for a moment. "Okay—you may be right. But then, how do we stop the cyber-attack?"

"Didn't you tell me Henry Ives has the code to stop it? Get a message to him. Let him know we've been following him, and the game is over."

"Um, well..." stuttered Senator Bly. "I'm not sure I can find Henry right now. He seems to have disappeared."

"Disappeared? When?"

"Yesterday. I was tracking him as usual, and suddenly everything went blank. He has vanished and wiped his equipment clean as well."

"Find him!" Geraldine stormed. "We need him to stop this attack! We didn't spend the last six months tracking him to have him evaporate now!" With that, she slammed down her phone and suspended the Virtual Reality platform.

"ATTENTION ALL BETA TESTERS. PLEASE LEAVE NOW. THIS SYSTEM IS GOING INTO MAINTENANCE MODE. PLEASE EXIT IMMEDIATELY."

Cara noticed a shift in the room. People disappeared, the same way Brady had.

Uh-oh. Henry hoped Cara was still behind him. Though he had planned to stay in if the app went into maintenance mode, he didn't know what would happen and feared it would be bad for Cara. He had to get her out now. As a beta tester, he knew how to use his mind to exit, but Cara didn't have that skill. The only way out for her was through one of the emergency exits. He pointed her toward the sign. "Run!" he shouted.

Panicking, Cara ran, arriving just as the gate slammed shut. She pounded on the door, but it refused to open. Henry grabbed her hand. The lights flickered, then went out, plunging them into darkness and silence.

Thirty one

"WHAT JUST HAPPENED? WHERE are we?" whispered Cara, still clinging to Henry's hand.

"I think they put the platform into maintenance mode. Everything is still here, but there is no movement or animation." They peered into the pitch-blackness, unable to see anything.

"What is this place?" whispered Cara.

"Fascinating," said Henry, with a slight Australian accent. "It's not a place, actually. Technically, we're not in the site anymore—but we're not out of it either. It seems we're in a virtual space somewhere between reality and fantasy. Physically, we are each sitting in front of a computer looking at a frozen screen, but somehow, our minds are trapped here, together."

"I heard them announce all beta testers should leave. Why didn't you go? And what's with your accent?" Cara had so many questions bubbling to the surface.

"One question at a time! Once I saw you, I couldn't leave you alone. I was afraid you weren't here voluntarily, and you wouldn't know how to leave." Henry explained.

"So... how *do* you leave? And where did Brady go?" Suddenly, Cara realized she hadn't given Brady's disappearance a second thought until now. Clearly, her mind was scrambled. Her stomach flipped as she felt panic rising within her. "Tell me what's going on, Henry. All of it!"

"Wait—that man who disappeared—that was your brother, Brady?" Henry asked.

"Yes! He got in here and then sent me a link and told me to click on it! Come on, Henry, tell me what this is all about!"

"Calm down, Cara. I'll explain as best as I can," Henry began. "It's making more sense now. As you know, I've been monitoring Majority Rules for a long time. I watched them develop this platform, Pairadice. They wanted beta testers—people to do final testing of the site before its public launch. I applied using a fake identity, and they accepted me into the program."

"Wait... so you have *another* identity?" Cara asked in amazement.

"I do. As far as Majority Rules knows, I am officially Samuel Evans and grew up in Queensland, Australia. About two months ago, I became a regular on this site."

"You've been doing this for months? Why didn't you tell us?"

"I didn't want to compromise your work. If Senator Bly was watching me, there was no way for me to communicate with you all safely about this. I had to remain silent about it with everyone, including you. And it's a good thing I did, because it turns out he *was* watching every move I made as Henry Ives, though I don't think he knows I am doing this. Samuel Evans is not on his radar."

"What have you been doing in here?" she asked.

"I've been gathering information. As a beta tester, I can enter and leave the program at will, and I've seen some terrifying things. You were only here a short time, and you can see how incredibly real it looks. But there is crazy stuff going on behind the scenes."

"Like what?" asked Cara.

"They're setting up a massive illegal money-making operation."

"You mean they're doing more than just luring people in and keeping them gambling with devious practices?" Cara was having a hard time comprehending the enormity of all this.

"That's right. A key component of this platform is to make it impossible to discern reality from fiction. Experienced gamblers know that in most online gambling sites, they're playing against a bot, and they temper their bets accordingly. But here, the animations are so sophisticated that even the most skeptical observer can't tell the difference. That makes an enormous difference in how much risk people will take. And since the house controls the bots, you can guess who wins 90% of the time."

Cara pondered this. "Making it hard to tell reality and fiction apart would also keep people in here longer. You didn't answer my question as to how to get out."

"When I started as a beta tester, they instructed me to always keep a token with me—they called it a talisman.

It could be anything, as long as it was something with a strong association to the physical world. They suggested actual money—preferably coins—that I could keep in my pocket, but I prefer these beads." He reached into his pocket and brought out four tiny magnets. Cara gasped. Those were the worry beads he had shown her months ago.

"To come out of the site, I hold the beads and imagine using them outside of this space. That image brings me out, as it is something powerfully connected to reality for me. It also helps that it's linked to a person. My brother gave me these beads, and I had a solid connection with him, so even though he died, the beads focus my mind."

"So, if I want to leave, all I need to do is hold something real and focus on using it in reality? Is that what you're saying?"

"Sort of, but it isn't quite that easy. The longer you're in here, the more real everything in here seems, so just focusing on reality doesn't work. You need to ground yourself to the outside world. The talisman works as a tether, and unfortunately, you don't have one with you. That makes me wonder if they intended for you to stay in here. Though, when the game was live, they had 'emergency exits' which they told us to use if we lost our talisman or if it didn't work and we felt trapped. That's where I was trying to take you. Once the game froze, however, the exits closed. I don't know how you can get out right now. I mean, physically, you're at your office, but your mind is stuck here until the game resumes and the emergency exits open up. And even then, I'm not really sure how those emergency exits work. I've never tried them myself. They might be just a gimmick."

"How did Brady get out?"

"I'm not sure," admitted Henry. "I wonder if something from the outside world intervened. They warned us beta testers to always be somewhere private when using the app. They made it clear we should have no interruptions. It's possible someone saw him staring at his computer monitor, turned it off, and touched him. That might have been enough to bring him out."

Still clutching Henry's hand, Cara shivered in the darkness. "If the site shut down, wouldn't we have been ejected? We'd be staring at a blank screen right now, right?"

"Theoretically, yes, but when they put the site into maintenance mode, they locked it down. I suspect they want you trapped in here right now. You were wandering around for a while before the site shut down, so they may fear you learned too many secrets. Also, I imagine they don't realize I'm here with you. If you were alone in here, your mind might go a little crazy."

She squeezed his hand, grateful for his presence. He was right—being in here alone would be truly terrifying. She peered through the darkness. If she looked hard enough, she thought she could spot a few shapes, which she assumed were bots, though she didn't really want to investigate. Yet she knew they couldn't stay put and do nothing. Or could they? How long had they been in here, anyway?

As if reading her mind, Henry stood and pulled her toward one of the slot machines. "We should move a bit," he said. "We may be here for a while. Moving will help us stay in our bodies, so we're not entirely in our minds. And while we're stuck here, we may as well do a little exploring. One important thing, though... let's not let go of each other's hands. I'm not sure, but that connection might be the only reason we can communicate with each other here." With his free hand, he reached out and touched a woman bot seated at the machine. "Incredible!" he said. "She is so cold. This is one thing I was trying to figure out. As beta testers, we had strict rules, and one of them was to keep our hands off the bots. At no time were we allowed to touch them. And now I see why."

"I don't understand," said Cara.

"If the app was live, and I touched someone, I would suddenly realize it wasn't real. Here, feel her arm." He took Cara's hand and ran it over the arm of the bot. Cara shivered once again and jerked her hand away.

"Ew! She feels dead!" Cara cried out.

"You're right. And I imagine that would be the same, even if the site was live. If you touched her, you might very well get confused enough to question the surrounding reality. And that could really mess up your mind if you didn't know what was going on."

Cara shivered again. All this talk of messing up her mind was grating on her. "Tell me about your brother," she said, pulling him away from the robotic people. She needed a change of subject. "What was he like?"

"My brother was one of the most easy-going people you'd ever meet," replied Henry, as they sat down at one of the blackjack tables. "Nothing bothered him—at least as far as he told us. But I came to understand that underneath that sweetness, he was a pathological liar. Now that I think about it, he probably lied to himself most of all."

Cara's breath caught. As Henry spoke of his brother, she thought of her father. She might have described him in exactly the same way.

"I could never trust him. Sometimes I wonder if that scarred me for life. I can't trust anyone, ever. I always expect people to let me down. I guess I learned at a very early age not to expect the truth. If you don't have high expectations, you're less likely to get hurt. I've trained myself not to expect anything from anyone. That way, they can't disappoint me."

Henry's words hit Cara like a punch in the gut. She recalled the countless times her father didn't show up for things—birthday parties, concerts, school plays—and how her mother always made excuses for him. It was the norm of how she grew up.

"Maybe that's what growing up with a gambling addict does to you," she said slowly.

All at once, she understood. Despite the pitch-darkness surrounding them, she felt like her eyes were open for the first time. She desperately needed to talk to Ron. "Henry, we need to get out of this place," she whispered. "I still don't understand how we're trapped in here. Now that I *know* none of this is real, I should be able to just go back to reality, right?"

"Yes... and no." said Henry. "The whole point of this site is to separate people from reality. It's designed to keep people from connecting with the outside world. For an addict, there is nothing more dangerous."

"But it's shut down, and I'm not an addict!" she cried. "There must be a way out!"

"Remember, you've been in here a long time now. Your brain is getting used to this. Intellectually, you know it isn't real, but what does that matter? Can you simply will yourself to wake up from a dream? Your mind is deep into this, and it will not come out on its own. You can't think your way out of this, Cara. You need a tie to the outside world."

For a moment, they were both silent, lost in thought. "What about my phone?" she asked.

"Your phone?" Henry asked. "What about it?"

"Could that be a talisman? I mean, it's something from the outside world that I have with me. And I got two phone calls in here *from* outside."

"That's impossible," said Henry flatly. "There's no way you could have communicated by phone *in here* with someone *out there*."

"But I did!" insisted Cara. "I got two phone calls, one from my mom just before Brady disappeared, and one from Ron just after."

"But did you talk to them?" asked Henry.

Instinctively, Cara squeezed her eyes shut, trying to re-member. Even in the complete darkness, closing her eyes gave her some control over her mind. The call from her mom had come right as Brady was pleading with her to allow him to play one game. She was about to stop him when her phone rang. Her mom told her to let Brady play! How did her mom know? It made no sense! "I don't understand!" she cried. "Somehow, my mom knew I was here with Brady, and he wanted to gamble. How could she have known that?"

"Did you actually talk to her?" repeated Henry.

"No, she hung up before I said anything. I looked down at my phone, and when I looked up, Brady was playing."

"What about the second call?" asked Henry.

"It was from Ron, a minute later, after Brady disappeared. He also said something about letting Brady play. But by then, I was so distraught that I didn't know what I was hearing. Then my phone went dead."

"Think for a minute, Cara. How long were you staring at your phone for each call? Is it possible that you left the app briefly to answer and then came right back in?"

Cara replayed the scene in her head. Had she come out just long enough to field those calls? Had she looked around at all when that happened? She couldn't remember. "I don't know... I suppose it's possible. But why? How did they know to call at that exact time, and why did I go back in?"

"I have a theory," said Henry slowly. "And if I'm right, it might be a way to get you out of here. I believe Senator Bly and Geraldine Major brought you and Brady into the platform to convince you to suspend the cyber-attack. It's possible they wanted to trap Brady in here by getting him to gamble again. They may have planned to use him as a pawn to force you to listen to their demands. If that's the case, then the timing of the two phone calls was not a coincidence. They engineered those. Someone from outside got your mom to call you at that moment and Ron to call you a few moments later. They *wanted* to hook Brady.

In the darkness, Cara nodded slowly. It sort of made sense. "But that still doesn't answer the question of how my mom and Ron called me in here."

"They didn't exactly. They called you on your phone in your office, and you picked up *in your office*. Remember, your mind is here, but your body is in your office. For a moment, you were back in your office, answering your phone. And your entire focus was *on your phone*. As soon as you glanced up from the phone and looked back at the computer monitor, you were back here. When you tried to respond from here, it didn't work. Somehow, you came out just long enough to answer the call and hear a sentence, but your mind was still here. It's like a ringing phone might partially pull you out of a dream, but then you go right back into the dream. Since you were already deeply embedded in this alternate reality, you had no knowledge this wasn't real. You had no reason to question it."

"Okay, that's possible," Cara said slowly. "But how would that help get me out of here now?"

"You have your phone with you, right?

"I do, but you said it's impossible to call from here to there."

"I did. But you're not going to make a call. You're going to *receive* a call, which you already said you can do. Here's my idea: You can't leave, but I can, since I have my talisman with me." He held up the worry beads. "It may be risky in that you'll be here alone for a while, but it's the best I can come up with right now. I'm going to leave. Once out of here, I can contact Ron and tell him to call you. If your phone is on, you should be able to hear it, and if my theory is correct, you may come out of the app long enough to answer. Then the trick will be to keep you out. I think it may work this time, because now you're aware of what's going on, and you won't be pulled back in the way you were when the animation was turned on. You will just need to focus your mind on what's real in your life—on the office, on Ron, on the house. Whatever you can think of to get you back to reality."

"Okay," said Cara. "If you think it will work." She didn't relish being left alone, but she also desperately wanted to get out of there.

"I can't guarantee it will work, but we have to try. Just remember, being alone here will be extremely disorienting. It might even drive you mad if you didn't understand it. That may be part of Geraldine's plan, but I don't think she realizes I'm in here with you. If I can get hold of Ron, it should only be a few minutes from the time I leave until you get that phone call. Just make sure your phone is on."

Her face fell as she remembered more. "I can't turn on the phone," she whispered. "The battery is dead."

Henry pondered this for a moment. "That may not be a problem," he said. "Ron should be near you when he calls. Your office is in his house, right? If he's there, he can plug in your phone to charge it up. Once it has sufficient charge, he can call. In fact, if you watch your phone, you may even notice when he plugs it in and it starts charging. That's the value of a talisman. It maintains its essence wherever it is. If the phone charges in reality, it should charge here as well."

Cara clutched her phone, hoping this would be enough to take her home. "Okay, let's do it," she said with as much gumption as she could muster.

She felt Henry loosen his grip on her hand as he prepared to go. "Wait!" she cried out, still holding onto him. "If Ron's there, can't he simply pull me away from the screen? You said you thought that's what happened to Brady..."

"I don't think so," he replied. "There's nothing to pull you away from. You're not focused on the game anymore, the way you were when it was live. Your mind is trapped in between. It's like you're in a different dimension altogether. It's kind of like when someone's in a coma and can't wake up just by being shaken." Cara shivered as she thought back to when Brady was in the hospital, and she had wondered if he could feel her touch.

"Using the phone will help ground you. Just remember—even coming out under normal circumstances can be tricky, especially the first time. It's incredibly jarring and you will be completely disoriented. Be prepared for that."

Thirty two

RON WAS FRANTIC WITH worry as he sped toward his house. He didn't know what to expect when he got there. He had set his phone on autodial to keep calling Cara. Why wasn't she answering?

His phone rang, and he realized it was an incoming call from Henry. "Cara's in trouble," Henry confirmed.

"Wait—how do you know? Cara texted me last night saying you disappeared. What the hell is going on, Henry?"

"I had to get away. Someone hacked my credit card account, and I'm afraid Bly is after me. So... today I went into hiding and visited a VR site—and somehow, Cara did as well. She's trapped in there now and needs our help to get out."

"What does that even mean? How does someone get trapped in a VR site?"

"Majority Rules is about to launch their new platform, Pairadice. I secretly signed on with them a few months ago, and I've been a beta tester—"

"Just tell me about Cara, Henry! Is she okay? I'm on my way to my house right now. What will I find when I get there?"

"Cara will be sitting in front of her computer, staring at a blank screen. Before you do anything else, plug in her phone. Charge it for a few minutes before calling her."

"So, her phone's out of charge? Is that why she hasn't responded? I've been calling her every minute for the last hour!"

"I think her phone died right after you called her. So, yeah, that's partly why she hasn't responded," Henry said.

"What do you mean, partly?"

"I'm not sure she could hear the phone right now, even if it was charged. She's in a deep trance. But this is the best plan I could come up with to get her out. If I'm right, when you plug in the phone, she may become aware it's charging and be ready for your call. It all depends how deeply immersed she is."

"Christ, what if nothing happens?" Ron wiped the sweat from his forehead as he sped even faster down the highway.

"Just do as I say. Let the phone charge for a few minutes, then call her. Stay with her. It may take a while, but she should hear the phone. Be patient. You may need to call two or three times. When she stirs, hold her tight and keep talking to bring her fully out. She will be very disoriented. The first time I went in, it was only for a few moments, and I had a tough time afterwards. It's an intensely confusing experience, and she's been in there a long time."

"Are you sure she'll wake up?"

"I'm not sure of anything right now, but this is the only solution I could think of. Remember, she must fully wake up so she won't slip back. Give her something sweet to eat—chocolate if you have it. That is very grounding. I'll be in touch with you soon... but don't contact me. I'm sure I'm still being watched! Good luck!"

Ron pulled into his driveway and raced into the house, steeling himself for what he might see when he entered Cara's office. As Henry had predicted, Cara was sitting upright in front of a blank computer screen. His heart skipped a beat. Was she even alive? She seemed glued to the screen, her phone on the floor alongside her, as if she had dropped it. Gingerly, he picked it up and placed it in her hand. He looked at it. As Henry had said, the battery was dead. He curled her fingers around it and plugged it in. The phone beeped once and lit up. Cara flinched and gripped it tighter. *Did he imagine that?* He couldn't tell because as he looked again, she remained hypnotized by the screen. Gently, he turned her away from the monitor and placed her hand on her lap, with the phone facing up. Then he knelt down and wrapped his arms around her. He murmured to her, but got no response.

"Cara, I'm so sorry. I know I pushed you when you weren't ready. I want you back here. Please... don't leave me. I need you. My life was in shambles before you came along. Stay with me... Please!"

He let the phone charge for about five minutes, then sat down on the floor and pulled her onto his lap. Holding her tightly, he called her on the phone.

ALONE, CARA WAITED IN the darkness for what seemed like ages. With each passing minute, she felt the panic rising within her. What if this didn't work? How long could she last here? Where was "here" anyway? What had Henry said? *"It might even drive you mad."* She had brushed that off, thinking she could handle it. Now she wondered if he might be right. Slowly, she felt her mind unraveling as she became more and more unhinged from reality. She was alone. Why did her father abandon her? It wasn't only that one time at the casino, she realized now. He was never there for her. He chose gambling over her—he even died for it. It was true, she thought with a sob. What kind of relationship was that?

She looked down at her phone and let it clatter to the floor. It was no use. She was trapped here forever, somewhere between reality and fantasy, whatever that meant. Neither of those words held much meaning for her anymore. She was slipping away into oblivion. Was this what Brady experienced when he was in a coma? The thought of Brady filled her with sadness. Would she ever see him again? And what about her mom and Ron? All that was rapidly disappearing as she sat in the darkness. Perhaps she should move, she thought. Hadn't Henry said something about moving to stay in her body? She felt something in her hand, and through the haze of her mind, realized she was holding her phone. But she had dropped it. How did it get there? Her fingers curled around it, and for a moment it felt as if someone was moving them for her. She looked down and, in the darkness, saw a faint glow. Her phone was charging! It was working! Was that a good thing? She tried to remember what it meant. Was she supposed to do something? Since she couldn't recall, she simply sat and waited, her hands clenched around her phone like a lifeline. A moment later, she fell to the floor.

CARA DIDN'T RESPOND AS the ringtone on the phone pierced the silence. Ron squeezed her tightly and held his breath. If this didn't work, he had no clue what he would do. Suddenly, he felt her shift. Her hand gripped the phone, and he saw her fingers relax. Gently, he guided her finger to press "accept" and brought the phone to her ear. Henry had told him the phone was like a tether, holding her in this reality, and that he should use it as long as necessary.

"Cara, it's me, Ron," he whispered into the phone. "Come back to me. It's time to come home." He held her on his lap, all the while talking to her to rouse her out of her stupor. Her eyes were open though unfocused, and slowly, he felt her move. Henry said the first minute was critical. He had to keep her connected to this reality. He hugged her to him. "Come back, Cara. I love you. You belong here, with me."

The phone clattered to the floor and Cara froze for an instant. Then she looked at Ron and sobbed as she clung to him.

"I've got you. You're home. You're safe here," he whispered. "Just stay with me, okay?" He grabbed a piece of chocolate and gingerly placed it in her mouth. As she tasted the sweetness, she blinked a few times, then opened her eyes once again and looked around. She was back in her office. Ron held her. She wrapped her arms around him, burrowing her head deep into his chest. His heartbeat was fast, echoing her own. For a few moments, the two of them sat there in silence, wondering what had happened. Cara sighed. There would be plenty of time for questions later, she thought. For now, she just wanted to soak up the reality of Ron and her life here.

How long did they stay like that on the floor? Cara had no idea. She simply knew that this, here, was real, and she was ready to tell Ron the truth. She trusted him. Slowly, she brushed her lips against his. This time, there would be no turning back. She was ready to go all in with him.

As their lips touched, Ron pushed her away. Hands on her shoulders, he held her at arm's length. "No," he said. "Not now. You've just been through an incredibly traumatic experience. This isn't the time." She looked at him questioningly.

"It's not that I don't want you. You know I do, desperately. I want to be sure it's your free choice. You can stay here and I'll hold you all night, but that's as far as it goes. If we're going to be together, we need to start off the right way."

"Just one kiss?" she asked, gazing into his eyes.

"One kiss, and then you're going off to take a nice hot bath. There are many ways to return to reality. I want to be sure you're fully back here before we go any further together."

She sank deep into the kiss, knowing it was a promise of many more to come.

Thirty three

CARA SAT IN EM'S apartment, reflecting on how much had changed in the past month. "Ron asked me to move in with him," she said.

"What do *you* want to do?" Em asked.

"I want to, but I'm scared. I'm crazy in love with him, but there's a part of me that says it's too fast. What if it doesn't work out? I just don't know what to do."

"It's a gamble, but so is life. For what it's worth, I think you should go for it," said Em. "You seem happier than I've ever seen you before, and he's good for you. Think of it this way—if things fall apart, you can always come back here. I'm not going anywhere for a while. We can continue to work together, even if you're not living here. Promise you'll stay in close touch?"

Cara smiled at her friend. Em was always so supportive, but Cara worried about her. She wondered if Em ever got out socially. If Em had a love life, she kept it completely private.

"I promise," said Cara, giving her a hug. "But eventually, I may need to break another promise I made to you."

"What's that?" asked Em.

Cara stepped back and took a breath in. "Ron wants to meet you in person. He's tired of the phone calls and keeps asking me how I knew you before all this started. It's clear to him we were more than just casual friends in college, as I originally told him. I want your permission to reveal your true identity to him. I don't want to keep any secrets from him, Em!"

Em's face clouded over. "I'm not sure..." she stammered. "I understand what you're saying, but I have to be so careful. Given the people I write about, my identity has to remain a secret. I just don't know if I can risk it. Especially meeting in person."

"I want to give him your actual name and tell him we were college roommates! And I want you to be part of our lives, as a friend, separate from the work we've done together. You need to get out, Em, and I want you to visit us at his house. Why can't we do that?"

"I'm afraid, Cara. Every time I go out, I worry someone has figured out I'm Libby Lewis. She has written some damning articles during the past year and gets a lot of hate mail. I have to keep my personal life separate from that. You're the only one who has crossed that line." She paused and looked away. Finally, she turned back to Cara. "Okay. I get this means a lot to you. If I visit you there, Ron has to understand my need to keep things separate. He's known me for a while now as Libby, because we have a professional relationship, but if he sees me in person, I'm Emiline Jackson. Does that make sense?"

"It makes perfect sense. Thank you!" said Cara, giving her friend another hug. "Let's plan on you coming for dinner next weekend! It'll be great for the three of us to be together, in person!"

"I suppose," said Em, laughing. "Though I feel like seeing him might be a letdown for me after the way you've described him. You let him know I'm expecting to see a Greek God when I walk in!"

"I don't think I've put him on that much of a pedestal," said Cara.

"Uh-huh," Em crossed her arms and smirked. She had a way of looking at Cara that said far more than words. "On another note," she said, "I want to show you my latest article. I wrote it early this morning. Look." She opened her laptop and pushed it toward Cara.

Senator Bly Gambled and Lost

"Senator Richard Bly, former chairperson of the Senate Appropriations Committee, resigned yesterday as a result of growing public concern about his involvement in a massive money laundering scheme coupled with false advertising. Bly has been under investigation by several watchdog agencies, and confidential documents obtained by the *Post* suggest he conspired with other prominent casino owners to launder billions of dollars, hired scientists to publish papers with false information, and blocked researchers from publishing accurate data. According to an anonymous source, 'These records clearly show Bly gambled on the gullibility of the American public.' A spokesperson for Bly's office said, 'While the Senator maintains his innocence, he feels he can no longer serve the best interests of his constituents.'"

"Bly was a major stakeholder in the Majority Rules corporation, which suffered a major financial setback last month after an internet security breach compromised the website. The FCC has advised the public to avoid visiting the Majority Rules website or using any of its affiliated apps until further security measures are in place. This comes amid increased public awareness of illegal practices carried on by the company for the past five years."

"Despite this warning, a spokesperson for the company announced Majority Rules will continue to operate, declaring, 'Online gambling is here to stay.' Ms. Geraldine Major, CEO of Majority Rules, was unavailable for comment and has not been seen for the past month."

"Em, this is terrific!"

"It should be in the paper tonight. And Henry and Gloria agreed to release the recording of that Gibraltar meeting. Bly will probably face criminal charges."

"It sounds like Bly, at least, will no longer be a threat to us."

"From what we've been able to piece together, Bly is having personal problems. Rumor has it his wife is in recovery from addiction to online gambling, and she is in a posh rehab facility right now. If so, he could be ruined financially and professionally. That's a nice little twist of fate, wouldn't you say?"

Cara sighed. "I suppose I feel vindicated in some ways, though it brings up another issue that needs to be addressed. The CDC still doesn't recognize gambling addiction as a true disease. Until that happens, there won't be enough federal or state funds for treatment programs. Bly's wife is lucky if he can afford an expensive treatment facility for her. But most people can't do that. I look at Brady and wonder how he's ever going to beat this if he can't find an appropriate program to help him."

Em nodded. "How's Brady doing, by the way?" she asked. "You said he was pretty shaken up by that last Virtual Reality experience."

"He was, and he says he's fine now, but I still worry about him. He claims to know he screwed up and swears it'll never happen again, but I don't believe him. It's the same old story. He hasn't been willing to get professional help, and a big reason for that is because help is not easily available. Very few therapists have experience with online gambling addiction. And forget about group programs. Resources for this are so limited right now unless you want to spend hundreds of thousands of dollars as Senator Bly may be doing. It's a major problem."

"Well, we have our work cut out for us, then," said Em.

Thirty four

GERALDINE COUGHED AS SHE stood once again in her penthouse office overlooking the city and the bay. Her empire, she mused. Such a beautiful place. She had worked so hard to get here. And now it was crumbling before her eyes.

She looked at the newspaper article once again. "Damn Bly!" she whispered. How could he have been so stupid? He had told her the recording was destroyed, but what other "confidential documents" would they be referring to?

Her phone beeped, and she looked at it idly. Another call from Senator Bly. But he wasn't even a senator anymore. For a month now, he had been sending her message after message. Emails, texts, voicemails. How much longer should she put him off? Irritably, she grabbed the phone and accepted the call.

"What part of 'stop contacting me' don't you understand?" she yelled into the phone.

Bly cleared his throat. "I assume you read the news," he said. He sounded defeated, but she had little compassion for him.

"Of course! How could I miss it?" she asked.

"I need help," he said hoarsely.

"Really? What kind of help can I possibly give you?"

"I need money," he whispered.

"Money? And you dare to ask me? Why the hell would I give you money?"

Bly hesitated, then erupted. "Because I have a problem, and you are to blame! My wife is in rehab now, thanks to a gambling addiction that *you* pushed on her. You did this to her. And now, I'm facing bankruptcy and need to come up with thousands of dollars to cover her treatment! She would never have gotten into this if it wasn't for you!"

"Oh, for Christ's sake, Bly! It's not my fault your wife is addicted to gambling. How dare you blame me!"

"You talked her into it, you bitch. I remember the day you introduced her to it. You told her how much fun it would be and showed her how to get started. And once she started, she couldn't stop!" Bly was screaming now. "She tried to kill herself last week!"

"And that's my fault?" she asked icily. "No, Bly, I refuse to take responsibility for your wife's weakness. I'm simply running a business, and if a client keeps playing, that's up to them. I never forced her."

"Right, but you kept inducing her to play. I know what you did. You kept sending her messages and links. You pushed this on her!"

"Like hell I did!" she exclaimed. "Those were all auto-mated messages, which *you* approved! We talked about this years ago. You knew what we were doing to gain customers and keep them playing."

His voice was steely. "You should never have interfered with my family. But since you did, you're going to make this right, or else..."

"Or else, what? Are you threatening me, Bly?" she asked. "Because I don't respond well to threats. Especially ones that come from someone who betrayed me."

"That wasn't my fault!" he exploded. "How was I supposed to know our meeting was being recorded?"

"I don't know, but since you weren't careful enough, our entire industry is suffering. That includes me. I've lost millions of dollars in the last month. Even if I wanted to help you, I wouldn't be able to."

"Oh... you have plenty of money hidden away," he retorted. "What I'm asking for is nothing compared to what you have. If you wanted to help me, you would."

"Well, guess what? I don't and I won't. Goodbye, Bly!"

She slammed down the phone and sank into her chair. It was not supposed to play out like this. Still furious, she glowered at the empty pack of cigarettes on the desk, mocking her. *Damn the tobacco industry!* That ought to have been her salvation. Was it just a few hours ago she sat in that damn doctor's office while he calmly told her she had untreatable stage 4 lung cancer and needed to get her affairs in order? She had been so sure of her plan. It should have worked. It *did* work—for a while. She had amassed billions of dollars while others gambled away their lives. Yet what did it matter now? Sales had plummeted in recent weeks as people became more aware of the dangers.

Keeping the business going was exhausting. And now, this.

"How long?" she had asked the doctor. He shrugged. "A month, maybe two at best."

Geraldine burrowed deeper into her plush chair, wondering if there was someone she should call. She had no one. No family. No real friends to speak of. Her business had always been her constant companion, and since the infamous cyber-attack last month, the company revenue had plummeted. As the business faltered, numerous news reports citing the perils of the much-touted Virtual Reality platform surfaced. That damn reporter, Libby Lewis, was nipping at her heels, uncovering more and more scams. Once the veil was lifted from her clients' eyes, they no longer fell for all her marketing ploys. People closed their accounts in droves as dangers involving Virtual Reality became more widely publicized, and she was powerless to stop it.

How dare Bly blame her! This was all his fault! He had been in lockstep with her for years. She knew he didn't care about his wife. It was a bond they shared—the inability to care about anything except for money and power. His wife was a token for him, but one he was now risking bankruptcy for. What a fool he was.

What did *she* care about? Was there anything she would go into bankruptcy for? She looked at her computer monitor. *If you can't beat 'em, join 'em.* Her father had told her never to gamble, but maybe it was time to stop playing by his rules.

She paused, about to enter her newest site. She didn't care if she stayed in there forever. As her hand hovered over the mouse, a thought occurred to her. If she was going on a gambling spree, she may as well take someone else down with her. She looked at her latest pop-up ad—the one specifically designed to lure back players who had been away for a while.

She sent the link to Brady's computer. *He will come,* she thought. *They always do....*

Brady sat alone in his room, trying not to think about gambling. After the incident with Cara, he was mortified at the thought of what he had done. He had put his sister in danger, and for that, he was ashamed. That shame, though, was short-lived. Cara forgave him, his mom forgave him—shit, everyone forgave him! He promised he would stay clean and told them he had it under control. And at that time, he even convinced himself. He was done with gambling.

Yet, he could not shake off the memory of walking into that Virtual Casino. He desperately wanted to go back. What did he have to live for here? He was stuck in a wheelchair for the rest of his life and unable to function on his own. He had nothing, really, except a toxic relationship with gambling.

He opened a file on his laptop and looked at the letter he had written, re-reading it for the hundredth time:

Dear Gambling –

I wish we'd never met.

I remember the day I first learned of you...

It was innocent enough at first. A few poker games with friends broke the monotony of growing up in a small town where everyone knew everyone else's business. It didn't take long for me to figure out that poker involved much more skill than luck, and, boy, was I skilled! I studied hard and you rewarded me with your riches. I was unbeatable... or so I thought.

I loved you! You waited patiently for me to grow up, promised me the world. And I believed you. I couldn't wait to turn eighteen and play in a casino. Enough of this small-town shit. I was ready for the big leagues!

I was flying—unstoppable. Soaring in the space you created for me. Time no longer existed. There was only this moment. This bet. Anything was possible. Until it wasn't...

I hate you! You lured me in, and then you threw me out like I was a worthless piece of shit. How is it you have such a grip on me? I wish I could say we were done, but even now, I feel your pull. Why are you doing this to me?

Will I ever be free of you? I go for months without you, and I'm happy—and then, in a moment of weakness, I'm pulled back in. You hijack my brain, blocking out all other worries or thoughts. I become trapped in a mindless place, and your promise of another win keeps me stuck there. It feels like paradise—until I come back to reality.

Get out of my life and stay out! I'm through with you! You destroyed my life! You don't own me. You are scum and I hope you rot in hell...

Hey... I hear you have a cool new site. I know I cut you off, but sometimes I wish you'd contact me. Others get to enjoy you... why can't I? One little visit... I won't stay long. What would be the harm?

He knew the harm now. And yet...

As he stared at his screen, a familiar icon flashed once again. He had blocked that site! Gambling was stalking him. But that was impossible! Or was it? His mouse hovered over the link. One piece of his mind screamed, "No! Don't do this!" even as the part of his brain that controlled his fingers clicked on the icon. He was in! And the first 30 minutes were free! He could set a timer, and once his time was up, he would stop. No problem. Surely he could do that. *What would be the harm?* He stared at the screen, and felt himself walk into the casino. In that moment, nothing else mattered.

Afterword

If you're wondering "Is this the end?" that's intentional. Gambling addiction, like most other addictions, doesn't always have a neat and tidy ending.

I wrote this book to shine a spotlight on an often-overlooked problem. People rarely talk about gambling addiction, and the legalization of online gambling is on the rise. The story is fictional; however, the framework contains many factual elements.

Gambling addiction used to be considered an impulse-control disorder, which had ramifications in terms of treatment options and insurance coverage for various programs. Until recently, it was not recognized as a disease in its own right and was often lumped in with substance abuse, in part because many problem gamblers were also diagnosed with substance addiction and/or mental health issues. That has changed, and it is now considered a disease, called Gambling Disorder. When it was under Impulse Control, it was not billable, but currently it is billable through most insurance plans, and many states are now funding councils to educate the public on prevention, treatment, and research. Public understanding is growing as well. The month of March each year is now gambling awareness month.

All the data and statistics in Ron's report are factual. The gambling industry has skyrocketed in recent years, primarily due to the development of online platforms, and there has been a concurrent rise in teen and young adult suicides over the past 20 years. Gambling addiction (now Gambling Disorder) has the highest suicide rate of any other disorder. Is this coincidental? One could argue there are many causes of suicide, and often it is difficult to know the direct cause in any given case, yet there is growing evidence that this correlation is real and is something worth paying attention to.

Given that the CDC is the premier organization responsible for Public Health in the U.S., I chose to highlight that organization as the one most responsible for research into the connection between gambling and suicide. However, the role of the CDC in covering up that link is a fictional part of this book.

The Gambling Industry Research Institute is fabricated, but the Tobacco Industry Research Committee was an actual group dedicated to promoting the health benefits of tobacco in the 1950s and 60s. While the gambling industry has not organized to this extent, this model of duping the public through targeted advertising and governmental lobbying has been a blueprint for several other corporate industries—the pharmaceutical industry for one, the sugar industry (attempting to lay the blame for obesity on fat), and the coal/oil industry (regarding climate change) for others.

The name "Pairadice" is fictional, though Virtual Reality is a rapidly evolving technology, and gambling sites are already capitalizing on it. Although most VR sites require the use of headsets in order to get the full sensation, there are smartphone apps which closely mimic the VR experience. While this section of the book is fiction, one can easily imagine a scenario in which a compulsive gambler can become "trapped" in a website, especially if every time they pick up their phone or open their laptop, targeted pop-up ads immediately draw them in.

The concept of creating the feeling of being in a real live casino while in the privacy of one's home is a lucrative venture for corporations and a potentially scary one for the end user. The use of these sites to blur the distinction between fantasy and reality is chilling and may have ramifications that go way beyond online gambling.

How do we combat this? Awareness of the problem is the best starting point. Online gambling can be hidden; it's not like alcohol where you can smell it on someone's breath or see how they can't walk a straight line. Since most people spend hours engrossed in their phones, it's often difficult to know what sites they're visiting and what they're doing there. Technology has its benefits, but we, the public, need to be aware of how that technology may manipulate us into believing things that are not true.

Acknowledgments

This book would never have been written without the support and encouragement of SIPA, my writers' support group. The group membership has evolved over the past two years, but you all know who you are, and I appreciate the contributions each one of you has made to my writing. Having a space to talk about the writing process each week kept me motivated and energized.

To my early Beta readers: Laura Fedolfi, Regina Walter, and Joanne Hyatt. I can't thank you enough for your input and advice. I know how hard it is to critique someone else's writing, and I so appreciate the effort you all put out to help me bring this book to life. I also wish to acknowledge Esther Wikander, Donna Harrington, and Carol Waite who read later versions of the manuscript and gave me valuable feedback.

Much of the book is fiction, and as such, it is a creation in my own mind. However, I wanted it to be based on fact and would like to give a special thank you to Dot

Duda for providing me with professional expertise and encouragement along the way.

I was fortunate to work with an amazing editor, Karen Salemi. Your hundreds of comments and suggestions were spot-on, and this book is so much stronger as a result. Thank you for seeing the things I couldn't see, and showing me how to make this book shine!

And finally, I could not have written this without the support of my family. Thank you to Dave, Andy, and Scott for believing in me and putting up with the times when I disappeared into my writing cave. Your support has meant the world to me.

Book Club Discussion Questions

1. The author began the story and separated some chapters with italicized text in a letter addressed to "Dear Gambling." Did you guess or know who wrote those letters?

2. Does the story have a villain? Who/what is it?

3. Could you identify with any of the characters? Could you put yourself in that character's place?

4. How culpable are those around an addict? What, if anything, are they obligated to do?

5. Were any characters "enablers" in the story? Did any characters change during the story?

6. How did the author foreshadow some of the events in the story?

7. Could you visualize the casinos Brady visited?

8. Did you wonder why Cara was prevented from investigating gambling?

9. What did you think about the plan to corrupt and shut down computers and "cripple" the gambling companies?

10. What did you learn about addiction? Is addiction anybody's fault? Whose? Why?

11. Did you know about the tricks, such as no clocks, no windows, or pumping in oxygen, employed by the gambling industry?

12. Are addictions always bad? Are there any that might be good? Why?

13. Were there any surprises in the story? Were you surprised by the real evidence the author provided in Ron's report?

14. Are you spurred to take action about gambling addiction? If so, what action would you take?

15. Who is responsible for informing society of potentially dangerous behaviors? What is the role of the government? The media? The education system? Other?

16. What are some of the major themes of this book?

Made in United States
North Haven, CT
11 July 2022

21210493R00205